lullaby

Diane Guest lives in Connecticut, USA.

DIANE GUEST
lullaby

Fontana
An Imprint of HarperCollins*Publishers*

First published in the United States by G. P. Purnam's Sons in 1990

This edition first published in 1991 by Fontana,
an imprint of HarperCollins Publishers,
77/85 Fulham Palace Road,
Hammersmith, London W6 8JB.

9 8 7 6 5 4 3 2 1

Photoset in Linotron Trump Medieval
by Input Typesetting Ltd, London
Printed and bound in Great Britain by
HarperCollins Manufacturing, Glasgow

for my children
Anne, Barry, Matthew and Allison

prologue

In late spring some afternoons seem to last forever; shadows move unseen, chilling so stealthily that no one notices until it is too late. This was such an afternoon.

The white-haired woman sat unmoving in her rose garden beneath a row of trellised arches that in summer would be opulent with perfume and color. But not yet. Now the rose vines were little more than a tangle of gray and brown, with only a few sprigs of green to prove that they weren't all dead. The warm sunlight had long since left the terraced garden and a cold breeze had come up off the ocean to stir through the budding irises, making soft, mysterious sounds as it passed. A huge white cat came out of the hedges, meowing, and began to rub impatiently against the woman's legs but she remained motionless, head tipped back, eyes closed.

It wasn't until the younger woman came down the shadowed path into the garden and spoke to her that she finally opened her eyes.

'Mother?' The voice was full of concern. 'I've been

looking everywhere for you.' She bent over and picked up the sweater that had slipped to the ground beside the chaise. 'I thought Doctor Adelford told you to stay indoors.' Gently she draped the sweater around her mother's shoulders.

The older woman didn't look up, nor did she speak.

The younger woman paused, then she held out a pale blue envelope. 'I've a letter for you.' Her voice dropped almost to a whisper. 'It's from Rachel.'

The older woman's head snapped up and her face, void of expression until now, came to life. It was a thin-lipped, aristocratic face where an after-image of past good looks still lingered, but her blue eyes were dull and sunk deep in the sockets, and her skin had the sallow, waxen pallor of the terminally ill. With a shaky hand she reached out and took the letter. 'Leave me, Elizabeth,' she said in the curt voice of one who is used to being obeyed.

'But, Mother . . . '

The older woman didn't speak again. Instead she waved one hand in imperious dismissal.

The younger woman hesitated for a minute, then turned and walked quickly up the path that led back to the main house. The cat followed.

Priscilla Daimler looked down at the letter she held in her hand. 'Rachel,' she whispered. 'My dearest Rachel. After all this time, are you still punishing me?'

As if in answer, the sea wind blew cold through the trees around the garden, casting shadowy patterns of light and dark, and the woman stiffened, lifting her head, alert to something but not sure what. 'Who's there?' she snapped.

Again, a feeling more than a sound, sensed but not heard.

'Who is it?' she said, suddenly afraid. She listened intently, but the sound – if indeed it could be called a sound – was still too indistinct to be identified. Her heart was pounding now but she forced herself to stay calm. 'You're imagining things,' she whispered. 'It must be the medication.' But real or imagined, whatever it was terrified her.

'Priscilla, don't be an ass,' she said crisply and the sound of her own voice reassured her. She shrugged her shoulders, exasperated with herself, then looked down at the letter she still held in her hand. There in the center of the envelope was her name, written in that round, childish curve that could only belong to one person, her daughter, Rachel. The only person she prayed to see before she died.

She forced back acid tears. She never cried, not even when she was alone, but if anything ever brought her to the brink, it was the thought of Rachel. No one else mattered. No one else ever had.

She closed her eyes and prayed that this would be good news. That Rachel had forgiven her and was coming home. No matter what the cost, Priscilla wanted her child to come home. She drew a labored breath into her ravaged lungs and with stiff fingers she opened the envelope. The letter was short.

'Mother,' it read, 'Elizabeth tells me that you are dying, so in spite of all that has happened between us, I am coming. Your daughter, Rachel.'

With a whimper, what little strength she had left went out of her and she collapsed like a rag doll against the back of the chaise. For a moment the letter fluttered in her hand, then caught up by a sudden gust, it blew out across the flower beds and down the shaded paths toward the old summerhouse.

'My letter,' she cried. She struggled to her feet, intending to go after it, but all at once she couldn't walk. She sank back down, conscious of a terrible chill in the air. She pulled her sweater tight around her shoulders but it did little good. The cold seemed to penetrate to the very marrow of her bones. You'd better try to get in, Priscilla, she told herself. Before you freeze to death out here.

And then she heard it again, but this time there was no mistaking what it was. A look of disbelief crossed her face, then one of pain, finally one of terror, for across the garden and down the sculptured paths, rising and falling above the whisper of the wind came the faint but unmistakable sound of a child crying.

The woman pressed her hands to her ears, trying to block it out, denying it, but it was no use. The sobbing was all around her now, touching her, insistent, pathetic, pleading, infinitely sad.

'You're hearing things,' she insisted but in her heart she was filled with the profoundest fear that what she was hearing was in fact real.

An hour later, Elizabeth found her mother still sitting in her garden, eyes staring, hands pressed tight over her ears.

'Mother?' Elizabeth said, alarmed. 'Whatever is the matter?'

And for the first time in years, Priscilla Daimler began to cry. 'Forgive me,' she sobbed, collapsing in her daughter's arms. 'Dear God, forgive me.'

one

Just before noon they stopped for lunch. Judd was starving but Rachel ate next to nothing. He watched her play with a piece of lettuce on her plate, then put her fork down and turn away to stare off into space.

'You okay?' he asked softly.

She nodded but her face was ashen, and when she looked across the table at him he could see the tiny lines of tension moving around the corners of her mouth.

'Are you sure you want to do this? Go back to Land's End?'

She looked away again. 'I have no choice,' she said. 'My mother is dying.'

'If you could just tell me . . . ' He stopped in mid-sentence, wishing he'd kept silent. He knew well enough that his wondering about her past only upset her. He was right.

She put her hands over her face. 'You know I can't talk about it,' she said. 'It's bad enough that I have to go.'

'I'm sorry, sweetheart,' he said, and he was. He hated to see her like this.

She dropped her hands. 'I'm the one who's sorry,' she said, trying to smile. 'For putting you through this.' She sighed. 'We'd better go. I want to get there before dark.'

Once back on the highway, they headed north and with each passing mile, Judd felt his wife slipping deeper and deeper into her own secret thoughts. Once, just to hear the sound of someone's voice, he said 'I love you,' but she didn't answer. No matter. He loved her anyway. He had always loved her.

The first time Judd Pauling ever saw Rachel Daimler he loved her. When he thought about it later, he realized that the feeling had come to him as simply and naturally as drawing a breath.

She was standing in the gallery entrance, and he would never forget how he felt when he turned and saw her there, so pale and ethereal. She might have stepped out of one of his own watercolors, an exquisitely fragile creature with a cloud of silver hair and classic, perfectly sculpted features. Her eyes were the color of turquoise, the color so often described by poets, yet so rarely ever seen in real life. But it was the expression in those eyes that paralyzed him, a look so filled with loneliness that it took his breath away.

At thirty-nine, Judd Pauling had known a number of beautiful women. In fact, he'd been married to one of them for almost ten years, and since his divorce from her three years earlier, he'd never suffered from a lack of female companionship. Judd was a handsome man, endowed with a keen wit but full of good humor, an unbeatable combination, a man as successful in his per-

12

sonal life as he was in his work. But from the first there was something about Rachel Daimler that captivated him, something that went beyond her extraordinary good looks. There was an unmistakable air of tragedy about her, and a rare, childlike vulnerability that made him want to protect her forever.

Judd Pauling, the man, admired her beauty; but it was Judd Pauling, the artist, who was held spellbound by the deep, unexplained pain he saw in her eyes.

Had he ever known what was to come, he might never have spoken to Rachel Daimler that day in the gallery. Indeed, he might have turned and run. As it was, he crossed to her side and held out his hand. 'I'm Judd Pauling,' he said. 'And I think I'm in love with you.'

She flushed, then smiled the sweetest smile he'd ever seen, but it was one that didn't diminish the sadness in her eyes. 'I'm Rachel Daimler,' she said in a low voice, so soft, so melodic, unlike any voice he had ever heard. 'And I admire your work, Mr Pauling, more than I can say. I've been waiting for months for your exhibit to open here in New York.'

He took her by the arm and led her through the crowd. 'Are you an artist?'

'I paint,' she said, 'but we all know that it takes more than paint to be an artist.' She paused in front of one of his most recent works, a bold, impressionistic treatment of the New York skyline. 'Now that,' she said with the wonderful, breathless quality that he later learned came when she was genuinely excited, 'that is a masterpiece.'

'It's yours.' He said it. He knew he had said it, but at the same time he couldn't believe his ears.

This time she laughed out loud, a delightful, infectious trill. 'You can't be serious.'

'But I am,' he said, laughing himself. Still he was astonished. Judd Pauling was not a man who normally went around giving his paintings away. Not that he couldn't afford it. It just went against the grain. He knew exactly what his ex-wife would have said if she had heard him, giving a painting worth tens of thousands of dollars to this total, albeit gorgeous stranger. One of the main causes for their growing apart had been his reluctance in the early days even to sell one of his paintings, never mind give one away. They were his children. His creations. Even now, it hurt like hell to part with some of them.

Admittedly, in the early days, right after he left the newspaper and began painting in earnest, not many people wanted his work. Nicole had had good reason to complain when someone did offer to buy one and he refused. They had lived a meager existence, not for long, true, but long enough to leave scars that never healed. Not even his two children could save their marriage.

Now, as he stood beside Rachel Daimler, he could hear Nicole as clearly as if she, too, stood beside him. 'Judd Pauling, you are a flaming horse's ass.'

Then he looked down at the lovely enchantress beside him and all doubt left him. To hell with Nicole. To hell with everything. Of course he'd given Rachel the painting. He'd had no choice. He was bewitched. 'Will you have supper with me?' he said.

'I'd love to.' She answered without looking up at him. Instead she moved along just ahead of him and he could almost feel the intensity of her concentration. She never took her eyes off the row of canvases.

They reached the end of the exhibit and were turning back when, all at once, she stopped dead in her tracks.

Her breath began to come in short, painful gasps. She was standing in front of one of his earliest paintings, a haunting landscape of a salt marsh, simple almost to the point of abstraction. He had done it years ago on the coast of Maine and it was one of the few he refused to sell.

'I loathe it,' she said.

Now it was Judd's turn to be surprised. Not so much by her words as by the vehemence of her tone. Her voice was so full of emotion that he had to look twice to be certain it had been she who had spoken. She was pale and shaking, but she recovered almost at once, blushing to the roots of her hair. 'Forgive me,' she said softly. 'It's just that I hate the ocean. Don't you?'

Puzzled, he shook his head. 'I think most artists are fascinated by it.'

'Of course, you're right,' she said. 'I, for one, hope I never have to see it again.' She turned away and he had the oddest feeling that he had been dismissed along with all of his paintings. She made her way to the door and he thought she was going to leave without another word, but at the last moment she turned and the smile on her face was dazzling. 'I'll be ready at eight,' she said and gave him an address on East Seventy-second Street. Then she was gone.

Judd Pauling saw her three more times before he asked her to marry him. Twice more and she accepted. Now, four months later, he had no regrets. Rachel Daimler was everything a man could want, and of all the men in the world, she had chosen him. He knew that for some reason she had never trusted a man before, never loved one. He didn't know why. She wouldn't tell him. And he didn't

15

care. All he knew was that she was his, and he vowed that he would never do anything to betray the trust she had placed in him.

He did wish that his children could spend more time with them. His two precious daughters, Emma and Addy. Emma, so smart, so solemn, so full of old-woman wisdom for someone just turned ten. And Addy, his effervescent, irresistible five-year-old. Colored confetti and a party hat. That was Addy. He wanted them to get to know Rachel, to love her the way he did, but it was impossible with them living hundreds of miles away in Colorado with Nicole. He had seen them only once since his marriage to Rachel, when they had come East for a week just after Easter. Rachel had turned herself inside out to make them feel welcome, and Judd had loved her all the more for it. Still, the girls lived so far away and he had so little time with them.

But besides that, something else really bothered him. It was his wife's inability to share with him. Not things. Rachel was generous to a fault with things. It was her thoughts that she kept exclusively to herself. Her thoughts and the reasons for the deep pain he saw in her eyes. Someone, sometime had done something terrible to Rachel Daimler. He only wished he knew what.

As they drove along the highway, he glanced at his wife out of the corner of his eye but her face was turned away. She sat like a stone, perfectly still except for the clenching and unclenching of her hand on the seat beside him. 'You okay?' he asked.

She nodded but continued to stare out the window.

Just outside of Portland they left the main highway and headed east. Earlier Rachel had given him general directions but now he needed help. He looked over at her. Her head was tipped back against the headrest, her eyes closed. She seemed to be asleep and he hated to wake her. She'd barely slept at all since the letter had arrived begging her to come home.

He came to an intersection and pulled to the side of the road. 'Rachel?' he said softly. 'Sweetheart, I need some directions.'

'Just keep going,' she said without opening her eyes. 'I'll tell you where to turn.'

Perhaps it was because he was preoccupied with concerns about his wife, or perhaps it was because there really was no warning, but all at once the road ended and the ocean began, stretching as far as he could see, gray and lonely and limitless.

'Bear left,' she said, eyes still closed tight.

He followed her directions, taking the dirt road that wound up along the shoreline. Every once in a while she would tell him where to turn. Sometimes north, sometimes east, and just as he was certain that they had moved away from the sea, they would come around a bend and there it would be again, vast and restless.

Suddenly she said, 'We're here,' and for the first time in hours, she opened her eyes and pointed. They turned onto a narrow road that climbed up along the bluff overlooking the tidewater. Here the pine trees were thick, crowding the road, and it occurred to Judd that maybe they were lost and Rachel was afraid to admit it. He was about to ask when, all at once, the road straightened out and there before them on a point of land high above the tidewater stood the house.

It was a huge but beautifully proportioned, three-storied structure with white clapboards and black shutters and a high-pitched gambrel roof dominated by four massive chimneys and six dormer windows. What must originally have been a carriage drive leading up to the front entrance was now a hedge-lined walk, bordered on both sides by elaborate gardens and smooth, manicured lawns just now turning green.

Judd let out a low whistle. He wasn't exactly sure what he had expected, but in view of his wife's aversion to her place of birth, he could not have been more surprised. He had half expected a run-down Gothic house of horrors. As it was, he decided that this was one of the most majestic-looking houses he had ever seen. He stopped the car and sat for one minute, letting his artist's eye roam over the perfect symmetry of the landscape.

Beside him, Rachel sat looking at the same scene, but her face was pale and she was leaning back into the seat as hard as she could, her feet braced rigidly against the floorboards, as if by sheer will she could make the car move backward, away from the place.

'It's spectacular,' he said, breaking the silence.

She didn't answer.

'Honey,' he said, turning her face with his hand so he could see her expression, 'are you sure you want to go through with this? It's not too late to go back.'

For one moment he thought she was going to say yes. She opened her mouth, then snapped it closed. 'She's my mother,' she said. 'And she's dying. I have no choice.' With that she opened the door and got out of the car.

At the same time, a woman appeared on the front steps. 'Rachel?' the woman said with obvious emotion. 'Sweet little Rachel. It's been so long!' She ran down the steps and threw her arms around Rachel.

'Yes, it has,' Rachel said, her voice low, betraying

nothing. She moved out of the woman's embrace and turned to Judd. 'Darling, I'd like you to meet Elizabeth. My sister, Elizabeth.'

Judd hid his surprise behind a quick smile and held out his hand. Rachel had never mentioned a sister, but then Rachel had not mentioned much of anything about her family. 'Judd Pauling,' he said.

Elizabeth looked puzzled but she took his hand in a cool, firm grip. She was a tall woman, much taller than Rachel, but slender, and she moved with the easy grace of a natural athlete. He didn't think that anyone would have described her as beautiful. Her features were too angular, too well-defined. But when she smiled back at him, even though the smile was an uneasy one, the resemblance to her sister was astonishing. He guessed that she was older than Rachel, not only because there were streaks of gray in her blonde hair but because of the fine lines around the corners of her eyes and mouth.

'Welcome to Land's End, Mr Pauling,' she said in a low, pleasant voice. 'Rachel didn't tell us she was bringing a guest, but we're delighted to have you.'

Judd threw a startled glance at his wife. Was it possible that Rachel hadn't told anyone they were married? 'Rachel?' he said, but she had turned away and was staring up at the house. He could see a stiffening of her shoulders, as if she were gathering what small reserves of strength she had left. 'This is my husband,' she said without looking at either one of them. 'Judd Pauling. He was kind enough to come with me.'

Judd turned back to Elizabeth, who looked as if she had been slapped across the face. Two high spots of color appeared on her cheekbones. 'I'm sorry, Mr Pauling . . . Judd,' she said. 'I didn't realize.'

Judd smiled, still without a clue as to what the hell was going on here. 'Rachel and I were married four months ago,' he said. He turned back to his wife but she was walking toward the house, quickly, her shoulders set as if against a strong wind. 'Well,' Judd said, feeling somewhat like an ass. 'I guess she's eager to see her mother.'

Elizabeth didn't answer. Her face was pale, and as she watched her younger sister climb the stairs to the front entrance Judd heard her whisper, 'God, help us all.'

As if in answer, a shutter on one of the upstairs windows suddenly broke free and, moved by the wind, began to bang rhythmically against the side of the house.

two

Dinner that evening was a peculiar affair. Rachel was transformed and he couldn't believe the change. He had never seen her so animated, and for the first time since he had known her, the sadness had vanished from her eyes, leaving her looking radiantly happy.

The table had been set for eight but only Elizabeth, Rachel and Judd were seated. 'But where are the others?' Rachel asked.

'I'm sorry, sweetie,' Elizabeth said. 'Mother had invited the Hadleighs and the Lesters. Sort of a homecoming for you.' She laughed and it was a nervous laugh. 'But when we discovered that you hadn't come alone, we thought you might like some time to get settled before you were besieged by old friends.'

Rachel was clearly disappointed. 'But Elizabeth, I would've loved to see them all. I want everyone to meet Judd.'

'Of course,' Elizabeth said. 'We can make plans for another evening. Perhaps on Friday?'

Rachel clapped her hands. 'Oh, Elizabeth, I can't wait to see their faces when I introduce them all to Judd. Won't they just be green?' She turned to him and all of a sudden she was as serious as he had ever seen her. 'You are the best thing that ever happened to me,' she said softly. 'The very best.'

Judd could only stare, still astonished at the change in her. Earlier, after the car had been unpacked, Elizabeth had shown him to their room, but Rachel was still nowhere to be found. He had just decided to go and look for her when she appeared at the door, flushed and breathless.

He did not ask how her visit with her mother had gone. He knew from experience that it was better to let Rachel tell him in her own time. She had busied herself unpacking, making small talk as she worked, but she made no reference to her mother.

It was not until later as they began to dress for dinner that he finally could resist no longer. 'How'd it go?' he asked.

She looked at him blankly as if she had no idea what he was talking about. 'How did what go?'

'The meeting with your mother,' he said.

She did not look at him. 'I haven't seen her yet.'

He was incredulous. 'You haven't? But I thought . . . Then where were you this afternoon?'

'I went to see Harold and Maude.'

'Harold and Maude?'

She flushed. 'Harold and Maude are my cats. My beautiful Persian cats. I haven't seen them in such a long time.' She looked up at him, begging him to understand. 'I had to, don't you see? All the time they thought I'd abandoned them.' Then she sank down on the bed and lay back against the pillow, her eyes full of tears, and opened her robe. 'Do you still think I'm beautiful?' she whispered like a child, desperate for reassurance.

As always, the effect of her nakedness on him was profound. No matter how often, he never quite got used to seeing the absolute perfection of her body, the flawless silk of her skin. Everything about her excited him. But the real key to Rachel's magic was the wild, unabashed streak of sensuality that lay behind the childlike, Victorian purity. When they made love, Rachel was a devil.

So he made love to her then, dazzled as always by the fierceness of her passion. 'You do love me, don't you, Judd?' she asked afterward.

'You know I do,' he said. 'More than life itself.'

She jumped up from the bed, and the sweet, vibrant woman-child he had fallen madly in love with suddenly appeared before him. 'Come then,' she said, pulling him up. 'The time has come for you to meet my mother.'

'You mean you don't want to go alone?'

The change in her was instantaneous. Her face crumbled. 'I can't,' she whispered. 'Please, Judd.' Her voice was pleading and the tears turned her eyes into pools of liquid sapphire. 'Please come with me. I need you.'

He pulled her close, smoothing the silk of her hair. He didn't understand any of this. Why was she so afraid? What terrible thing had the woman done to her? 'Hush, my darling,' he said gently. 'Of course, I'll come with you.'

She looked up at him, so grateful that he felt ashamed. 'Thank you, Judd,' she said. 'I can't go alone. You understand, don't you?'

But he didn't. The only thing he understood was that she was clinging to him now like a drowning woman clings to a piece of driftwood, fighting for the strength to survive. And if his presence gave her courage, then so be it.

But once they stepped outside the bedroom door and began the long walk down the gallery leading to the main hall, he felt certain that she would never go through with it.

The room Rachel had insisted they use was in the north wing, about as far from the main house as they could get, Judd realized, and still be at Land's End. And no one but Judd had seemed surprised when Rachel had declined to stay in her old room.

Arm in arm they passed down the long gallery where all the Daimler ancestors hung in portrait. He would have liked to linger, to ask about these people who lined the walls, to examine the paintings, to admire them, but Rachel was moving quickly, looking neither right nor left, and Judd could feel the tension building in her body with each step they took.

By the time they reached the broad steps that led to the main hall, Judd knew he had lost her.

They were almost to the grand staircase when Rachel stopped suddenly in front of a closed door. She took a pained breath, then knocked.

'Come in.' A faint voice.

Rachel opened the door and went in, leaving Judd to follow.

Unlike the rooms in the north wing, this one was open and spacious, with tall windows almost touching the floor, windows that during the day would flood the room with sunlight. Now it was dimly lit, the only illumination cast by a low fire on the marble hearth. Like the rest of the house – at least as much as Judd had seen – the room was exquisitely furnished with handsome period pieces dominated by a magnificent, eighteenth-century canopy bed. The colors in the room were dramatic, rich reds and blues, skillfully woven into tapestries on the walls and draperies and carpets on the floor. On the table by the window was an enormous bowl filled with brilliant red roses and their perfume almost masked the dark smell of sickness that hung in the air.

Priscilla Daimler sat in a chair by the fireplace, a fragile woman but obviously as meticulously cared for as the room in which she sat. At first glance, Judd thought she was asleep.

Then Rachel spoke. 'I'm here, Mother,' she said, so faintly that Judd barely heard.

Her mother didn't speak, nor did she turn. She simply held out her arms and after one, long, shattering moment, Rachel flew across the room, threw herself on the floor in front of her mother, and buried her face in her lap. Her sobs were so full of anguish that Judd felt a lump come into his throat.

Priscilla put one hand on her daughter's head, a beautifully shaped hand with long, delicate fingers, flawlessly manicured. 'Hush, my darling,' she said softly. 'It's time to forget, to heal, to get on with our lives. Together. What's done is done. We can't change it, my darling, so please don't cry.'

Judd stood silent, holding his breath, watching the scene. He was overwhelmed by the intimacy he could feel between the two women, and shocked that he could have misread Rachel's feelings about her mother so badly. Clearly his wife did not hate the woman. But if the guilty party had not been Priscilla Daimler, who then

25

had hurt Rachel so terribly, and what had driven her so far from Land's End?

All at once, Priscilla Daimler seemed to realize that she and her daughter were not alone. 'Who is this you've brought with you, Rachel?' she asked quietly.

Rachel looked up at her mother, her face tear-streaked, and for a moment, Judd had the strangest feeling that she had forgotten all about him. Then she jumped to her feet and with a small, self-conscious laugh she rushed to his side. 'This,' she said, and when she looked up at him her face was radiant, 'this is Judd Pauling, Mother. My husband.'

Priscilla's reaction was almost the same as Elizabeth's had been. One of shocked disbelief. 'Your husband?' She leaned her head back against the chair. 'That is impossible.'

Rachel crossed to her mother's side and knelt again. 'Oh, but it's not, Mother,' she whispered. 'And I'm so wonderfully, blissfully, unbelievably happy. Please be happy for me, Mother. Oh, please.'

Priscilla pulled her daughter close and held her, rocking her as if she were a small child. 'Of course I'm happy for you, Rachel.' She sounded suddenly exhausted.

'Everything is going to be just fine, Mother. Now that I'm home. You'll see.'

Her mother didn't answer. Instead, she stared over Rachel's silver head straight at Judd but without seeming to see him, and the look on her face was full of grim determination.

Finally she spoke, at the same time pushing Rachel gently away. 'You'd better get down to dinner, children,' she said. 'You know how temperamental Kate is about serving on time.'

26

'But aren't you coming?' Rachel asked, and she seemed as frightened now to be leaving her mother as she had been to see her.

'I'm tired, Rachel,' her mother said quietly. 'You two go along. Tell Elizabeth to have Kate send me a tray.'

'But . . .'

'No buts. We'll talk tomorrow.' She paused, and again, Judd became aware of the intense bond between the two. 'You *will* be here tomorrow, won't you?'

'Of course we will, won't we, Judd? We'll be here as long as you need us.' She turned to him. 'We will stay, won't we, Judd?' she asked with an urgency that he couldn't ignore.

'Whatever makes you happy, Rachel,' he said gently. Then he took his wife by the arm. 'I'm glad we finally met, Mrs Daimler,' he said.

'I am, too, Judd,' she said, but somehow he didn't think she was. Not at all.

Later, he was so engrossed in his thoughts that he hardly realized that dinner was being served. The food was superb, expertly prepared, and the conversation, even though there were only three of them, was spirited.

'So, Judd,' Elizabeth was saying, 'what business are you in?'

'I'm an artist.'

She raised her eyebrows. 'Oh, *that* Judd Pauling,' she said with genuine surprise. 'How stupid of me not to have made the connection. We have one of your paintings, don't we, Rachel?'

Rachel looked up and smiled sheepishly, as if she'd just remembered. 'Why, yes. We do.' She turned to Judd. 'I guess I forgot to mention it. Didn't I?'

'You did,' he said. 'But you're forgiven. Which one is it?'

'It's called *October Country*,' Elizabeth said. 'It's one that Peter . . . ' She stopped short, and at the same time Rachel dropped her glass of wine, splashing ruby liquid across the tablecloth.

'Now look,' she said, and Judd thought he saw a quick glance pass between the two women. 'Thank heaven Mother wasn't here to see *that*.'

'Who's Peter?' Judd asked but no one seemed to hear.

Elizabeth picked up the service bell and rang. 'Don't worry. It's not the first time someone's spilled something, and I'm positive it won't be the last.' She said it calmly enough but underneath Judd could hear a nervousness in her voice that he suspected had nothing to do with the spilled wine.

'Shall we go into the library for coffee?' Rachel stood. 'It's so much more comfortable. Besides, the echoes in this room are depressing.'

'Echoes?' Elizabeth asked.

Rachel smiled. 'You know, Elizabeth. The echoes of all the people who should be here but aren't. You really ought to have let the Hadleighs and the Lesters come. We would've had such fun.'

'We certainly would have,' Elizabeth said. 'I can hardly wait until Friday night.'

Judd was dreaming about Emma and Addy. They were all living in the old beach house in Waltham – Judd, Nicole, Emma and Addy, and they were outside building castles in the sand. It was a happy dream and he was enjoying it, out in the warm sun with his children. He wasn't even bothered that Nicole was with them.

But all at once the dream changed, suddenly, without any warning, the way dreams do. The day turned cold and the tide began to rip in. Much faster than he knew it should. He called for the children to gather their pails and shovels, to come quickly, but everyone was moving in slow motion, and they kept falling down. He tried to help them but he couldn't get his eyes open wide enough to see.

He felt the wall of water hit him before he ever saw it and he heard Addy cry, the terrified, helpless cry of a child who doesn't understand what's happening, who doesn't understand that this is only a dream.

He sat straight up in bed, heart pounding, trapped somewhere between sleep and waking. And he could still hear Addy crying.

It's only a nightmare, he told himself, but he could still hear it, softer now but still audible, a lost, pathetic sound that broke his heart. I can't stand this, he thought. Someone is hurting Addy. 'Stop it!' he shouted. And the sound was gone.

But one thousand miles away, five-year-old Addy Pauling was still crying. Not because the waves had engulfed her but because her mother had just been killed.

three

It was the twentieth of May and it was raining. Ten-year-old Emma Pauling sat beside her sister, Addy, in the front seat of their father's car, waiting for him to fill the tank with gas. Together the three of them had flown east from Colorado. From her mother's funeral. Now they were heading north from Boston to their step-grandmother's house in Maine. A place called Land's End.

Emma had mixed emotions about the whole thing. She had met Rachel once before and she really liked her. Not only was she beautiful, but she was nice. She played with them and when they told her things she really listened. In fact, it was almost as if she and Addy and Emma were all the same age. All children under the skin. When Emma thought about her stepmother she had no bad feelings at all and that, Emma knew, was weird. After all, you weren't supposed to like stepmothers.

The only reservation Emma had had about Rachel was one of loyalty. Would it hurt her mother if she liked her stepmother? Emma didn't know, but now, with her mother gone, she guessed it didn't matter one way or the other.

She blinked back a tear and forced herself to think about Addy. Addy liked Rachel, too, so it had come as a shock when Addy told her she didn't want to go to Maine. In fact, her little sister said she hated Maine, even though she had never been there.

'Hate is a bad word, Addy,' Emma had told her. 'You should never say hate.'

'Well, I hate Maine all the same,' Addy had said. 'And that's that.'

'You're just being silly because you want to stay in Colorado.'

'I'm not silly,' Addy had insisted.

'Are so.'

'*Am not!*'

After a time, Emma had given up but she still hoped that Addy was going to behave herself.

'Are you sure I've never been in Maine?' Addy was asking.

Emma nodded.

'Have you?'

'I think so. When I was real little. At the ocean.'

'Did you like it?'

Emma pressed her face against the window. 'I'm not sure. Probably.'

'I know *I* won't like it,' Addy said and put her thumb in her mouth.

Emma reached over and pulled it out. 'You're not supposed to do that,' she said. 'It'll make your teeth all crooked. Mommy said.'

Addy's face suddenly got all scrunched up, the way it did just before she cried. Emma put her arm around her sister and hugged her. 'Don't worry, Ads,' she said, trying to distract her. 'You'll *love* the ocean. It's so much fun, with big waves and lots of sand.'

Addy snuggled up beside Emma and her mood brightened as Emma had hoped it would. 'Are there slippery slides?' she asked.

'No, Ads,' Emma said patiently. 'This is the ocean, not a swimming pool.'

'Will I be able to touch bottom?'

'Of course you will. Where it's shallow.'

To Emma's surprise the thundercloud look came back. 'Why do we have to live with Rachel's old mother, anyway?'

Again, the infinite patience, answering the same question for the hundredth time. 'Because Daddy is married to Rachel, and Rachel's mother is very sick so we're going to live there for a while.'

'I hope she doesn't stink,' Addy said.

'Just because old Mrs Eldridge stinks doesn't mean that all old people do. Besides I don't think that Mrs Daimler is that old.'

Addy wasn't convinced. 'I wish we could go home,' she said mournfully, and Emma could tell it wasn't going to take much to start her sister bawling again.

'What's the matter, Ads?' she asked softly. Usually Emma could make Addy happy because, by nature, her sister was a very happy person. But lately things were different. And for some reason, Emma didn't think it was all because their mother had died. Somehow Addy just seemed different. Not just sad but really different.

Emma stared out through the rain, thinking hard about horses. She loved horses and when she felt bad, she always tried to think about them. It kept her from bursting into tears like a baby. It wasn't that she didn't feel like crying. It was just that she wasn't little anymore. She was ten and everyone knew that ten-year-olds shouldn't cry. Emma remembered when she was seven and her parents got their divorce. She had cried a lot then. But no more. Now she was ten.

She pushed her glasses back up on the bridge of her nose and tucked her straight, dark hair behind her ears. Daddy had said that she was going to have to help him with Addy now, and she would. Not that it would be anything new. She had been keeping Ads out of harm's way since the day she was born.

She watched her father pay the man for the gas, and she relaxed a little. If there was one bright spot left in her life it was her father. She loved him as much as she loved anyone, even though she hadn't seen much of him in the last three years. She frowned. She never knew just why he and her mother had started not to like each other, but one thing she did know. Her father loved her. And he loved Addy and was trying to do his best to make them all a family again.

Judd opened the door and jumped in. 'Great day for ducks,' he said, throwing his rain-soaked slicker into the backseat.

'Does Mrs Daimler stink?' Addy asked.

Emma sighed. 'I tried to tell her that all old people don't stink but she doesn't believe me.'

'Mrs Daimler doesn't stink, Addy,' Judd said, smiling. 'Not at all. In fact she smells sort of like flowers.'

'Well, where will we sleep?'

'You'll have your very own rooms,' Judd said. 'Rachel is getting everything ready, and I know you'll think they're beautiful.'

'Rachel is beautiful,' Emma said.

'Yes, she is,' Judd said, turning out onto the highway. He wondered how his wife had been coping since he left a week ago. He had spoken to her on the phone every day and she sounded calm enough, but remote somehow, and he could visualize her with that lost look in her eyes again.

When he had first told her the children would be coming to Land's End, she had gone all to pieces, as if she hadn't imagined for one minute that such a thing would ever happen. She had been almost incoherent, giving one reason after another why he should make other plans for them. 'Land's End is no place for a child,' she had stammered finally. 'It's full of death, can't you see that?' And it wasn't until she realized that he had no choice, that he either had to bring them here or go back to New York with them, that she conceded.

He'd thought the crisis had passed, and then he told her he was going to Colorado to get them. She had begged him to stay. 'Can't we just send someone for them? Does it have to be you?' He had seen the fear in her eyes.

'What is it?' he had asked. 'What are you so afraid of?'

She had turned away and covered her face so he couldn't see her expression.

'Tell me,' he had pressed, angry with her, angry with himself for not being able to help her. 'Tell me why you're so afraid.' He watched her struggle, her face distorted by emotions he couldn't begin to understand. And then she threw herself against him, crying, out of control.

'I'm afraid you won't come back,' she sobbed.

He was stunned, not knowing what she might say but certainly never expecting this. 'My God, Rachel,' he said, holding her, soothing her. 'I love you. You are my life. Why would you ever imagine I wouldn't come back?'

'Because I'm such a nothing,' she had whispered. 'Because nothing I love ever lasts.'

'I hate Maine,' Addy said suddenly, jolting him back to the present.

'Addy, be quiet,' Emma said quickly. 'She's just being a grouch, Daddy. Pay no attention.'

'I'm *not* being a grouch,' Addy said, her face scrunching up. 'I'm only saying the truth.'

'But you've never been there, Ads,' Judd said patiently. 'How do you know you hate it?'

His younger daughter turned and looked at him, her eyes welling up with tears. 'I'm not kidding you, Daddy,' she wailed. 'I hate it. I really do.'

'You're not supposed to say hate, Addy,' Emma said sternly.

'Only not about a person, Emma,' Addy said. 'It's okay to say it about a place.'

'Time out,' Judd said. 'Now let's hear all about it, my little Adelaide. What makes you think you won't like it?'

'I just know it, that's all.' Then Addy began to cry in earnest.

Emma put her arm around her sister. 'Shhhhh, Ads,' she said gently. 'It's okay. We're going to have a wonderful time, aren't we, Daddy?' In desperation she turned to Judd.

'We are,' he said cheerfully. This thing with Addy would pass, he was sure. After all, she was only five and her mother had just died. He couldn't expect her to absorb it all without any problem. But once she got to know Rachel, she'd come around. She wouldn't be able to help herself. 'And I'll tell you something else.' His voice dropped to a conspiratorial level. He'd been keeping this information for just such a crisis. 'Rachel has two cats. And one of them is going to have babies.'

Addy's sobbing stopped abruptly and she looked up at her father, incredulous. Cats were her favorite animals, but she'd never been allowed to have one because Mommy was allergic. She had a whole collection of cat figurines and cat pictures and stuffed cat toys, but never had she ever lived anywhere where they had real live cats. 'Two cats?' she said. 'Two real live cats?'

'Yep. White ones. Fluffy white ones. Harold and Maude.'

All at once the storm passed. Addy clapped her hands together. 'I'm so happy, I could just die,' she said, bouncing on the seat.

Emma threw her father a look of adoration mixed with one of relief. He had managed the impossible. This was the first time since their mother's death that Addy seemed almost like her old self. 'See, Ads?' she said. 'I told you things wouldn't be so bad.'

But Emma's sense of relief was to be short-lived. As they wound around the last bend in the road approaching Land's End, Addy fell strangely silent. So silent that, at first, Emma thought she had fallen asleep, but when she peeked around to look at her sister's face, she saw that Addy's eyes were wide open. She started to ask if she were all right, then stopped short, sucking her breath in, for they had come within sight of the house, and at that moment Emma forgot all about Addy. In fact, she forgot all about everything. Never in all her life had she ever seen such a magnificent mansion. It looked like a house right out of one of her picture books, with tall, sparkling windows that reflected the sky and the clouds and the smooth, velvety lawns. 'Oh, Daddy,' she breathed. 'It's a real palace!'

'It is, isn't it?' Judd said and opened the car door.

Emma opened the door on her side and slid out, never taking her eyes off the house. So enchanted was she that she forgot all about her sister. 'Can we go in?' she asked her father, still breathless, still unable to believe that they were actually going to stay in this enchanted place.

She looked up at the high dormer windows and let her imagination take control. There was a beautiful princess hidden up there in one of the rooms, just like in *The Secret Garden*, only a girl instead of a boy, and Emma would discover her and they would become best friends.

And then she heard it. Far off at first, faint, but clear enough to identify. The pathetic, pleading sound of a child crying. Emma cocked her head to one side, unable to tell where it was coming from, but it was the eeriest sound she had ever heard. It seemed to be coming from somewhere near the house, drifting close, fading, then coming close again, soft, unbearably sad, like someone lost forever.

Frightened, bewildered, she turned to her father, but he wasn't looking at her. He was staring at Addy, who knelt huddled on the ground beside the car.

And all at once, to her horror, Emma realized that the wretched, unearthly cries weren't coming from the house at all. They were coming from her sister. They were coming from Addy.

four

Judd left Addy upstairs asleep in bed, Emma keeping vigil. He found Rachel in the solarium, playing with one of her cats and having tea with Elizabeth.

'Surely you're going to tell him, Rachel,' Elizabeth was saying in a hushed tone. 'Surely he has a right to know.'

He couldn't hear the response. 'Tell him what?' Judd asked.

'Isn't Harold the most gorgeous cat you ever saw?' Rachel said, ignoring the question. Gently she put him down on the floor. 'Go along now, you rascal,' she said. 'I'll play with you later.' She poured Judd a cup of tea. 'How's Addy?'

He sat down heavily. 'Doctor Adelford thinks she's finally reacting to the ordeal she's been through. Her mother's death, the move. It's a lot for anyone to absorb, never mind a five-year-old.'

'Is Henry still here?' Elizabeth asked.

'Yes,' Judd said. 'He's gone upstairs to see your mother.'

'Where's Addy now?' Rachel asked.

'Upstairs,' Judd said, 'Emma's with her.' Solid, dependable Emma, so frightened by Addy's strange outburst, yet so determined to stay with her in case she woke up.

'She'll be scared if I'm not here,' she had told her father. 'Don't worry, Daddy. I'll be fine. I'll just sit here and read.' And looking across at his skinny, bespectacled daughter, Judd thought he had never loved anyone quite so dearly.

'You know something, Emma?' he'd said. 'You are some kind of super little kid.'

She hadn't answered. She had just smiled her wise, old-woman smile, pushed her glasses up on her nose, and settled herself in the chair beside the bed. She opened *The Secret Garden*.

'Are you reading that again?' he asked.

'This is the third time,' she admitted, 'but it's still the best book ever. Besides, this place sort of reminds me of Misselthwaite Manor. It's so big and everything.' She looked up at her father, embarrassed to be asking but unable to resist. 'Do you suppose there might be a place like the secret garden here?' she whispered. 'Where me and Addy could play all by ourselves?'

'I wouldn't be surprised,' Judd said. 'Tomorrow, if the weather is good, you and your sister can explore.'

Emma had nodded, then dropped her eyes and began to read.

'Would it help, do you think, if I sat with them for a while?' Elizabeth was asking.

'You're kind,' Judd said, grateful for the genuine concern he heard in her voice. 'But I think they're fine for now.'

'Did Henry give Addy anything to calm her down?' Rachel asked.

Judd shook his head. 'He says she's exhausted, that sleep's probably the best thing for her right now. He'll come back in the morning if we need him.'

'Perhaps we ought to move both girls into one of the north bedrooms,' Elizabeth said. 'Then they could stay together. And be closer to you two. At least until Addy feels more confident.'

Rachel's face fell. 'But I worked so hard to make their rooms comfortable,' she said, then immediately retreated. 'I'm sorry, darling,' she said. 'Of course we'll move them if you think it would help.'

'Maybe it would be better if they did sleep together,' Judd said. 'I'd hate to have Addy wake up in the night and be alone.'

'It's too bad Nellie isn't here. She would've known what to do,' Elizabeth said, and Judd heard Rachel gasp. He looked over and saw that all color had drained from her face.

'Who's Nellie?' he asked.

'Nellie was our nanny,' Rachel said, a bit too quickly, Judd thought. But then perhaps it was just because Rachel was so uptight. She had been ever since he had arrived with the children. 'She took care of us when we were little,' she added. 'But she's gone now.'

'Gone?'

'She went back to England,' Elizabeth explained. 'I never did know why. I guess she just wanted to go home. Although I'd always thought she considered Land's End her home.' Her voice drifted off and she fell silent, lost in some memory of her own.

No one spoke for several minutes. Finally Elizabeth said 'Well, I'll just have one of the servants open the blue bedroom. The one next to yours. It's a bright, airy room with twin beds. The children will be very comfortable there, don't you think so, Rachel?'

'Of course.' Judd could tell she was still upset but then, all at once, she brightened. 'And when Addy feels better, they can move back,' she said.

Judd took a sip of tea that scalded his lips. 'Jesus,' he whistled.

Rachel laughed, her mood changing like magic. 'It's hot, silly,' she said. 'I can see I'm going to have to take better care of you.'

'Impossible,' he said, looking across the table at her, thinking how very beautiful she was when she was happy. He wondered if he would ever understand her.

'How long do you two plan to stay at Land's End?' Elizabeth said.

Rachel looked surprised at the question. 'Why as long as Mother wants us here, of course.'

'And you've no need to go back to New York?' Elizabeth asked Judd.

He shook his head. 'I can work here just as well. At least for a while.' He looked over at Rachel. 'If it makes my wife happy, then so be it.'

'Lucky you,' Elizabeth said. 'I wish I could afford to be so independent. I have to leave in two weeks.'

Judd was astonished. 'I thought you lived here.'

She laughed. 'Not since I was fourteen years old and went away to boarding school. Now I live in College Park. Just outside of D.C.'

'What do you do?' Judd asked.

'I teach. Political science. And when I'm not doing that, I teach riding.' She smiled then, the first genuine smile he'd seen from Elizabeth. It was a smile that made her look just like Rachel. 'My two specialties,' she said. 'Horses and horses' asses.'

Judd laughed, and looking across the table at her, he decided that he liked her. His first impression had not been flattering. He had her pegged as a nervous spinster whose life for the most part revolved around her mother. A woman who was having a difficult time adjusting to her sister's re-entry into the family. Now he realized he'd been wrong. Clearly, Elizabeth Daimler was her own person. Good going, Judd, he said to himself. You certainly have a knack for understanding what makes people tick. First Rachel, then her mother, now Elizabeth. Who's next? he wondered.

'Elizabeth is the bright one in the family,' Rachel said quietly. 'She always was and I suppose she always will be.'

'Hogwash!' Without warning, Priscilla Daimler had appeared in the doorway, looking every inch the lady of the manor. The magic of makeup concealed the deathly pallor of her skin, and her hair, though pulled back in a bun, was stylishly coiffed, framing her face, making her look far less formidable. Only her eyes betrayed her, showed how very ill she really was. Sunk deep in the sockets, hooded, they gave her a secretive look, making it impossible to read her expression.

'Hogwash,' she said again and crossed behind Rachel's chair. 'The only reason Elizabeth has been so successful is that she never had a problem in her life.' She bent and

42

kissed the top of Rachel's silver head. 'You, my darling, have never known anything but adversity.'

Rachel flushed and looked down into her teacup. Elizabeth had turned away so Judd couldn't see her face. Priscilla sat down, and at once, servants materialized out of nowhere, ready to obey her slightest command. There was no doubt here as to who was mistress of the castle. Without a word, but with a wave of her hand, she made it clear what her pleasures were. Then, as quickly as they had appeared, the servants disappeared to do her bidding.

'Surely you aren't going to eat that, Mother,' Elizabeth said, pointing to a pastry on Priscilla's plate. 'Henry would be furious.'

'Henry isn't the one who's dying,' her mother said. Then she turned to Judd. 'The doctor tells me your little one has had quite a bad time of it.'

'She has,' Judd said.

'What happened?'

Judd told her the story.

Priscilla Daimler listened but she seemed curiously detached, as if she really weren't hearing. Or she didn't want to. When Judd was finished, she said, 'Well, anything we can do . . .'

For a moment no one spoke. Then Elizabeth said, 'Would you like to approve tonight's menu, Mother?'

'Is there something special?' Priscilla asked, pouring herself a cup of tea, and Judd couldn't help but notice her hands: slender, graceful aristocrats, clearly pampered, but with an intrinsic strength that he found curiously familiar.

'Do you play the piano?' he asked suddenly.

Priscilla Daimler's fine eyebrows arched up. 'I used to,' she said. 'Why do you ask?'

'Your hands,' Judd said. 'You have the hands of a pianist. My ex-wife had hands like that.'

'Ah, I see you have an eye for detail. The eye of an artist,' she said. A simple enough observation, but behind the hooded gaze her expression was guarded, watchful, and Judd wondered why.

'I'd love to hear you play sometime,' he said.

'Mother is a brilliant pianist,' Elizabeth said.

'Mother used to have potential,' Priscilla countered. 'But she was never brilliant.'

'I didn't know Nicole played,' Rachel said quietly, and Judd detected hurt in her voice.

'There was never any reason to mention it,' he said softly. 'Never any reason to mention Nicole at all.'

There followed a long awkward moment when no one spoke. Then Elizabeth said, 'Could we please talk about the menu? Please? Before Kate has a coronary in the kitchen?'

Priscilla turned to her daughter with a look of quiet exasperation. 'What, dear girl, are you going on about?'

'The dinner party. That we're having tonight. To welcome Rachel home. Has everyone forgotten?'

Rachel brightened. 'Oh, Elizabeth, I had. Wait until you see, Mother. Elizabeth and I have carried on in the finest Daimler tradition. This party is going to be fabulous.'

Priscilla leaned back, relaxing for the first time. 'Well then, let me see what you girls have come up with.'

Judd smiled to himself, watching his wife come to life. She was like a little girl around her mother, so eager for her approval, so vulnerable, so dependent. Yet it had been Rachel who had left Land's End, and seeing her now, he couldn't believe that anything could ever have driven her away.

After her father left the room, Emma sat still for several minutes and tried to read, but it was impossible. She could hear the sound of Addy's steady breathing, but she wanted to hear beyond it. To see if there was something else. Like maybe someone crying, like Colin in her book. She listened but she heard nothing, so she got up, tiptoed to the door and peeked out.

The room they were in was at the end of a long corridor, with an arched window at one end and broad steps at the other, leading who-knew-where. And all along on both sides there were closed doors with tapestries and paintings hanging in between.

Emma stood still as a statue and listened. She knew well enough from her reading that most mysteries began with strange sounds. Still she heard nothing.

She pulled her head back in and closed the door, not the least dismayed. After all, she'd only been here for a short time. There would be plenty of time for exploring, for discovering mysteries. Daddy said they were going to stay here for at least a month, maybe longer. That would be more than enough time to check everything out. And even though she was eager to explore, Emma had decided that it might be better if she took Addy with her. At least at first. Not because she was nervous. That wasn't it at all. It was just because . . .

Well, she wasn't exactly sure why. But once she got to know her way around a little bit, she would explore on her own. By nature, Emma was a solitary child, intelligent, imaginative, and unusually independent for her age. But something about Addy's weird outburst this morning

45

had really shaken her. She couldn't get rid of the feeling that even though the terrible sounds had ended up coming out of Addy's mouth, they hadn't started there. So maybe it might be better, she thought, if I am a little careful. It certainly can't hurt.

Emma crossed to the bed and stood, shifting from one foot to the other, watching her sister, wishing she'd wake up; but Addy slept on.

Finally, Emma sat down on the edge of the chair and took a piece of string from her pocket. She had been trying to master cat's cradle ever since school let out, but there was one part that she always messed up on. Humming quietly under her breath – not loud enough to wake Addy if she really was asleep, but loud enough for her to hear if she was only dozing – Emma busied herself with the string, weaving it in and out, making a tangle, starting over.

So intent was she on her game that at first she didn't realize that she wasn't the only one humming. 'Ads?' she said softly. She stuck the string back in her pocket and crossed to the bed, but her sister's eyes were closed and her breathing was still deep and steady.

'That's funny,' Emma said to herself. She cocked her head to one side, listening, and to her delight she could still hear it. A faint humming sound, but now she realized it was coming from outside.

She went to the window and looked out. From where she stood she could see the broad green lawn curving back from the house, and just beyond the crest of the hill, the sea, all gray and white-capped and sparkling. The sight of it so close made her suck in her breath. She'd never imagined that they were so near. 'Oh, Addy,' she whispered. 'Just wait until you see. We're almost on top of the ocean.'

In her excitement, Emma forgot all about the humming. She opened the window wide and stuck her head out. She could actually hear the sound of the waves crashing on the shore.

And then, above the sound of the sea, she heard it again, this time more clearly. A soft, mindless kind of tune, as if a child were humming and not really paying attention. But as Emma listened, the tune changed and the child began to sing out loud. A sweet, wistful song that sounded like a lullaby.

Emma stretched her neck out the open window as far as she could, looking in every direction, but she couldn't see a soul. Just deserted walkways and tall hedges and flower beds. Still she could hear the melody clearly. There really is a mystery, she thought. Just like in my book.

'Where are you?' she whispered. 'Don't be afraid.'

The singing stopped.

Emma frowned. 'I know you're out there,' she said, searching the wide lawn for some sign of the little girl. 'Why are you hiding?'

But the only answer came from a flock of gulls, circling just above the top of the bluff. Then they swooped away toward the open sea, and all was quiet again.

Emma shrugged and was about to turn away when something weird caught her eye. The grass on the lawn seemed to be getting greener, a deep, summer green, almost black. She pushed her glasses up on her nose and squinted in disbelief. Was she seeing things?

And all at once there *was* something out there. A dark spot – not a shadow exactly but a dark spot. She watched, wide-eyed now, as it began to move slowly across the lawn, pressing the grass down as it passed.

Frozen, Emma stared.

And then the singing began again, faint at first but coming closer and closer until suddenly, the sweet, light sound was all around her. For one terrible, unbelievable minute she thought it was actually going to touch her. But how could that be possible? She shook her head back and forth. It couldn't be, it just couldn't. She felt dizzy but she didn't fall down. Instead she closed her eyes tight, paralyzed, and incredibly, she felt the singing brush past her and into the room.

Now the little girl was terrified. All she could think of was to get away from the window, to jump into bed with Addy and pull the covers over her head. She jerked around, stumbling, then opened her eyes wide in fear and disbelief.

Addy was sitting up cross-legged in the bed, picking little feathers out of the eiderdown quilt. And she was humming. The same, soft, haunting lullaby that Emma had just heard outside the window.

Moments later, when Judd opened the door to check on the children, he found Emma standing by the bed, crying her eyes out, and Addy sitting up, staring at her sister in complete astonishment.

'Sweetheart,' he said, going to Emma, pulling her over to sit beside him on the bed. 'What is it? What's the matter?'

'I don't know, Daddy,' she wailed. 'I heard someone singing, and then I opened the window and looked out, but there wasn't anyone there, and then all of a sudden . . . ' She burst into a fresh flood of tears.

'Emma got scared,' Addy said.

Gently Judd held his daughter at arm's length and tipped her face up so he could see her expression. 'First of all,' he said, taking her glasses off, 'let's clean the tears off these so you can see.' He wiped them carefully, then put them back on the bridge of her nose. 'Now,' he said sternly, 'have you been scaring yourself again? Using that wild imagination of yours?'

Emma didn't answer.

'You know how you've done it before?' he said softly. 'Thinking up all kinds of mysteries and sometimes scaring yourself to death? Like when you thought up the story about the teeny tiny woman, and you had to sleep the rest of the night with Mommy?'

Emma looked up at her father in surprise. 'How'd you know about that?' she asked, then flushed. 'Mommy told you.'

He nodded.

'She promised she wouldn't.'

'She had to, Emma. Because she was afraid you might let your imagination run away with you when she wasn't there to help. She wanted me to be aware of it, that's all.' He hugged his daughter. 'She just didn't want you to scare yourself because she knew what a crazy little storyteller you are.'

Emma nodded but she didn't feel relieved. True, she did have a vivid imagination. And she'd scared herself before. But this was different. This she hadn't imagined. At least she didn't think she had.

She took the tissue her father offered and blew her nose, but out of the corner of her eye, she cast a sidelong glance at the open window and shivered. Her father could think what he liked, but she knew one thing for sure. Someone had been singing and it hadn't been just Addy.

49

Maybe she hadn't seen the grass change color. Or the dark spot moving on the lawn. But somewhere out there was another little girl. Emma didn't know who she was or what she wanted, but deep down in her heart of hearts Emma was afraid of her.

five

The house was ablaze with lights and each room a blaze of color, filled with flowers of every description. It was as if somehow Land's End had been at rest, waiting for winter to pass, waiting for Rachel to come home, and now it was alive again and happy.

Everything had been expertly prepared, a blend of all those ingredients required to create a perfect backdrop for a perfect party. And like her house, Priscilla Daimler seemed to be gathering strength and purpose with each hour that passed, so that when she appeared at the head of the stairs, Judd, who had been downstairs waiting for Rachel, was astonished.

Priscilla was dressed in an elegant black tunic over oriental-styled trousers, and she exuded a confidence that Judd could only marvel at. For the first time, Judd saw a kind of raw power in the woman, a feeling that he found curiously disquieting. 'You look incredible,' he said as she came down the stairs.

She smiled, took his arm and let him lead her into

the drawing room. 'I feel incredible,' she said. 'And I'll feel even more incredible after you fix me a dry martini. Bone dry. Straight up.'

Before he could answer, she said, 'I know, I know. I'm not supposed to have it. Henry would have a fit.' Her voice dropped and he thought he heard a hint of uneasiness. 'But I need it,' she said. 'Just don't tell Elizabeth. You'd think she was the mother and I was the child.'

He did as she asked and was just about to fix one for himself, when he heard Rachel call from the stairs. 'I think my girl wants to make a grand entrance,' he said. 'She insisted that I make myself scarce until she was ready.'

'I'm sure you won't be disappointed. Rachel is perfection.' Priscilla said. 'Go along. I have things I must attend to.'

Judd left the room, but not before he saw Priscilla Daimler drain her glass.

Rachel was standing at the head of the stairs and for a moment, Judd was speechless. She was wearing a dress that looked as if it had been spun from glass and it gave the impression that she wasn't really there, that she was simply a breathtaking illusion. The only jewelry she wore was a single diamond bracelet high on her upper arm. As she started down the stairs, it seemed to him that she had just stepped out from behind a cloud into the moonlight.

'You are a vision,' Judd said, moving up the stairs to meet her.

Later, Priscilla Daimler greeted her guests at the door of the living room, the perfect hostess, speaking quietly to each in turn, gesturing, then ushering them over to the piano where Judd and Rachel stood, sipping their drinks. As he watched, it almost seemed as if Priscilla were standing guard, making certain that no guests came into the room until she had prepared them. Prepared them for what? he wondered. Were they all going to be as taken aback by Rachel's marriage as her family was? He supposed so. He shrugged. He didn't really care because he had never seen his wife so vital, so enchanting. She was genuinely happy to see all these people, and they in turn seemed delighted to have her back. 'Things haven't been the same without you, Rachel,' said one elderly gentleman as he came across the room. 'You and your father were the only Daimlers who ever knew how to throw a good party.'

Rachel laughed, an easy, contagious sound. 'And you, my dear Philip, are the only man I ever knew who could keep up with us.' She turned to Judd. 'This is Philip Winter,' she said. 'One of my dearest and oldest friends . . .'

'You didn't need to say old,' he interrupted.

'You know I didn't mean *old*,' she said. 'Anyway, darling, besides all that, Philip is also probably the most eligible bachelor on the East Coast.' She put a slender hand on Judd's arm. 'And this, Philip, is Judd Pauling. He *used* to be the most eligible bachelor on the East Coast. But no more. Now he's my husband.'

'So I've been told.' Philip smiled and held out his hand. 'My heartiest congratulations to you, Judd. I only wish Rachel had let me know she was available. I've been begging her to marry me since she was ten years old.'

'I can well understand your devotion,' Judd said, looking across at his wife, loving her, loving to see her so happy. It was going to be much easier to concentrate on helping Addy and Emma adjust if he didn't have to worry about Rachel, too.

Earlier, Emma and Addy had eaten a light supper, then had begged to watch a rerun of *Gilligan's Island*. Judd had seen no harm in it, but clearly television viewing was not something Priscilla Daimler considered appropriate for children, and she told him so.

Judd had to admit that he had never given it a great deal of thought. That had been Nicole's province, and it had never become an issue because most times when they were with him, Emma had preferred to read and Addy had been happy to play games.

In any case, he decided to ignore Priscilla's comments. He didn't think that this was the time to create any more disruption for his children than was absolutely necessary. He settled the two girls in front of the set, leaving them to escape with Gilligan for a half hour. Then he took them upstairs, heard their prayers and tucked them in. In the same room, in beds almost touching.

Judd knew that Emma prided herself on being quite grown-up, and very independent, but he suspected that she was still shaken over what had happened that afternoon. Not that he understood it. She had told him about some humming outside that all of a sudden was inside, coming out of Addy's mouth. In any case, he was almost sure that she really didn't want to sleep in a strange room all alone. So while Addy was in the bathroom brushing her teeth, Judd had taken Emma aside.

'Emma,' he said. 'I have to ask a huge favor.'

She looked at him so gravely that he almost laughed. 'Of course, Daddy.'

'I know you really want to have your own room, but

your sister is having such a rough time of it . . . Well, I was wondering if . . . '

'You want me to sleep with her, right?'

'Right. The servants have opened a room right next to Rachel's and mine. Are you sure it's okay?'

'I don't mind,' she said quickly. 'It'll make Addy feel better.'

'It sure will, Emma,' he said. 'And me, too.'

Now, as he stood watching Rachel with her friends, he said a silent prayer of thanks for his good fortune, his adorable wife, his two precious children. He watched Rachel move among the guests, smiling, animated, clearly the belle of the ball. And Priscilla, circulating graciously through the crowd, behaving for all the world as if there were nothing whatever the matter with her.

'Penny for your thoughts.' He turned to see Elizabeth standing just behind him. Like her mother, was was wearing evening pants under a black tunic that posed a striking contrast to the pale peach of her complexion and the soft blonde of her hair, and Judd suddenly realized that Elizabeth was a very attractive woman. It was only when she was standing next to Rachel that she seemed plain.

He covered his surprise with a quick smile. 'I was just thinking what an extraordinary woman your mother is. You'd never know she wasn't in the peak of good health.'

Elizabeth nodded. 'It's the nature of the beast that's killing her to be kind at times. At other times . . . ' She frowned. 'If you stay here long enough you'll understand what I mean. Besides, my mother is a great actress and she wanted this night to be perfect. Having Rachel home is the answer to her only prayer.'

Judd smiled. 'My wife certainly is enjoying herself.'

'Rachel always loved a party,' Elizabeth said. 'Just like her father.'

Judd perked up his ears. Except for Philip Winter, this was the first time anyone had mentioned Nicholas Daimler. 'Where *is* Mr Daimler?' he asked.

'Rachel never told you?'

He shook his head.

'He died. When Rachel was twelve. I was away at school, but I know it was a terrible blow to her.' She became pensive. 'Rachel was the apple of his eye. He adored her and she adored him. They were inseparable. Not that she was any less important to Mother. But at that point, Mother was very busy with her music.' She stopped and took a sip of wine. 'After Father died, Mother gave up the piano. From then on she devoted herself to one person. Rachel.'

As she spoke, Judd watched her carefully, trying to detect some trace of resentment, but he heard none. 'Didn't it ever bother you? All the attention to your sister?'

She looked surprised, then thoughtful. 'I suppose. At times. But I was never neglected. Besides, I was six years older. I went away to school when Rachel was only eight. She was still such a baby.' She smiled then, remembering, and a dimple appeared in one cheek, making her look almost impish. 'Anyway, even when she was being the worst brat, Rachel was always adorable.'

Judd laughed. 'Rachel? My Rachel? A brat? You can't be serious.'

'Serious about what?' Priscilla Daimler cut in. 'Come now, Elizabeth, our Judd is supposed to be mingling, getting to know his wife's friends.' She took him by the arm and led him away. 'I want you to tell the Graysons

56

what you were telling me earlier. About those rascals at the Guggenheim.'

'Are you going to play for us, Priscilla?' David Graves asked as they moved around the piano.

'Not right now, darling,' she said, waving a hand. 'Perhaps a little later.'

'I'd love to hear you play,' Judd said.

'I haven't touched the piano in years,' she said quietly, 'and I have no intention of ever touching it again. Ah, here we are.' Together they moved into a group of people, three of whom Judd had just met. The fourth was Dr Adelford.

'Behaving yourself, I hope?' he said to Priscilla.

'Of course, Henry. Don't I always?'

'Never,' he sighed. 'Never, never, never.'

'Poor Henry,' she said, 'trying so hard to keep me alive.' She turned to Judd. 'Now, my dear, tell these ignorant people what you were telling me about the latest scam in the art world.'

Judd told them all he knew about the ingenious operation that had resulted, much to the horror of the museum's directors, in the purchase of an undisclosed number of fakes, and after some spirited conversation about the decline of Western civilization, he caught his wife's eye and excused himself to join her. 'I'm starved,' she whispered. 'How about you?'

Judd realized suddenly that he hadn't eaten since breakfast. 'Lead the way, m'dear. Lead the way.' They made their way to the dining room where a magnificent buffet had been laid out. Judd piled his plate none too delicately and was just about to follow Rachel into the drawing room when Henry Adelford stopped him. 'How's the youngster doing?' the doctor asked.

'She seems to be much better, thanks.' And she did. Now it seemed it was Emma's turn to freak out, but Judd didn't mention that.

'Well, patience and lots of love,' Adelford said. 'That's the ticket. There's a lot of security that's been lost. Just remember that.'

'I will,' Judd smiled. He decided he liked Henry Adelford. He was a nice guy. 'And thanks.'

'Anytime,' the doctor said and moved off.

Judd looked for Rachel but she had disappeared down the hall. He was just crossing the foyer, heading in the same direction when faintly, above the sounds of people talking, he thought he heard someone playing the piano. Damn that Priscilla, he said to himself. Telling me she'd never play again.

He crossed to the living room door and looked in. There were several people gathered there, but curiously no one was talking. They were all turned toward the concert grand that stood alone at one end of the room. From where he stood he couldn't see, but almost immediately he realized that it couldn't possibly be Priscilla Daimler playing. Whoever it was was struggling. Not making mistakes exactly, but laboring, playing with such pathetic determination that it made him cringe. And then he realized it had to be a joke. It couldn't be for real. Judd chuckled. Someone's got a weird sense of humor, he thought.

He moved into the room. The other guests were all standing around, watching quietly but fidgeting, clearly uncomfortable with the situation. It was obvious from their reactions that this was no joke. So what was going on? He was almost to the piano when he stopped dead in his tracks and stared, unable to believe his eyes.

There, in her nightgown, sitting all alone on the bench was Addy. And she was playing the piano with such agonizing effort that it was painful to listen.

His first instinct was to stop her, make light of it, and get her back to bed, but something held him back. A caution. Something that told him to be careful, that something here was terribly wrong. Slowly he put his plate on an end table and walked to the piano, easing himself down onto the bench beside his daughter.

The tears were streaming down her cheeks, but she didn't seem to realize he was there. Her little fingers kept going over and over the same notes, trying desperately to get them right.

'Ads?' he said quietly. 'Sweetheart?'

At first she didn't seem to hear, then all at once she dropped her hands in her lap. 'I'm sorry.' Her voice sounded so small, so tired. 'I didn't do good.' Then she looked up at him and her eyes were full of despair. 'It's all my fault,' she stammered. 'I should've practiced harder.' Then she burst into tears.

Judd picked her up in his arms. 'Sshhh, Ads,' he whispered. 'It's all right.' Only dimly aware of the others in the room, he carried his sobbing child to the door, but just as he was about to go out into the foyer, he turned. And that's when he saw Priscilla Daimler. She was standing in the shadow to one side of the door, and it seemed to Judd that he had never seen a face quite so full of fear.

Emma was fast asleep when he carried Addy into the bedroom. He sat down on the edge of the bed, cradling her, rocking her. She'd calmed down considerably and seemed to be content now just to lie still in his arms and be soothed. She was alternately hiccoughing, sniffling and sucking her thumb.

'Daddy?' Emma said, struggling to wake up. 'What's the matter? Did Addy have a bad dream?' She sat up and rubbed her eyes.

'I'm not really sure, Emma,' Judd said. 'She came downstairs just now. To play the piano.'

Emma giggled. 'She did?' She jumped out of her bed and came over to snuggle close to her sister. 'Ads, you silly. What did you do a thing like that for?'

Addy shook her head.

'What did she do that for?' Emma asked Judd.

'I guess she wanted us all to hear how well she can play,' Judd said quietly.

Emma seemed to find the whole thing hilariously funny. 'But Daddy,' she laughed, 'Addy doesn't know how to play the piano. She hasn't ever played in her whole life.'

Judd suddenly felt sick. 'I know she doesn't play very well,' he said. 'But your mother did give her some lessons.' He paused. 'Someone did.'

Emma shook her head vehemently. 'No way, Daddy. Mommy wanted her to try, but Ads never would. Never once. She couldn't even play "Chopsticks".'

Judd stared at his daughter. She had to be mistaken. Addy hadn't played very well. In fact, he didn't know when he'd ever heard anyone in such agony. But there wasn't a doubt in the world that she had played.

And all of a sudden he was chilled to the bone. Jesus Christ, he thought, what in hell is happening to my baby?

six

'But both children agree that Addy doesn't know how to play the piano. Not even one note.' It was early morning and Judd was sitting in the solarium across from Henry Adelford, having coffee. At the doctor's request, Rachel had left the two men alone.

She hadn't wanted to. After the incident in the living room, Rachel was devastated. While Judd was upstairs trying to settle his children down, the gay, vibrant Rachel had vanished, leaving the other Rachel, the lady with the lost, tormented soul.

For the rest of the evening, she had clung to him, refusing to leave his side, and the party had gradually broken up. But later, after they had gone upstairs, she had pulled away from him.

'What is it?' he had asked. He was exhausted but he could tell that she was terribly upset. He held her.

'Why did Addy want to ruin my party?' she asked quietly but he could hear the hurt in her voice. 'Does she dislike me so much?'

Judd couldn't believe his ears. 'Addy doesn't dislike you, Rachel,' he said. 'I don't know why she came downstairs tonight, but I'm sure it had nothing whatever to do with you.'

She shook her head. 'I think somehow she believes that if I weren't here, maybe her mother would come back. I think Addy wants me out of your life. I think . . . Oh, I don't know what I think.' She began to pace back and forth, wringing her hands. 'What have I done to be so tormented?' she whispered more to herself than to him. 'I'm so afraid. I'm so afraid.'

Judd pulled her to him and held her, trying to stop her trembling. 'It's all right, Rachel. There's nothing to be afraid of. Nothing.' He wondered if it would help if she knew that Addy didn't even know how to play the piano, but something told him not to mention it. At least not until he talked to Henry Adelford.

He made love to her then, with the tenderest passion, hoping she would be reassured, and finally she slept. But Judd didn't. Rachel's words kept going through his head. She couldn't be right about Addy, he was sure of it. But then wasn't Rachel's explanation for Addy's bizarre behavior as plausible as any other?'

When morning finally came, Judd felt as if he hadn't even closed his eyes. On the other hand, Addy and Emma had bounced out of bed at the crack of dawn, full of energy, as though nothing out of the ordinary had happened the night before. And when Elizabeth offered to take them down to the stables to see the horses, they went without a backward glance. So much for lack of confidence, Judd thought wryly.

'The mind is a strange and wondrous mechanism,'

Henry was saying. 'It has an incredible system of checks and balances.'

'Are you trying to say in a kind way that you think Addy might be nuts?' Judd said.

'I'm not saying any such thing. What I am telling you is that the child has suffered a terrible loss. And it's a difficult task to assess the true impact of that loss on a five-year-old. If it's even possible.'

Judd took a deep breath. 'So what do you think I should do?'

'Well, first I want you to let me check her over. Make sure there's nothing wrong physically that might be causing trouble. Then we'll take it from there. Assuming there are any more incidents.' He took a sip of coffee. 'To tell you the truth, Judd, I think you've seen the last of Addy's performances.'

Judd put his hands over his face. 'Jesus, Henry, I hope to hell you're right. She's so little. She's just lost her mother and her home. She doesn't deserve any more pain.'

'We'll make it as easy on her as we can. But if what I suspect is true, Addy may have been suffering from simple depression. Perhaps in a way she views herself as wicked for having lost her mother. Guilty. The what-have-I-done kind of thing.'

'You mean that maybe she played the piano because she hoped it would please Nicole, maybe bring her back?'

Henry shrugged. 'Could be. It's not at all out of the realm of possibility. We've had cases of people who've done stranger things.' He leaned across the table and poured himself a fresh cup.

'Rachel thinks that Addy did it deliberately. To ruin her party,' Judd said quietly.

Henry raised an eyebrow. 'Whatever for?'

'She thinks Addy wants her out of my life. That maybe if Rachel is gone, Nicole will come back.'

The doctor mulled that one over for a moment, then to Judd's surprise he nodded. 'Could be,' he said. 'I hadn't thought of that angle, but it's no more implausible than any other. But again, Judd, if that's it, she'll get over it.' He paused. 'Provided you can do a mighty fancy balancing act.'

'Like what?'

'Like making sure Addy knows you love her. But not exclusively. There's the key. You have to make sure she understands that Rachel is a critical part of your life. And a permanent one.' He held up his hand. 'But all this is premature. A doctor never prescribes a cure before he knows the nature of the illness. Tell me. What does Addy say about all this? About the scare she had when she first got here, and then last night?'

Judd threw up his hands. 'She doesn't remember anything about it. All she says is that she woke up and didn't know where she was.'

'But she was frightened.'

'You bet she was. Who wouldn't be?'

Henry nodded. 'Where're the children now?'

'Elizabeth took them down to the stables to see the horses.'

'Has Addy seen Rachel this morning?'

Judd nodded.

'And how did she behave?'

'Like any ordinary happy five-year-old. It was Rachel who was the basket case. She tried to seem natural, but you could cut the tension with a knife.'

'Do you think Addy noticed?'

64

Judd shook his head. 'Addy was just regular, bubbly old Addy.'

'That's good. The quicker she gets back to normal, the more likely something like last night will never happen again.' He looked at Judd over the top of his glasses. 'I'll tell you another thing, though, and I hope you won't misunderstand. This episode hasn't done my patient any good.'

'You mean Priscilla.'

Henry nodded. 'This has really thrown her for a loop, Judd. I'm not sure why but it has.' He paused, choosing his words carefully. 'You must know that the last thing I can have her subjected to is stress of any kind.' He leaned across the table and lowered his voice. 'And I certainly wouldn't let it become public knowledge that Addy performed without benefit of any musical training. Mental disturbances are difficult for most people to understand. Why create more anxiety here than is absolutely necessary?'

'I agree,' Judd said quietly. 'For now we'll keep this strictly between us.' He stood up. 'Now if you can spare me, I think I'd better go and see how Elizabeth and the kids are doing.'

He met Rachel coming down the stairs. 'Where are you off to now?' she asked. She looked terribly tired.

'To the stables. Elizabeth took Addy and Emma out to see the horses. Want to come?' He didn't know why he asked. He knew how afraid she was of horses.

She looked confused, as if she had no idea what to do. 'I can't,' she said finally. 'I promised Mother I'd supervise the rose pruning. She's not feeling very well this morning.' She held out her hand. 'Come with me? Please?'

'I can't honey, he said. 'I really have to see what Addy is up to.'

The color drained from her face. She said nothing but Judd could tell that he had hurt her, that she felt rejected. He put his arm around her and kissed her softly on the cheek. 'You're still my best girl,' he said. 'I love you, Rachel. My children being here hasn't changed that and it never will.'

She flushed. 'Pay no attention to me, Judd. Please? I'm just tired.' Still, there was something in her tone he hadn't heard before, something that made him uneasy. 'You'd better go check on your children.' Then she stood on tiptoe and kissed him, his sweet, gentle wife once again.

Judd was halfway to the door when something occurred to him. He turned. 'Rachel?'

She was still standing on the stair. 'Yes?'

'Why is your mother so upset about Addy?' He'd suddenly remembered the ghastly look on her face last night.

'My mother has always loved children,' Rachel said quietly. 'She hates to see them hurt.'

'Of course,' he said. 'I just wondered.' Then he left the house.

He wasn't exactly sure where the stables were, but the grounds keepers were out in full force on this perfect morning, and he had no trouble getting directions. He followed one of the hedge-lined paths that ran parallel to the sea, to a spot high above the tidewater. Here there were no tall pines, no tangled underbrush. Only masses of pale-pink azalea and crimson rhododendron just now coming into bloom. Everywhere he looked there were beds of snowdrops and crocuses and daffodils in all the misty, watercolor shades of violet and yellow and white.

66

He stopped. It was almost painful to look at, it was so beautiful. 'What Monet would have done with this!' he thought and decided that it would be here that he'd do his first sketches. He made a frame with his fingers and held it up, trying to get some feel for the composition, when, all at once, he saw something that struck him as odd.

There, at the crest of the hill, just where the path curved down toward the open meadow, he could see a small stretch of underbrush beyond the neatly trimmed hedge. Once noticed, it stuck out from the rest of the scene like a sore thumb.

He walked back up the path, looking over the hedges and beyond. Now he could see that, at one time, the path had branched off here, the existing walkway leading to the stables, the other down toward the sea. But now, the second walkway had almost disappeared; its opening was filled in with boxwood and the path itself was overgrown, choked off with thick tangles of briars twisted together in such a way as to make passage virtually impossible.

He frowned. There was something about this that set his teeth on edge, something that anywhere else would have gone unnoticed. Why, in this Garden of Eden where nothing unsightly was allowed to exist, why had this single path been left untended, encouraged to return to its wild state, thus rendering it impassable? He made a mental note to ask Elizabeth about it. Probably a perfectly simple explanation, he thought.

Suddenly he felt a coldness against the back of his neck that had nothing to do with the weather. He pulled the hood of his sweatshirt up over his dark hair and turned away, heading down the gentle slope toward the open meadow.

At the foot of the hill the path ended, and at the same time he heard Emma call.

'We're over here, Daddy. Come quick.' He walked across the field toward a large fenced-in pasture. Emma was sitting on top of the fence, Addy and Elizabeth were standing close by.

'Look at that mare, Daddy,' Emma pointed. 'Isn't she gorgeous? Her name is Clarissa, and Elizabeth's going to let me ride her.'

'Well, that is exciting news,' he said.

'Emma tells me she's had several years of riding lessons,' Elizabeth said. 'Is that right?'

'True enough. Emma's quite the little horsewoman.'

'Just checking,' Elizabeth smiled, and the dimple appeared in her cheek. 'Clarissa can be balky at times.'

Addy came over and threw her arms around her father's legs. 'Guess what, Daddy?'

'What?'

'Elizabeth says if I wait here very quietly, maybe Harold and Maude will come by. She says they like to hang around the stables because sometimes there are mice.'

Judd looked over at Elizabeth. 'I take it Maude hasn't had her babies yet?'

'Not yet,' Elizabeth said. 'But any day now. I've already told Addy that she may have one. They're really Rachel's cats, but I'm sure she won't mind.' She frowned. 'I suppose I shouldn't have said it without checking with you first, though. In case you have an objection. Stupid of me.'

Judd looked down at his daughter. Addy's eyes were sparkling and he could see the excitement bubbling up. 'Well . . . ' he said, considering.

Addy sucked in her breath and held it.

'Okay. You can have one. If Rachel says it's all right.'

Addy let out a squeal and began to bounce up and down like a yo-yo; watching her, Judd felt as if he were in the *Twilight Zone*. How could this plump, jolly little jumping-jack of a child be suffering from fits of depression? Or more unbelievable, could she really want Rachel out of his life? Impossible. There had to be a better explanation.

'Do you ride, Judd?' Elizabeth said, breaking into his thoughts.

He nodded. 'I haven't for a long time, though.' Not since he'd known Rachel, at any rate.

'Perhaps we could ride sometime? Before I go back to D.C.'

He smiled. 'I'd like that.' He leaned against the fence, watching Emma feed apples to one of the horses. He couldn't believe how normal everything here seemed, and for the first time since coming to Land's End he felt hopeful. 'It would be fun to ride again,' he said aloud. 'Rachel will probably have a fit, though. She's a basket case around horses.'

'I know,' Elizabeth said quietly. 'She used to ride, you know. Better than I did, in fact.'

'You're kidding.'

'No. But after the fire, when Father was killed, Rachel never got on a horse again.'

Judd shook his head. Again he realized how little he really knew about his wife.

Elizabeth motioned to Emma. 'C'mon, kidlet,' she said. 'Let's get this bridle on Clarissa and see what you can do with her.' She took Emma by the hand and together they walked through the gate and across the pasture toward one of the horses who was grazing peacefully under an old apple tree. Watching them go, Judd smiled. Emma certainly had taken to Elizabeth.

'Let's go look for Maude,' Addy said, tugging at his sweatshirt.

'Okay, let's.'

'I'll show you where the horses sleep.' She took him by the hand and led him to the stable door.

Inside there was room for a dozen horses or more, and like everything else at Land's End, the place was meticulously maintained. Addy led him between the rows of stalls.

'Each horse has his own place to sleep,' she said seriously. 'See? The signs tell you who lives where.' She pointed. 'Who lives in that one?'

Judd looked at the quarter board. 'Vanilla,' he said.

'Vanilla the horse,' Addy chuckled. 'That's a riot.'

They had almost reached the end of the row when, all at once, Addy let out a squeal. 'Look, Daddy. There she is over there by those buckets!'

Judd turned. There, curled up on a pile of empty burlap bags was a huge Persian cat.

Addy's fingers flew to her mouth and she stood staring, wide-eyed, not quite so confident now that the cat was within range.

Judd took her by the hand and together they crossed the few feet to the spot where the animal slept, unconcerned.

Addy dropped to her knees. 'Could I touch her?' she whispered.

'Sure you can, Ads. As long as you're very gentle.'

The child reached out a shaky hand, and with soft,

timid touches she began to stoke Maude's luxuriant white coat.

The cat opened her pale-green eyes and stared lazily back at the little girl, then yawned, stretched, and allowed the child to continue her petting.

Addy looked up at her father, enchanted, unable to believe that she was truly touching this magnificent creature. Then she looked back at Maude and began to talk to the cat in a small, singsong voice. 'I love you, Maude,' she crooned. 'You are the prettiest cat I ever saw. And I would never hurt you. Not ever, ever, ever.'

From somewhere outside, Judd could hear Emma calling. 'You stay right here, Addy,' he said. 'I'll be right back.'

'Don't worry, Daddy,' Addy said. 'I won't move an inch.'

Judd went to the stable door and looked out. At first he didn't see Emma or Elizabeth, but he could hear them. He walked around the corner and there, cantering around the riding ring on Clarissa, looking every bit the professional equestrian, was Emma.

'That's it,' Elizabeth was saying. 'Now you've got it.'

Emma made two more circuits around, then slowed to a trot and posted over to where Elizabeth was waiting.

'Marvelous, Emma,' Elizabeth said. 'You're a natural.' She held the bridle while Emma slipped off. 'She's very good,' Elizabeth said to Judd, leading the horse into the yard. 'I wish I had more time to spend with her.' She frowned. 'Well, we'll see.'

'Where's Ads?' Emma asked, catching her breath. 'I wanted her to see, too.'

'She's in the stable with Maude.'

Elizabeth smiled. 'She found fat Momma.'

71

'She did.'

Can I go see?' Emma asked.

Judd nodded. 'Sure. Just don't scare the cat away or your sister will be furious.'

Emma stopped to scratch Clarissa on the nose, then she crossed the yard to the stable door. She couldn't remember when she'd had such a wonderful morning, and she decided that riding was at least as exciting as looking for mysteries, and a lot less scary. Yesterday's episode had faded into a memory, blurry, indistinct, like ink letters on a blotter. In fact, she'd almost convinced herself that even the humming hadn't been real. Daddy had said it wasn't, and Emma wanted desperately to believe him. But still . . .

She walked quickly behind the stalls, looking for her sister, but no one seemed to be there. 'Ads?' she called. 'Where are you?' She walked to the end of one row, then turned and started up the other side. She was almost back to the door when she saw Addy kneeling on the floor, the huge cat curled up in her lap.

'Hi, Ads,' she said, flopping down beside her.

'Isn't she gorgeous?' Addy whispered without looking up. 'But you have to be very, very careful with her, because Elizabeth says she's going to have babies.'

'Where's the other one? Harold.'

Addy shrugged. 'I'm not sure. But maybe he'll come around if we're quiet. Cats don't like noise, you know.'

'Can I hold her?'

Addy frowned. 'I don't think she likes strangers so I'd better keep her on my lap. But you can pat her. Right here.' She pointed to a spot behind Maude's ears. 'She likes it right here.'

Gently Emma began to scratch the cat. Maude closed

her eyes and continued to purr. 'Wow, she's so fluffy,' Emma said.

'She sure is. And just wait until she has her kittens. I'm going to get one.' She looked up at Emma. 'And you know what I'm going to name her?'

'What?'

'Clementina.'

'But what if it's not a girl?'

Addy paused. 'Well if it isn't, I'll just think up another name. Maybe Mr Freddy.' She put her face down almost on top of Maude's head. 'Would you like Mr Freddy?' she whispered to the cat.

Maude didn't move. She was the picture of content-ment.

'I think she likes Mr Freddy,' Addy said.

'If I had a kitten,' Emma said, 'I'd name it Melody, but I'd rather have a horse.'

'Not me. I don't want anything in this whole world except one of Maude's babies.'

Emma nodded and smiled to herself. Addy sure was acting normal. Maybe later they'd even be able to go exploring. She sat back on her heels and thought about it. Where should they begin, she wondered. Inside the house? No. That would be better saved for a rainy day. The obvious place to start on a sunny day like this would be outside, following one of those mysterious, winding paths. But just in case, she'd make sure they steered clear of the place where she'd seen the dark spot. If she'd really seen it, that is. So intrigued was she with her plans that at first she didn't realize how cold it had become. And dark. A funny, deep kind of dark. She shivered. 'Ads,' she said. 'Did you bring your sweater?'

Addy shook her head.

'I wish I brought mine. I'm cold.' She wrapped her arms tightly around herself. It seemed as if icy little fingers were moving up and down her back. 'Let's go see what Daddy's doing,' she said. All of a sudden she couldn't wait to get outside.

But Addy shook her head. 'You go. I have to take care of Maude.'

'But Addy . . . ' Emma began, then stopped short. Someone was coming. 'Daddy?' she said. 'Elizabeth?'

Silence.

Shivering, she threw an uneasy glance over her shoulder, but she couldn't see anyone. Still she was sure someone was there, hidden, breathing softly, watching. And somehow she knew it wasn't a grown-up. She knew it was a child. Maybe the child she had heard yesterday.

She turned back to her sister who was still crooning happily to the cat. 'Come on, Addy,' she said, trying to sound casual. 'Let's go exploring.'

'You go,' Addy said. 'I'll stay here.'

'Please, Addy,' Emma said, and, all at once, there were tears in her voice.

Addy raised her eyebrows in surprise. Emma was acting scared again. Emma who was always so brave. 'All right,' she said. 'Just a minute.' Carefully she moved the cat back to her perch on top of the burlap bags. 'Good-bye, Maude,' she said. 'I'll be back, but first I have to go take care of my crybaby sister.' Then she took Emma's hand and together they left the stable.

Once outside, Emma's fear began to subside in the glow of the warm sunshine. Even so, she couldn't help glancing over her shoulder toward the stable door. Something bad had been in there, she knew. Something very bad.

'What scared you?' Addy asked.

Emma shrugged. 'Nothing,' she said. She wanted to tell Addy, but she didn't know how to explain, didn't know the right words to express her creeping sense of horror. 'Let's go look at the baby horses,' she said and together the two children began to skip across the yard toward the paddock.

Judd watched his children come out of the stable, hand in hand, and cross to the paddock where a coal-black mare stood patiently nursing her colt. Elizabeth was standing just inside the fence, brushing the dried mud off of Clarissa's legs. 'They seem to be doing just fine, don't they?' he said more to himself than to her. He could feel the tight knots of tension across his shoulders beginning to loosen up.

'They do,' Elizabeth said. 'And once they find their way around, I'm sure your troubles will be over. Land's End is an endless enchantment for a child.'

Judd looked over at her. 'Rachel doesn't think so.'

Elizabeth frowned. 'I know. She doesn't now, but she didn't always hate it.'

'What happened?'

Elizabeth shrugged and stopped brushing for a minute. 'I'm not sure,' she said noncommitally. 'Maybe she just grew up.'

He thought about that for a minute. 'Surely that's not why she left Land's End.'

Elizabeth patted the horse on the rump. 'All done, Clarissa,' she said and the horse trotted off. She turned back to Judd, and when she spoke her voice was constrained. Clearly she was uncomfortable talking about her sister. 'I'll be perfectly honest with you, Judd,' she

75

said. 'I'm not really sure what happened to Rachel. But even if I knew, I wouldn't tell you.' She paused, looking at him with those clear, turquoise eyes so much like her sister's. 'Why don't you just ask her?' she said quietly.

'She won't tell me, either,' he said.

Elizabeth turned away. 'Maybe it's for the best,' she said. 'Sometimes it's better not to know.'

seven

For the second time that day, Judd found himself sitting across from Henry Adelford, talking about Addy, only this time they were in the doctor's office. Henry had just finished giving Addy a complete exam, and she and Rachel had gone down the street to get an ice-cream cone.

'Well?' Judd held his breath.

'I can find absolutely no evidence of anything physically wrong with the child,' Henry said.

Judd exhaled, but he wasn't sure whether he was relieved or not. 'So what does that mean?'

'It simply means that there is no physical reason why Addy has behaved so . . . well, so strangely for lack of a better word. She seems to be a perfectly healthy five-year-old.'

'Seems to be?'

'Well, we both know that something's been going on in her head that we don't understand.' He paused. 'But as I said this morning, I think you've seen the last of her episodes.'

'So she doesn't seem depressed to you? Neurotic?'

'No. Not at all. She seems like a normal five-year-old who doesn't like strange people poking at her. And you were right. She seems perfectly at ease with Rachel.'

Judd was silent for a minute. Then he pressed. 'What if something else happens?'

Henry shrugged. 'Why not wait and see? At this point, you may not have anything to worry about.' He stood up. 'If I were you, Judd, I'd let sleeping dogs lie. If Addy's mother hadn't just died I might feel differently. I might even suggest you take her to see a neurologist. Consider the possibility of a brain tumor.'

'Jesus,' Judd said. 'A brain tumor? She's only five.'

'I know that,' he said. 'I just said if, Judd. If. I don't think for a minute she has a brain tumor. I think she's been making a difficult emotional adjustment that may or may not have something to do with Rachel. I know it's been a struggle but I have a feeling that from now on, Addy's going to be just fine.'

Judd took a deep breath, finally relaxing. 'Thanks, Henry.'

At that point there was a knock on the door and the nurse stuck her head in. 'Rachel just wanted me to tell you two that they're back. And Mrs Schiller is here.'

'We're almost finished,' Dr Adelford said. 'Just give me a few more minutes.'

She nodded and closed the door.

'One more thing, Judd,' Henry said.

'Shoot.'

'It's about the conversation we had this morning.'

'Priscilla?'

Henry nodded. 'I can't stress how important it is that she be kept out of this as much as possible.'

Judd nodded, but still there was something he wanted to make perfectly clear. 'Look, Henry,' he said. 'I know your concerns. And it's not that I'm unsympathetic to Priscilla. But I have two very vulnerable children and a very nervous, insecure wife to deal with. You said this morning that I was going to have to do a fancy bit of balancing, and no matter what Addy's problem is, that's the truth. If I told Rachel I was leaving Land's End with my children, I'm not sure she'd be able to leave her mother and go with me. And if she didn't, you might have more than just Priscilla Daimler to worry about.'

Henry looked startled. 'I'm sorry, Judd. Forgive an old man for being single-minded. I had thought Rachel was better.'

Now it was Judd's turn to be surprised. 'Better? What do you mean, better?' Clearly Henry knew something about Rachel that Judd didn't.

'I just meant that Rachel has always been a very sensitive young woman,' he answered in a matter-of-fact tone, but Judd wasn't fooled. Henry Adelford knew something about Rachel that he didn't want to discuss. Maybe he even knew why she had left Land's End.

'Maybe we can talk sometime,' Judd said, getting to his feet. And if the subject came up again, maybe he would push to discover the real reason Priscilla was so upset about Addy.

'Anytime,' Henry said, moving to the door, clearly anxious now for Judd to be gone. 'Good luck.'

'Thanks,' Judd said, but somehow he didn't think he'd need it. Somehow he felt that things were finally going to go his way.

Rachel and Addy were waiting in the outer office. 'Wait till Emma finds out I got an ice-cream cone,' Addy said on the way out the door. 'I bet she'll be real mad she decided not to come with us.'

Six miles away, Emma was sitting on the floor beside Priscilla Daimler's chair, reading aloud from *The Secret Garden*, and at this place in the story she made her voice take on a mysterious, hushed tone. 'The mournful sound kept her awake,' she read, 'because she felt mournful herself. If she had felt happy it would probably have lulled her to sleep. How it "wuthered" and how the big raindrops poured down and beat against the pane!' Emma took a breath.

'You read very well,' Mrs Daimler said. 'And you were very good to take time to come and read to me.'

'Oh, I didn't mind a bit,' Emma said quickly, and it was true. She'd always loved to read aloud. 'Shall I keep going?'

Mrs Daimler smiled but it was a tired smile. 'I'm afraid I must take my nap. But perhaps another time when neither of us has anything more pressing? I do want to hear the part again when Mistress Mary discovers the garden.'

Emma closed the book and got to her feet.

'You go down to the kitchen,' Mrs Daimler said, closing her eyes. 'Tell Kate or one of the maids to give you a glass of lemonade and a ginger cookie.' Then she waved her hand in dismissal.

'Thank you,' Emma said. She turned and was almost to the door when Mrs Daimler stopped her.

'When your father and stepmother get home, Emma, please tell Rachel I'd like to see her.'

'Yes, ma'am,' Emma said. 'Well, see you later.' She closed the door quietly behind her and stood for a minute in the hall outside, thinking about the strange lady inside. When Elizabeth had first asked her if she'd mind reading to her mother, Emma had been nervous.

'Mother can't see well enough to read for any length of time,' Elizabeth had said. 'But she loves books.'

Emma had hesitated. She'd only seen Mrs Daimler twice since they had arrived at Land's End and that had been enough to convince the little girl that Rachel's mother didn't like them. That she wished Addy and Emma had never come here. It wasn't anything she said, exactly. It was more the way she looked, with her eyes dark and hidden. Like a nun. Or a witch. And then later Mrs Daimler hadn't wanted them to watch *Gilligan's Island* on TV, only Daddy said yes.

All in all, Emma felt very uneasy about Rachel's mother, so when Elizabeth asked her, Emma had been reluctant.

'Don't worry,' Elizabeth had said. 'She won't bite you. She's really very sweet. I usually read to her in the afternoon, or sometimes one of the servants will. But I'm sure she'd be pleased if you would today.'

Emma frowned. What if the book was too hard for her? What if she stumbled over the big words and made a fool of herself?

'I noticed you were reading *The Secret Garden*,' Elizabeth said. 'Mother read it to us when we were very young. I know she'd love to hear it again.'

Emma brightened. 'Do you really think so?'

'I know so. Come on.' She took Emma by the hand. 'I'll take you upstairs. And later, if it doesn't rain, maybe the two of us can get in some riding. How does that sound?'

'Fantastic,' Emma said, feeling a little better. She guessed she could survive anything if the reward had to do with riding Clarissa. Besides, Elizabeth had asked it as a favor, and Emma certainly didn't want to let her new friend down.

But once inside Mrs Daimler's room she decided she'd made a big mistake. The room was huge, like a room in a museum, and Mrs Daimler didn't look a bit friendly sitting there in her chair by the window.

But when she spoke, her voice was soft. And sad, somehow. 'Come here, Emma,' she said. 'Let me look at you.'

Emma crossed and stood just to one side of the window, holding her book tight in her hands, shifting nervously from one foot to the other.

'For heaven's sake, child, hold still,' Mrs Daimler said, not unkindly. 'Someone would think you had to use the bathroom. You don't, do you?'

Emma was taken aback, then blushed, realizing to her horror that she did have to go.

'Well, hurry along,' Mrs Daimler said, reading her expression. 'Right through there.' She pointed.

Emma was gone only a few minutes, but when she came back Mrs Daimler had moved to a chair by the fire. 'It's cold,' she said. 'But I don't suppose you children ever notice. Children never do. It's only when their mothers are cold that they wear their sweaters.'

'I never get cold,' Emma said, then shivered, suddenly remembering how freezing cold it had been in the stables this morning. She pushed the thought aside. 'At least not usually.'

'And where is Addy this afternoon?' Mrs Daimler asked.

'Oh, she went into town with Daddy and Rachel.'

'Oh?'

'Yes. They took Addy to see Doctor Adelford.'

'Doctor Adelford?' she said, looking for a minute like a cat that had spotted a mouse in the tall grass. Then she seemed to realize that Emma was staring, so she smiled. 'And why did they take her to see Doctor Adelford?'

Emma hesitated. 'Because of what she did last night,' she said finally.

'Sit down here and tell me all about it.'

Emma settled herself on the floor beside Mrs Daimler's chair. 'Addy played the piano.'

'I know,' Mrs Daimler said. 'I heard her. But what does that have to do with the doctor?'

Emma looked up at the old woman. She wasn't sure she ought to say any more. Maybe Mrs Daimler would think Addy was queer.

'Don't worry, child,' Mrs Daimler said, and she sounded awfully tired. 'It can't be that bad.'

'Well . . . ' Emma hesitated, but then she decided it could do no harm to tell. After all, it was a silly thing Addy had done, but she hadn't hurt anyone. It wasn't as if she'd sworn or spit or burped at the table. 'Addy doesn't know how to play the piano.' Even as she said it she couldn't help but smile.

Mrs Daimler narrowed her eyes. 'What do you mean?' she asked quietly.

'I mean that Daddy said she played the piano, but I told him she didn't know how to.' And as Emma thought about it, again the picture of Addy banging away, pretending to play, struck her as funny. She giggled.

But Mrs Daimler didn't laugh, and Emma realized suddenly that she was the only one who thought what Addy had done was funny. Daddy didn't. Rachel didn't. And now, looking at Mrs Daimler's white, pinched face, it was clear that she didn't either.

'You mean she's never had any piano lessons?' Mrs Daimler was saying, her voice almost a whisper.

Emma shook her head. 'Never.' All at once, her heart began to pound. Something about what Addy had done was scaring people. But why? 'She really didn't play a song or anything. Not a real song.' She said it more to herself than to Mrs Daimler. 'Did she?' She looked up over the top of her glasses, suddenly frightened.

Mrs Daimler didn't say anything. She just sat still in her chair and breathed in and out hard, as if it really hurt. Then she said, 'I'm sure Addy was just playing a trick on us, Emma. I don't think it's anything to worry about.' She leaned her head back against the chair. 'So tell me, what have you brought to read?'

Now, almost an hour later, Emma stood outside in the corridor and breathed a sigh of relief. Reading to Mrs Daimler had been no problem at all. In fact, Emma decided that she wouldn't really mind doing it again sometime.

She turned away from the door and headed down the hall, intending to go straight to the kitchen for her lemonade and cookies, but somehow she got turned around. She went to the end of the corridor, through a passage, down some steps and to her surprise she found herself in a long gallery with walls covered with paintings.

It was very quiet here, and, all at once, she felt as if she were the only person alive in the whole house. Still, she wasn't going to let it bother her. She wasn't going to let herself get scared. She deliberately took her time, looking carefully from one side to the other.

Some of the paintings were of people, others of places, but she had never seen so many in anyone's house before. In museums maybe. Or once in one of her father's shows. But never in anyone's house. She stopped in front of a large painting of Land's End that looked real enough to step into. There were some people picnicking on the front lawn, dressed in old-fashioned clothes and for a minute Emma forgot where she was. She let herself pretend that she was walking across the velvety green grass and everyone was so happy to see her. She smiled to herself and moved on.

Further along she discovered a picture of Mrs Daimler when she was much younger, and across the hall one of Elizabeth on a magnificent black horse. And finally there was one of Rachel, looking so young, so beautiful in a blue lace dress with flowers in her hair.

Emma was about to go on when, all at once, she noticed something odd. Between Rachel's portrait and the picture of an old man with a wart on his chin, there was an empty place. There was a nail and everything but no picture. 'I wonder who's supposed to be there?' Emma said aloud and suddenly, for no reason at all, she was scared.

She took a few more steps, walking in slow motion, the only sounds the *pad-pad-pad* of her sneakers on the carpets, and the quick, shallow puffs of her own breathing. She stopped and put her hands to her mouth; she could feel her teeth chattering. There was something following her. Something small and very, very cold.

She listened, and faintly from behind she could hear

a soft, padding sound, like bare feet on a hardwood floor. And then she heard the high, thin voice of a child singing the same eerie lullaby she had heard once before. 'Who's there?' she whispered.

The singing stopped. But she knew someone was still there. Just like in the stable. Someone was watching her.

She stood frozen. Only her eyes moved. High on the wall by Rachel's portrait she could see a spider, slowly spinning its web. A little ball of dust stirred along the baseboard. And somewhere far down some distant corridor a door slammed shut.

Emma looked at her sneakers, wanting desperately to run, but not daring for fear that whoever was there would chase her. She held her breath. 'What do you want?' she whispered.

No answer.

She waited, not knowing what to expect, not daring to imagine. Still there was no sound, and, all at once, the feeling that someone was there began to fade.

Slowly she exhaled. 'There now,' she said finally and the sound of her own voice gave her some courage. 'Just go down to the kitchen and have a glass of lemonade.'

She squared her thin shoulders and very deliberately began to walk back the way she had come, whistling 'Yellow Submarine' as loudly as she could.

At the end of the corridor she paused, confused because she couldn't remember which way to turn. She was almost certain that this was the way she had come with Elizabeth, so she went up a few steps and turned again. She was breathing easier now because she knew that the main hallway was just at the end of this passage. She remembered for certain.

But when she got there she found herself at the

bottom of a steep, narrow stairway, and she realized with a sinking heart that she was lost. Still, she didn't dare go back.

Slowly placing one small foot in front of the other, she started up the stairs; curiosity mixed with dread, part of her wanting to see what was up there, the other part praying she'd meet one of the servants or that one of them would find her. But no one appeared.

Up the stairs she went. Slowly. Five steps, turn, five more. With a thumping heart she took the last three.

At the very top was a closed door, and Emma stopped short, staring, wondering what lay beyond, not sure she really dared to find out.

With a final gulp, she swallowed the lump in her throat, reached out with her right hand and touched the doorknob. It turned. And then Emma let out a huge sigh of relief. The door was locked.

'You scaredy cat,' she said, rattling the knob back and forth, full of renewed confidence. 'You see? There's nothing here that can hurt you.'

She was about to turn back when, all at once, something happened that made her eyes snap open wide in horror. From behind the door she heard the sound of small, shuffling footsteps coming closer and closer, then a whimper, and finally a soft, scratching sound, as if someone were trying to get out.

Terrified, Emma whirled around and half-running, half-falling she flew back down the stairs, stumbling at the bottom, crashing to her knees, her glasses flying off her nose.

And then, from above, incredibly, she heard the slow, creaking sound of the locked door swinging open.

Emma let out a screech and jumped to her feet. She

didn't bother to pick up her glasses. She ran as fast as her legs could carry her back the way she had come, her only thought now to get away as fast as she could before it caught her.

Down the dark hallways she flew, up steps, around corners, scared out of her wits, and then, all at once, she was at the top of the main staircase, and Elizabeth was coming up.

'Why, Emma,' Elizabeth said. 'Where've you been? I've been looking everywhere. And where are your glasses? And what on earth have you done to your knees?'

'I got lost,' Emma wailed. And something awful was chasing me, she wanted to say but she didn't dare.

Elizabeth put her arms around the little girl. 'Hush, sweetie. It's all right. It's an easy thing to do in this big old house. But you'll see. In no time at all you'll be able to find your way around here blindfolded.' She brushed away a tear and took Emma by the hand. 'Come and show me where you lost your glasses. Then we'll go down to the kitchen and have some fantastic chocolate chip cookies. Kate just took them out of the oven.'

Reluctantly, Emma led Elizabeth back the way she thought she had come and there, at the foot of a back stairway that led to the third floor, they found her glasses, just where she had dropped them. Emma sneaked a fearful look up the stairs. Above, she could see that the door was firmly shut, but she felt the hair stand up on the back of her neck anyway. It may be shut now, she thought, but it wasn't. I know it wasn't. 'What's up there?' she asked in a small voice.

Elizabeth shrugged. 'Just some big old empty rooms that no one ever uses anymore.'

'Does anyone ever go up there?'

'No, Emma. No one ever goes up there. Why do you ask?'

Emma thought for a minute, then decided she had to tell the truth. At least some of it. 'Because I heard someone. Behind that door. Just a few minutes ago.'

Elizabeth looked puzzled. 'That's odd. I don't even think the servants clean up there anymore.' She looked up the stairs, then laughed. 'Look, Emma,' she said, putting Emma's glasses back on the bridge of her nose. She pointed. 'I think we've found the culprit.'

Emma squeezed a reluctant glance up the stairs, and there, sitting at the very top was one of Rachel's cats.

'You rascal,' Elizabeth called. 'Come down from there. Don't you know any better than to scare little girls?' Then she turned to Emma. 'Now what do you say we go have some cookies?'

Emma nodded. Still she wasn't at all convinced that it had been the cat she'd heard. Cats can't open doors that are locked, she said to herself. But what if the door hadn't really been locked? What if she'd just been too afraid to open it?

With a sinking feeling in her stomach, she followed Elizabeth, wishing desperately that she could tell her about the child hiding in the stable, and then again in the gallery. Maybe Elizabeth would even know who it was. But she didn't dare ask. She was afraid that Elizabeth would think she was queer. Just like they all thought Addy was. And she knew she wasn't going to be able to say anything to her father. He'd just be more convinced than ever that she was imagining things.

But Emma knew she wasn't. Something was bad in this house. Something too awful to imagine. And what made her even more frightened was the fact that she seemed to be the only one who knew it.

A mile away, Addy sat between Judd and Rachel in the front seat of the car, and she and Rachel talked nonstop all the way back to Land's End, all about Maude and what a beautiful cat she was. Judd could tell that Rachel was trying her best to act natural. She told Addy where the two Persians had come from, and how much she'd loved them when they were kittens. She told Addy funny stories about what they had done when they were little, and how Priscilla had yelled at them for scratching her precious furniture. It was almost as if Rachel were talking about her real children.

Addy was delighted. 'We love cats, don't we, Rachel?' she whispered, as if they shared the greatest secret in the world.

'I do,' Rachel said, quietly. 'As far as I'm concerned, if a person doesn't like cats, something's got to be wrong with him.'

Addy couldn't agree more.

Judd listened, watching his daughter out of the corner of his eye. She was bouncing up and down on the seat beside him, so unconcerned, so normal. 'I just made up a poem,' she said. 'Want to hear it?'

'Sure.'

'It goes like this. Daddy's Addy is Addy's Daddy.' She giggled.

Judd smiled. 'Great poem, Daddy's Addy,' he said. 'Really great.' Henry's probably right, he thought. Whatever was bothering her, she's worked it out. And with each passing mile he felt more and more relaxed.

But as they curved up the road toward Land's End, it

began to rain, and as the weather grew more dismal, so did Addy. 'Let's not talk anymore,' she said finally, then leaned her head back against the seat and began to suck her thumb. She'd been doing a lot of that lately.

Normally Judd would have told her to stop. Certainly, had Emma been in the car, she would have. But as it was, Judd decided to say nothing. If a little thumb sucking gave small comfort, then so be it. For that reason he was a little chagrined when Rachel said, 'You shouldn't suck your thumb, Addy. It will make your teeth crooked.'

But Addy gave no indication that she'd heard. She simply stretched out her legs and continued to suck.

Rachel flushed and threw Judd a glance that said, 'See? I told you she doesn't like me.'

By the time they reached the drive leading up to the house, it was pouring, and Judd had to squint to see through the windshield. 'Damn wipers,' he muttered.

'You should've had them fixed,' Rachel said quietly.

'I know.' That didn't help.

'Maybe you should go around in back so we won't get wet.'

'Good idea,' he said. They took the drive that made a wide circle around the grounds to the back of the house, and Judd pulled the car up under the portico at the rear entrance.

'Everybody out,' he said, but for some reason no one moved. He looked from his wife to his child and back but they both seemed paralyzed. And then, as if she were in terrible pain, Addy pulled herself to a kneeling position on the seat, and turned toward Rachel. She put both hands over her face so Judd couldn't see her expression but he heard her voice. An infinitely sad little voice, so lost, so bewildered that it broke his heart.

'Why do you hate me?' she whispered. 'What did I do? Why am I always such a bad, bad girl?' And she began to cry. 'Please don't send me away,' she sobbed. 'Please.'

Hearing her, Judd was filled with outrage that someone had dared mistreat his child, and horror because for some insane reason the voice speaking so pathetically didn't sound anything like Addy.

'Addy,' Judd whispered. 'Dear God, Addy. What in the name of heaven is happening to you?' In desperation, he turned to Rachel for help only to find that she, too, had covered her face with her hands and was trembling like a leaf.

The air around him was electric with emotion. Clearly, Addy was devastated by some terrible, subconscious injury, but as he turned from his weeping child to his wife he sensed something that he never would have expected. Not bewilderment or even hurt, but anger. Inexplicable, teeth-clenching anger.

Torn between fear for his child and shock at Rachel's reaction, he reached out to touch her. 'Rachel?' he said, but she jerked away and still shaking, she began to fumble with the door handle.

'Take care of your daughter!' she exclaimed, and as suddenly as the anger had come, it was gone, leaving her sounding mortally wounded. 'I can manage.' She opened the door, then all at once, as if she had lost the will to move, she slumped back against the seat in a dead faint.

eight

Judd tucked Emma in, then turned to his younger daughter. He leaned over and kissed her gently on the forehead. 'Good-night, Ads,' he said. 'Sweet dreams.'

"Night, Addy's Daddy.' He could tell she was almost asleep. He stood looking down at her, wondering how this child could look so peaceful on the outside and yet inside be so full of turmoil.

'Daddy?' Emma whispered from the other bed.

'Yes, honey?'

'I heard you talking on the phone to Doctor Adelford. Is something wrong with Addy?' He could hear the anxiety in her voice.

He sat down on the edge of her bed. 'She's really missing Mommy,' he said quietly.

'But I miss Mommy, too.'

'I know. But you're older. And braver.'

Emma didn't answer for a minute, then she said, 'How come Addy doesn't know there's anything wrong with her? How come she thinks she's perfectly fine? And how could she hum a song she doesn't even know? Or play the piano?' And now, underneath the anxiety, he could hear the fear.

Judd shook his head. 'I don't know. We're just going to have to wait and see what the doctor says tomorrow.'

'Doctor Adelford?'

'No. A new doctor. Doctor Roth.'

Again she was silent and Judd could tell there was something more, something she wasn't saying. 'What is it, honey? What's bothering you?'

'I just wish . . . ' She stopped.

'You just wish what?'

'I just wish that Mommy was here.' She said it so quietly that he hardly heard it, and for some reason he didn't think it was what she had really wanted to say. He wondered suddenly if Emma knew more about this than she was telling. If maybe she was the key. After all, Emma knew her sister better than anyone else. Maybe she knew what Addy really thought about her mother's death. And about Rachel. He frowned, realizing for the first time that he'd never asked either of his children how they felt about his remarriage. Tomorrow he would. He'd ask them both. Maybe then he'd have some clue as to what was happening to Addy. 'Give your old Dad a kiss goonight,' he said.

Emma sat up, put her arms around his neck and hugged him tight. A little too tight? he wondered. 'Now lie down and go to sleep,' he whispered.

She snuggled down under the covers. 'Are you taking Addy to the new doctor tomorrow?'

Judd nodded.

'Can I go?'

He frowned. 'But I thought you were all set to go riding with Elizabeth.'

'I think I'd rather go with you, if it's okay.'

'It's okay, Emma. Now go to sleep.' He kissed her again, then left the room.

Emma lay in bed for a long time, thinking. Earlier, she and Elizabeth had been in the kitchen, eating cookies and drinking lemonade when the door had opened and Addy had bounced in.

'Hi, Emma,' she said, crossing to stand beside her sister. 'Guess what? I just had an ice-cream cone. With sprinkles.'

'Well, I'm having chocolate chip cookies,' Emma said. 'Where's Daddy?'

Addy pointed toward the door. 'Rachel had a fit or something,' she whispered, 'so Daddy's helping her in.'

Elizabeth looked over at Addy. 'What?'

'Rachel had a fit or something, so Daddy's helping her in.'

Elizabeth got up and was almost to the door when Judd came in, supporting an unsteady, ashen-faced Rachel. 'My God, what happened?' Elizabeth said.

'Rachel fainted.' Judd was still stunned himself, not only by what Addy had said, but by Rachel's reaction to it. He helped her to a chair, where she sat trembling, her eyes filled with tears. He looked across the table at Addy who was talking to her sister as if nothing unusual had happened. He couldn't believe this. His daughter had just had another freak-out and this time she hadn't even cried afterward. She'd simply hopped out of the car and skipped into the house, leaving Judd speechless and Rachel in a state of total collapse.

He sat down beside his wife and passed his hands over his eyes.

'What can I do?' Elizabeth was asking.

Judd shook his head. 'I'm not sure.'

Elizabeth went to her sister. 'Can I get you something? Should I call Henry?'

Rachel shook her head. 'I'll be fine.' But she didn't look fine. She was still trembling and little beads of perspiration had broken out on her nose and forehead. She seemed bewildered, as if someone had dealt her a terrible blow and she didn't know why. But Judd knew who had done it. Addy.

He reached over and took Rachel's hand. For a moment it fluttered in his hand like a wounded bird, then lay still. He frowned. He wanted to tell her that Addy hadn't meant what she said. The problem was he wasn't sure himself. How the hell are you going to explain this one, Henry? he wondered.

Elizabeth sat down on Rachel's other side, and her voice was low, reassuring, almost as if she were talking to a child. 'It's all right, Rachel,' she said. 'I'll take you upstairs. Mother will know what to do.'

Rachel shook her head and began to cry. 'Mother will say it's my own fault.'

'What is?' Elizabeth asked. She looked over at Judd, her eyes full of question.

Rachel covered her face with her hands. 'Everything,' she whispered. 'Everything. Just like always.'

As confounded as he was, Judd suddenly became aware that Addy and Emma were watching this whole scene, wide-eyed. His instinct was to get them out of the kitchen, but he knew he couldn't leave Rachel in this condition. 'Elizabeth,' he said, 'do you suppose you could find something for the girls to do? I need to talk to Rachel.' He threw her a pleading look.

For a minute she hesitated, clearly reluctant to leave her sister, then she jumped up. 'Of course,' she said. 'Come on, you two. You haven't seen the game room yet, I'll bet. I'll teach you how to shoot pool.'

As she led the two children out of the kitchen, Judd flashed her a look of gratitude, but he wasn't the only one who was grateful. Emma had never been so happy to get out of a place in her life. And now, lying in her bed thinking about it, she was more nervous than ever. Something bad was happening at Land's End, she just knew it. Daddy thought Addy was sick, but Emma wasn't so sure. She'd begun to wonder if what was wrong with Addy had something to do with that other child. The one who hummed. The one who watched, hidden, while Emma and Addy played. The one who had scared Emma so badly this afternoon. But who was she? And what did she want? Emma shivered. Could it be possible that she was a . . . a ghost? She had read plenty of stories about ghosts, and although Mommy had always told her they weren't true, Emma had never been able to forget a book she had read called *Ghosts of England*. In it there were real photographs showing spirits walking upstairs and all kinds of scary things. Maybe tomorrow she'd look through Mrs Daimler's library and see if she had any books that might help Emma understand what was happening to them.

But ghosts weren't her only worry. Earlier she had overheard her father telling Dr Adelford that Addy had said some weird things to Rachel, that she had begged Rachel not to send her away. Emma couldn't believe it. Why would Addy say something like that? It was almost as strange as Addy humming that day, or playing the piano.

Unless . . . unless somehow this was all connected. Emma had kept that thought all afternoon. She couldn't shake the feeling. She kept hearing Addy crying in that voice that wasn't Addy's. And the lullaby. That awful, spooky lullaby. How could Addy have hummed it when she didn't even know it? And then there was the piano playing. And now her saying these queer things to Rachel. Emma decided the time had come to talk this all over with Addy.

So, right after supper, when the two little girls were alone in their room playing 'Go Fish,' Emma said, 'What did you say to Rachel?'

'When?'

'After you went to the doctor's.'

'We talked about Maude,' Addy said. 'Do you have any Jacks?'

Emma looked down at her cards. She had two. 'Addy, did you cheat? Did you peek at my hand?'

Addy shook her head vigorously. 'Don't be a bad sport just because I'm a good guesser.'

Emma pulled the two cards from her hand and gave them to her sister. 'Well?' she said.

'Well, what?'

'Did you say something bad to Rachel?'

Addy looked up, curious. 'Like what?'

'Like she thought you were a bad girl and she hated you. And she was going to send you away?'

Addy chuckled. 'No way. Why would I say something dumb like that?'

Emma shook her head. 'I don't know.' She looked over the top of her glasses at her little sister and watched carefully to see if she was fibbing. 'Do you like Rachel?' she asked quietly.

'Sure. I told you, she's going to let me have one of Maude's kittens.' Addy began to wiggle. 'Let me see. Do you have any fives?'

'Addy,' Emma protested. 'Now I know you're cheating.'

Addy leaned back on her heels, laughing as hard as she could. 'You do have some fives, don't you, Emma! Ha, ha, I knew it!'

'I'm not playing with you anymore,' Emma said, her eyes filling with tears. She threw her cards down on the floor.

Addy looked at her sister, absolutely disbelieving. Emma was never a poor sport, not even when Addy really was cheating. She put her hands on her hips. 'Emma,' she wailed, 'no fair. I didn't peek at your cards. Why are you being so mean?'

With a major effort, Emma pulled herself together. Addy was right. She was being mean, but she couldn't help it. It was just that she felt so scared and confused about all the junk that was happening. And Addy wasn't any help. She didn't remember anything.

Emma knew that she needed to talk to someone about this. But who? Would Daddy listen, or would he just think she was crazy?

She looked over at her little sister and felt a stab of guilt. Here she was taking it out on Addy, and Addy didn't even know what was going on. Besides, she was only five.

Emma took a deep breath and picked up her cards. 'Okay,' she said, 'let's finish the game.'

Later, when Daddy had come to tuck them in, she'd

almost blurted out everything, about being watched in the stable, about the child who cried upstairs behind the door, and about Addy. But at the last minute she stopped herself. Daddy was smart, but she wasn't sure that he would be able to understand this. Or believe it. And if he didn't, then what would he think of her? Daddy was already really upset about Addy. She guessed he didn't need to be upset about her, too. Besides, he thought Emma was being so brave. He even said so, so she guessed she'd have to be. She rolled over onto her stomach and buried her face in the pillow.

A cool breeze blew through the open window stirring the curtains as it passed. Outside she could hear the pounding of the waves on the sand, and for one minute she thought she heard it again. Someone crying.

'Stop it!' she shouted. She stuck her fingers in her ears and burrowed down under the covers until she couldn't hear a thing. But still she heard it. In her ears, in her head, in her bones. The sad, pathetic sound of that same child crying, only this time, as frightened as she was, it made Emma want to cry, too. So she did. Quietly, unheard, Emma cried without really being sure why. Was she scared or was she just sad?

'Emma?' Addy mumbled from the other bed. 'What's the matter?'

'Nothing,' Emma sniffed.

'Why are you crying?'

'I'm not.'

'Then how come I can hear you?'

'You're imagining.' She wiped her eyes on the corner of her sheet. 'Now go to sleep.'

''Night, Emma,' Addy said. 'I love you.'

''Night, Ads. I love you, too.' Then she lay stone still,

her eyes closed tight, holding her breath, and, all at once, she felt Addy's small hand slip into her own. She smiled. Addy had sneaked into bed with her to try to comfort her. 'You're a good little sister, Addy,' she whispered. She rolled over to kiss her good-night, then sat bolt upright, staring in horror and disbelief.

Across the way in the dim light she could see a mound that was Addy. Addy, still fast asleep in her own bed.

Emma sat paralyzed for one minute, her mouth open, her throat moving, but no sound came out. And then she began to scream.

Rachel was already in bed when Judd came in. He undressed quickly and got in beside her. He knew she wasn't asleep but she didn't move, nor did she speak. 'Honey?' he said softly. 'Are you okay?'

She nodded.

'I talked to Henry. He thinks I should take Addy to see a psychiatrist.'

No response.

'She didn't mean to hurt you, Rachel,' he said. 'She doesn't even remember saying a word. Surely you must believe that.'

There was a moment of silence, but when she finally spoke her voice was deadly calm. 'Whether she knows it or not,' she said, 'Addy's going to destroy us. She's going to take you away from me.' It wasn't a reproach. It was a simple statement of fact.

Judd pulled her to him and held her. 'That's the craziest thing I've ever heard. There's nothing in this world that means more to me than you do.'

She looked up at him, her eyes full of tears. 'Then

send them away.' Not a command. Not even a request. It sounded like a prayer.

He felt a sudden wrench of helplessness, as if he were trapped in an invisible web, unable to change what was going to happen, remembering only how much he loved her. 'Dear God, Rachel,' he said. 'You know I can't do that.'

She flinched, as if he had slapped her, then turned away, but not before he saw her expression change. The desperate look vanished, leaving one of grim determination. 'I know,' she said. 'But I had to ask.'

Judd got out of bed and went to stand by the window. He was stunned. Rachel was convinced that Addy hated her, that she was a threat to their marriage, and no matter what Judd said, she still believed it. She wanted him to send his children away. But why? What was she thinking of even to suggest such a thing? Sweet hell, he thought. Sweet bloody hell.

He looked out across the moonlit lawn that stretched down toward the sea and wondered what in the world, if anything, he could do to fix things.

All at once, he heard a soft rustle just behind him. He turned to find his wife standing there, and with one fluid motion she threw herself into his arms. 'It's all right, Judd,' she said through clenched teeth. 'Everything's going to be all right. I promise.'

He held her at arm's length, tipping her chin up with his hand, forcing her to look at him. 'What's going on here, Rachel?' he asked. 'Why did you ask me to send the children away?'

For a long moment he watched her, searching for something in her expression that might help him understand, and what he saw astonished him. The pain and the sadness were gone, leaving only a look of absolute resolve. But even as he was marveling at this new strength, she disintegrated, collapsing against him, burying her face against his shoulder. 'It's Mother,' she said. 'Emma told her that Addy didn't know how to play the piano. And it made Mother crazy. Now she wants you and your children to leave Land's End.'

Judd was speechless.

Rachel pulled away and stood staring out toward the sea. 'That's what she wants. But, for once, she isn't going to have her way.' Again the sound of determination, so uncharacteristic, so unexpected.

Judd found his voice. 'But why is she so upset? Addy's problem doesn't concern her in any way that I can see.'

She sucked in a breath and her next words, so quiet, were full of sadness. 'Because, for once, Mother agrees with me. She sees Addy as a threat to my well-being. She doesn't want me hurt ever again and she thinks you're going to hurt me.' She sounded tired, but for once she didn't sound beaten. 'She doesn't want Addy and Emma here. She doesn't want you here either.' She paused and when she spoke again there was a hint of triumph in her voice. 'I talked to her for a long time, and I think she finally understands. If you go, I go, too. I won't let her destroy my happiness ever again.' She straightened her shoulders, and he could almost feel her digging in her heels. 'I don't think Mother is going to make any more requests where you and the children are concerned.'

He held her then, saying nothing, but feeling a huge measure of pride in her for being able to stand up to her mother. And a deeper anger at Priscilla Daimler for having been so cruel. Had she no understanding of her daughter at all? In the morning he was going to pay that lady a visit, and dying or not, she was going to have to answer some questions.

Judd bent over and kissed his wife, feeling the soft curve of her body against him, feeling her warmth. 'I love you, Rachel,' he whispered. 'No one can ever change that, no matter what.'

She let out a long sigh, then began to move against him with that slow, irresistible sensuality of hers. 'Make love to me,' she whispered, her voice husky, promising infinite pleasure.

Judd lifted her as effortlessly as if there were no substance to her, and carried her to the bed. He had only one thought now: to lose himself in her, to let her ease his pain.

But his passion was short-lived, for in the next instant, from the neighboring room, there came a series of high, bloodcurdling screams.

For the next hour he sat on the edge of Emma's bed, calming her, reassuring her that it had all been a bad dream, until finally she fell into a fitful sleep.

In the other bed, Addy slept like an angel, smiling. Next door, Rachel lay on her back, eyes closed tight, but she wasn't sleeping. Her breasts rose and fell rapidly, and her hands clenched into tight fists at her side.

Outside, somewhere far across the tidewater, a dog howled. And toward morning it began to rain.

nine

First thing in the morning Judd let it be known that he wanted to see Priscilla, but by eleven she still hadn't sent for him. Elizabeth said she wasn't feeling well. 'Why are you so anxious to see her?' she asked. She and Judd were standing on the breakwater, watching Rachel rig the sails on her boat.

Over breakfast, she had told Judd without warning that she was going to spend the day sailing, and like so many other things about Rachel, it had come as a complete surprise. He had always thought that she hated the water, but watching her now, he could see that she was no stranger to the sea.

He glanced over toward the boathouse, where Emma and Addy were sitting on the dock, paddling their feet. 'Did you know that your mother wants us to leave Land's End?'

Elizabeth looked shocked. 'Who told you that?'

'Rachel.'

'I can't believe it,' she said. 'Why would Mother say

such a thing? Ever since she found out about her cancer, her remaining goal in life was to have Rachel come home. And now you're telling me she wants you all to leave?'

'She doesn't want Rachel to leave,' he said. 'Just us.'

Elizabeth frowned. 'Did Rachel say why?'

'She said that Priscilla sees Addy as a threat to our marriage. And she wants to save Rachel from any more pain.'

For a minute Elizabeth was silent and when she finally spoke she sounded sad. 'But how could your leaving possibly achieve any such thing? Rachel adores you.'

Judd shrugged. 'Maybe Priscilla views me as competition,' he said quietly.

Elizabeth was silent for a minute, as if measuring her words. 'If I were you, Judd,' she said finally, 'I'd check this all out with my mother.'

'I intend to.'

'Throw me that length of rope,' Rachel called to Judd from the deck, 'and then hop aboard.'

Judd hesitated. 'How long are you going to be out?' he asked, picking up the rope, tossing it to her.

'Oh, only a couple of hours. Just down to Kennebunkport and back,' she said, looking up at the sun. She laughed. 'As long as the fog doesn't roll in and swallow us up.'

'But I have to take Addy to Portland at one o'clock,' he said.

Her face fell. 'I forgot. Oh, well, don't worry. Another time.' She blew him a kiss. 'You go along with Addy.' She didn't wait for him to answer. She turned away, steering the boat along the breakwater and out toward the open sea.

'Be careful,' he called, feeling suddenly uneasy. He

wondered if Rachel had really forgotten about Addy's appointment with Dr Roth. Or if she'd been testing him and somehow he had failed. Could it be possible that Priscilla was right? That he and his children would end up causing Rachel untold pain? He sighed. Why, he wondered, did his wife have to be so fragile, so easily bruised? Please don't let anything happen to her, he prayed. Please.

'She'll be all right,' Elizabeth said, reading his thoughts. 'Rachel is as comfortable on the sea as she is on the land. Peter taught her everything there is to know.'

'Peter?' Judd tried to remember where he had heard that name before. 'Who's Peter?'

Elizabeth went pale. 'Oh, just someone we used to know,' she said quickly. She turned and began to pick her way across the rocks toward the boathouse. 'Let's go back to the house, shall we? Maybe Mother has put in an appearance.'

He called to Addy and Emma and together the four of them made their way back up the path toward the house.

At the top of the bluff, Judd turned back but Rachel's boat was only a small speck on the horizon, a speck being blown away by the wind, and for one terrible moment he felt as if he'd lost her.

Then Addy spied one of the cats, and with a squeal she was off up the path. 'Come on, you guys,' she called. 'Maybe we can catch her.'

They followed the cat along the bluff and Addy had almost caught up with her when suddenly she disappeared behind one of the hedges. Addy flopped to her knees, her face a picture of disappointment. 'Oh, Maude,' she wailed. 'Please come back.'

'She must've gone down to the old summerhouse,' Elizabeth said, pointing past the hedge toward the thicket beyond.

Judd stopped beside her, staring. This was the spot where he had noticed the abandoned path the day before. 'What's the old summerhouse?' he asked.

'It's where Rachel and I used to play. But no one uses it anymore.'

'I can see why,' Judd said. 'It looks almost impossible to get to. Unless you can fly.'

Elizabeth tipped her head to one side, considering. 'I've always wondered why Mother let it get so overgrown,' she said. 'Odd.'

'My thought exactly.'

'Oh, well,' she said. 'No point trying to figure out why Mother does what she does.' She turned to Emma. 'While we're in the neighborhood, do you want to go down and say hello to Clarissa?' She held out her hand.

Emma hesitated.

Judd frowned. Emma had been a bundle of nerves all morning, and he knew it was because of that awful nightmare she'd had. 'Go along, Emma,' he said. 'You know horses always make you feel better.'

Emma nodded but he could tell that she was still uneasy.

'But don't stay too long if you want to go to Portland with Addy and me.'

'I won't,' she said quietly. 'And don't worry. I won't go into the stable.' The last she said almost to herself. Then she turned down the path, following Elizabeth.

Judd raised an eyebrow. That was a funny thing to say. Why should he care if Emma went into the stable?

Still puzzled, he took Addy by the hand and together they made their way back to the main house.

'Well, for one thing, Addy wants to know if they have mixed-berry yogurt in Heaven, because it's the only kind her mother likes.' Dr Roth leaned back in his chair and took out a crumpled pack of Camels. He was a heavy-jowled man with watery, brown eyes, dressed in a suit as ill-fitting and crumpled as his cigarette pack, but Judd had liked him instantly. Dr Roth hadn't much going for him in the looks department, but when he first spoke to Addy, his manner was completely disarming. It was clear that he genuinely liked children and they liked him. 'Do you mind if I smoke?'

Judd shook his head.

'Most people do, you know,' the doctor said. 'Can't say I blame them. Some even question my ability to practice psychiatry. That old idea that if you can't help yourself how can you help anyone else?' He shrugged. 'Maybe they're right. But I keep trying.' He smiled. 'Anyway, let's talk about Addy. The reason I mentioned the yogurt was because it's one indication that Addy has accepted the fact of her mother's death. At least on the face of things.' He lit up, took a deep drag, then began to flip through some papers on his desk. 'Notes I took while I was talking to your daughter,' he said, pulling out one sheet. 'For instance she seems to have a very accurate understanding of the permanency of her situation. Which is a giant step for an adult, never mind a child.'

'You mean she realizes that Nicole is dead.'

'More than that. To some children, "dead" means being just asleep somewhere. Hiding in a closet perhaps, or under the bed. But Addy seems to understand the concept of "gone away forever." For some kids that's a tough nut to crack. Some insist that they can see the dead person, talk to him, play with him.'

'So you don't think she's doing these weird things to please her mother, hoping she'll come back?'

'I doubt it very much, Mr Pauling.'

Judd took a deep breath. 'So what do you think is wrong with her?'

The doctor put his cigarette in the ashtray and crossed his hands over the bridge of his nose as if he were praying. 'First, if you'll bear with me for a minute, I'd like to explain a few things you may or may not already know.' He put one hand down on the desk, palm up. 'Here we have the average five-year-old. On the whole a nice little person. Honest, direct, doesn't ask much, doesn't give much. What does he like to do best? Play. Simple. What's he afraid of? The dark. Maybe thunder. Big dogs.'

'Ghosts?' Judd asked, then wondered why. It wasn't Emma they were talking about. It was Addy.

'Oddly enough, no. Not ghosts. At least not to any great degree. Ghosts are too nebulous for most five-year-olds. If Addy were a little older, or even a little younger, I'd say sure. But not right now.' Dr Roth mashed the butt in his ashtray and lit another. 'Would you like to know what frightens the average five-year-old the most?'

Judd nodded.

'Loss of mother. The dread of abandonment.' He paused. 'Your little Addy lives in a here-and-now world. She isn't an explorer, she isn't interested in opening new frontiers. She likes the familiar. The routine. Her own chair at the table. Her bed. The corner of the yard where she always plays house. Her street. Her school. You get the idea.'

'And now it's all gone.'

'All gone. I'm saying this not because I know yet what's troubling her. There are a multitude of possibilities. I'm telling you these things to help you understand the depth of Addy's loss. It's not unusual that the child is experiencing distress. The question is, how deep does it go, and what are we going to do about it?'

Judd took a notebook from his jacket pocket. 'You don't mind if I take some notes myself, do you? I have a much better chance of remembering all this later on if I can see it in writing.'

'Write away.' Dr Roth ground out his cigarette and leaned back in his chair. 'Now. Let me tell you what I know so far about Addy Pauling.' He riffled through his papers, reading as he went. 'She shows no physical signs of depression or anxiety. She doesn't fidget. Doesn't bite her nails. Doesn't pick her nose. She's alert, answers directly. She's very excited about the new kitten that's on the way. She loves tuna fish sandwiches. But hold the celery. Sometimes she had to scold her mother for forgetting. She sleeps well.' Dr Roth looked up. 'Does she? Any frequency of nightmares, that kind of thing?'

Judd shook his head, again remembering last night's episode with Emma. 'No. Not Addy.'

The doctor continued. 'She knows her letters, and she's frantic to learn how to read. But even so, she loves to have her sister read to her.' He looked up again. 'You might try reading to her yourself. Maybe set up a routine time each day. Something she can count on. But I'm getting ahead of myself. Back to the sleeping. Does she wet the bed?'

'No. At least never when she's been with me.'

Roth nodded. 'She told me quite indignantly that only babies wet their beds, and she, after all, is nearly six.' He

111

paused. 'Still, you might ask Emma about it.' He flipped through a few more pages. 'Thumb sucking? She tells me she used to, once in awhile, but she assured me that she was giving it up, that I didn't need to worry about it.'

Judd smiled. 'So she says. But that's one thing I've noticed more of lately. Her mother told me months ago that Addy had made real progress in breaking the habit. But now she seems to have picked it up again.'

'Not alarming. If that were all we had to deal with, I'd be out of business.' He went back to his notes. 'She likes to sing, and isn't the least bit shy about performing. She sang me a wonderful little song about a puppy named Rags, complete with all the hand motions.' He sat back and lit another cigarette. 'So all in all, Addy seems like a very normal, happy five-year-old.'

'Did she have anything to say about her mother? Or Rachel?'

Dr Roth shrugged. 'Nothing spectacular. Neither one of the topics seemed to elicit the slightest hostility or fear. She doesn't seem angry at her mother for dying. Nor is there any evidence that she blames herself. She's just a very sad little girl when she talks about your ex-wife. On the other hand, she doesn't seem to have any strong feelings one way or another about Rachel. Except to say that she has two cats and she's very pretty.'

He stood up and crossed to the window. From there he could see Addy and Emma playing on the swing set in his backyard. 'A very nice little girl,' he mused, then turned back to Judd, frowning. 'And as I said before, basically a very honest, direct five-year-old. And therein lies the dilemma.'

Judd waited.

'From what you've told me, these episodes of hers

have been extreme. Whatever inspired her to play a piano without any musical training whatsoever, whatever is making her behave toward your wife in such a hostile fashion, it isn't the result of a simple reaction to the death of her mother, I'm afraid. It goes far deeper. And this amnesia thing. That's usually a defense. Her way of coping. The fact that she doesn't remember – and I don't think for one minute that she's lying – is symptomatic of serious psychological distress.'

Judd felt sick. 'So what does that mean?'

'Well, it depends on whether subconsciously Addy is feeling angry, or guilty, or frightened, or all three. If it's anger, then who is she angry at? You? Her mother? Your wife? Or perhaps she's angry at herself. And feeling guilty for being angry.' He sat back down. 'Another consideration. Has she been able to share her grief with anyone? With her sister perhaps. But has she shared it with you? Or does she see your wife as an impediment to that sharing? Does she feel that you really don't care that her mother is dead?'

'I don't have any answers for you,' Judd said quietly. 'None. And for that, I'm the guilty one.'

'I'm not here to lay any blame, Mr Pauling. Perhaps this has nothing to do with you at all. Perhaps Addy has some bizarre notions about her mother that are completely irrational. Children are great theory builders. They can construct the most elaborate defenses against their subconscious fears. Unfortunately, we won't know what's going on with Addy until we do some real digging.'

'What do you want me to do?'

'I'd like to see Addy again next week. That is unless something else happens to alarm you. In the meantime,

113

I want you to spend as much time with her as you can. Watch her. See if she seems restless. More withdrawn some times than at others. Question her gently. Gently, Mr Pauling. About her mother. Try to let her work through her grief. Listen to see if she blames herself. And whatever you do, don't try to offer her any answers. Listen but don't counsel. That's my job. Take notes. And Mr Pauling . . .'

'Yes?'

'Hug her a lot.' He looked at his watch. 'I hate to end it here,' he said, 'but I have another appointment at three-thirty.'

Judd stood up and held out his hand. 'Thank you, Doctor Roth.'

The doctor's hand was dry and scaly. 'I'm sorry I couldn't be more specific, Mr Pauling. But it's early in the game. I do think you've caught this thing before it's had a chance to do any permanent damage.'

'I hope you're right. Until next week then.' Judd turned and was almost out the door when the doctor stopped him.

'I'd really like to talk to Emma next time, too, so please bring her along. I think we may find that she has a lot of our answers already.'

Emma was standing on the floor of the glider in Dr Roth's backyard, pumping furiously, while Addy sat on one of the side seats, holding on for dear life. 'Not so hard, Emma,' she said. 'I'll fall.'

'You won't,' Emma said, but she eased off a little. 'It's no fun if we just go slow.'

'It is for me,' Addy said.

'How did you like the doctor?'

'He looks sort of like a lizard,' Addy said.

'But is he nice?'

'He has a dog. And a son named Spider.'

'Did he tell you what's the matter with you?'

'There's nothing the matter.'

'Did he say?'

Addy shook her head.

'Did he ask you if you were afraid of ghosts?'

'No. But he asked me if I sucked my thumb and I said no.'

'Oh, Addy, you fibbed.'

'I did not. I stopped.'

'When?'

'Yesterday. And I didn't even suck my thumb last night.'

'Did so.' Emma shuddered when she thought about last night. That small hand that didn't belong to anyone.

'Did not. Besides I'm not going to do it anymore. Only babies suck thumbs.'

'What else did he ask you?'

'Oh, lot's of stuff. He wanted to hear a song. And I did a puzzle. And I drew a picture of our family. Only I had to put Mommy up in Heaven.' She looked up at the blue, cloudless sky. 'What keeps her up there, Emma? How come she doesn't fall down?'

Emma looked up. 'Because she can fly, that's why. When you die and go to Heaven you can fly. Like the angels and God and everyone.'

Addy nodded solemnly. 'I don't think Doctor Roth knows about that stuff. He kept asking me if I knew where Mommy was. And did I ever see her.'

'How could you see her if she's dead?'

Addy shrugged. 'Maybe he thinks Mommy is a ghost.'

Emma opened her eyes wide. 'Do you think Doctor Roth believes in ghosts?'

Addy considered. 'Maybe. He kept asking and asking about dead people. He even wanted to know if Mommy ever talked to me, told me to do things.'

Emma felt her heart jump into her mouth. If Dr Roth believed in ghosts, then maybe here was some hope. Maybe he was someone she could ask about the ghost at Land's End. If it was a ghost. Maybe he wouldn't laugh, or tell her she was just imagining.

'Emma,' Addy yelled, 'you're pumping too hard!'

'I'm sorry, Addy,' Emma said and she slowed down, but her heart was still pounding. She was wondering if they were going to come here again. And if they did, how could she ask Dr Roth about ghosts without anyone hearing?

Moments later, her problem was solved when her father came into the backyard and told them it was time to go. 'You can swing again next time,' he said. 'Dr Roth has a few more things he wants to talk to you two about, so he wants us to come again next week.'

'He wants to talk to me, too?' Emma asked, almost breathless.

Judd nodded, looking hard at his daughter. 'Are you okay?'

Emma jumped off the glider. 'I'm fine, Daddy,' she said. 'Just fine.' She didn't know what the doctor wanted to ask her and she didn't care. All she knew was that maybe he believed in ghosts, and if he did, then maybe he could help her before something terrible happened at Land's End.

ten

By the time he got back to Land's End, all Judd wanted was a stiff drink, a hot shower and some quiet time with Rachel and the kids. But it was not to be. Priscilla had invited Henry Adelford, the Elliots, and a spinster named Jane Bogner in for a light supper and a few hands of bridge.

Judd had met them all earlier, and had found them pleasant enough, but tonight, besides spending some time with his family, he'd hoped to find a chance to talk to his mother-in-law. That was not to be, either. Priscilla stayed secluded in her room until after her guests had arrived, and didn't put in an appearance until supper was about to be served.

Rachel was almost as animated as she had been the night of the party, with one major difference. She barely spoke to her mother. On the other hand, Priscilla was making every effort to please her daughter. Clearly, she was penitent, Judd decided, and he wondered whether he needed to say anything to Priscilla at all. It seemed clear that for once in her life Rachel was in the driver's seat. Still he decided it wouldn't hurt to find out why his mother-in-law felt Addy was such a threat, and why she wanted him out of Rachel's life as well.

At supper, Judd found himself seated between Elizabeth and Henry. 'How did your appointment go?' Henry asked in a low tone.

'As well as could be expected,' Judd said. 'I liked him very much.'

'He's one of the best. Used to be on the staff at the Children's Hospital in Boston.'

'Do you play bridge?' Priscilla interrupted and Judd couldn't help but marvel at her tone. It was as if she were one of his most ardent admirers.

'I haven't played in years,' he said. 'Not since college.'

'That's all right, darling,' Rachel said quietly. 'You and I will show them all.'

Priscilla looked at her daughter with veiled eyes, her face a mask, revealing nothing. 'But I'd hoped you and I would be partners, Rachel. The way we used to be.'

'You and I have never been partners, Mother. Not really.' Rachel spoke softly, but there was an edge to her voice. 'Partners are equals.'

There was a moment's awkward silence, then Elizabeth jumped in. 'Rachel went sailing today, Henry. In *Windward*.'

'Good girl,' Henry said. 'Does she still handle as well as ever?'

'Better,' Rachel said, her face lighting up. 'I'd forgotten what a challenge it is to be out all alone on the ocean. It's almost like a religious experience.'

'You sound like Peter,' Margot Elliot laughed.

Rachel's face froze. She turned to Judd, pointedly

118

ignoring the woman. 'Will you come out with me tomorrow? If the weather holds? Please? You'd love it, I just know you would.'

Judd hesitated, remembering Dr Roth's words. Spend as much time with Addy as you can. 'I'm sure I would,' he said. 'I'll bet the kids will love it, too.'

Rachel's smile faded. 'But Judd, I'd hoped we could . . .'

'Rachel!' Priscilla spoke only the single word, but it was like a shot from a rifle, sharp, explosive.

Slowly, Rachel turned and stared at her mother. 'Don't say another word, Mother,' she said, her face grim, her eyes flashing. 'Not another word.'

Priscilla stared back, silent.

For what seemed an eternity, the two women stayed locked in some mysterious battle of wills, neither speaking, neither seemingly concerned about anyone else in the room. And finally, astonishingly enough, it was Priscilla who capitulated. She looked away. 'Why don't we have our coffee in the library,' she said, her voice shaking. 'I'll have Clarence get a fire going. There seems to be a chill in the air tonight.' She looked around the table. 'Or am I the only one who noticed?'

Henry stood up and went around the table. He pulled her chair back and helped her to her feet. 'You're not alone, my dear,' he said. 'It is chilly. But then evenings in June often are.' He didn't look at Rachel, but somehow Judd had the feeling that he was really angry with her.

With infinite tenderness he took Priscilla by the arm, and Judd couldn't help but notice how carefully he handled her, as if she were the rarest piece of porcelain. Could it be, he wondered, that Henry Adelford was in love with Priscilla Daimler?

119

He watched as Rachel's mother took the doctor's arm. Without a backward glance, the two left the room, the rest of the company trailing after, leaving Judd to wonder who, if anyone, had really won the battle.

'What was that all about?' he whispered to Rachel as they crossed the foyer.

'Nothing,' she said. 'Mother forgets that I am no longer a child to be silenced with a flick of her tongue.' She went into the library.

Judd followed, thinking again what a strange past these two women must have shared to cause such devotion at times, such open, such inexplicable hostility at others. He was definitely going to have to talk with his mother-in-law, no matter how unpleasant it might be.

Judd had never seen such rotten cards in his life, and for that he was eternally grateful. It meant that he didn't have to worry about making any stupid mistakes bidding in a game that Rachel and the Elliots seemed to be playing for blood.

Nor was there any casual conversation at either table. Except when they were bidding, no one spoke, and again Judd was grateful. He wasn't in the mood to make small talk. He had too much on his mind.

Addy had gone to bed without a murmur, falling into a deep, peaceful sleep almost as soon as her head hit the pillow. But Judd knew that Emma wasn't going to be so lucky. She'd hemmed and hawed, making every attempt to avoid the inevitable, that awful, scary moment when he would turn out the light and leave her alone. Long after Addy had fallen asleep, he sat on the edge of Emma's bed, telling her stories about when he was little, stories she'd always loved to hear.

But tonight he could tell that Emma wasn't paying attention. She seemed skittish. She kept looking past his right ear toward the window, and every little sound made her jump.

In the end, he'd left the door open and the light on in the adjoining bathroom. He didn't make an issue of it. He simply left it on, hoping it would give Emma enough peace of mind to allow her to fall asleep.

'Lay down your hand, Judd,' Rachel was saying. 'We're in it for four hearts.'

Judd put his cards on the table. 'Sorry I'm not more help,' he said. He pushed his chair back. 'And while you're struggling here, I think I'll check on the kids.' He stood up and was almost to the door when it opened, and there, just outside, stood Emma in her nightgown, teeth chattering, big, quiet tears rolling down her cheeks.

Everyone stared.

'Another bad dream?' he asked gently.

She shook her head. 'Daddy,' she said, her voice quavering, 'I can't find Addy. She's not in her bed. She's not in the bathroom. She's not anywhere at all.' She took a breath. 'And Daddy, her bed is all wet. I think she had an accident.'

Judd took her by the hand. 'It's going to be all right, sweetheart,' he said calmly. 'I'm sure she's just taken a wrong turn somewhere. We'll find her in no time.' But suddenly he wasn't so sure. He felt an unexpected stab of fear, and an irrational need to hurry. He dropped Emma's hand and walked quickly across the foyer, taking the stairs two at a time. He could hear Rachel and Emma following behind him but he didn't stop.

The door to the children's room was ajar, the light in the bathroom still on, and he could see at once that both beds were empty. 'Addy?' he called, scanning the room in a single glance. 'Where are you?'

Silence.

He crossed to Addy's bed. The covers were rumpled and in one motion he pulled them back. Emma was right. The sheets were soaked. Dr Roth's question came to him in a flash. 'Does Addy ever wet the bed?' And his own answer. An emphatic no.

He turned and headed toward the door at the same time Emma and Rachel appeared. 'Emma, you go with Rachel. Look in all the rooms in this wing. I'll check the main house.'

'I don't see what all the fuss is about,' Rachel said quietly. 'Addy obviously wet the bed and doesn't want anyone to know it. She's probably hiding somewhere.'

Judd frowned. That was the most ridiculous thing he'd ever heard, but all of a sudden he felt panicky. What if Rachel was right? What if Addy really had been afraid to tell anyone that she'd had an accident?

'Daddy, can't I come with you?' Emma whispered.

Judd hesitated but only until he saw the fear in his child's eyes. 'Sure you can. Come on, let's go.'

Rachel went in one direction, he and Emma in the other, down the dark corridors, opening doors on either side, calling Addy's name. But there was no answer. They checked every room on the second floor, then started down the main stairs. 'We'd better get some help,' Judd said. 'Maybe the servants can find her.'

He and Emma were halfway down when all at once he saw Priscilla Daimler standing at the bottom, staring up at them. Her face was half hidden in the shadow, but he could feel her fear. The air around her was electric with it. For some reason, his mother-in-law was terrified.

122

Slowly she came toward him up the stairs, and stopped, facing him, her face distorted, but she didn't speak. Then she took a deep, painful breath and continued up the stairs. At the top she turned and motioned him to follow.

Hand in hand, he and Emma went behind her down the main corridor, through the gallery, down another hallway, finally stopping at the foot of a steep, narrow stairway leading to the third floor.

Judd felt Emma jerk back, heard the sharp intake of breath. 'You okay?' he asked.

She nodded, but he could see that, like Priscilla, Emma was terrified. It suddenly occurred to him that they all were, but somehow he didn't think it was for the same reason.

He glanced at his mother-in-law who had stopped and was staring silently at a small, narrow door, almost hidden behind the stairs.

For a minute she didn't move, then with a trembling hand she lifted the latch and opened the door. 'Come out, child,' she breathed. 'No one's going to hurt you.'

Judd couldn't believe his ears. Did Priscilla really believe that Addy had crawled into this dark, musty cubbyhole? He bent over and peered into the dank recesses of the closet but he could see nothing past the steep angle of the stairway. 'Addy?' he said, incredulous. 'Are you in there?'

For a moment there was silence. Then to his astonishment he heard an almost inaudible whimper and a single word. 'Papa?'

Judd's jaw dropped. There *was* a child in there, cowering in the back of that dark, narrow crawl space, sobbing. But it certainly wasn't Addy. He squatted down. 'There's

123

nothing to be afraid of, little girl,' he said gently. 'Come out. No one's going to hurt you.'

Silence.

And then he became aware that Emma had knelt down beside him. Her head was cocked to one side as if she were hearing something he couldn't. 'Ads?' she called, tearfully. 'It's me. Emma. Come on out of there.'

'Emma, that's not Addy,' Judd whispered.

Emma turned and looked up at him through her tears, with the most peculiar expression on her face. It was full of reproach, as if he'd said something incredibly stupid. 'Yes, it is, Daddy. It's Addy.'

He stared at her, speechless.

'Addy?' she said again only this time her tone was sharp. 'I'm serious. You come out of there right this minute.'

And suddenly, to his great shock, from the recesses of the cubbyhole, he heard a soft, shuffling sound, and then a glassy-eyed Addy crawled out on all fours.

Judd swooped her up and cradled her against his shoulder. It was like hugging a rag doll. No resistance. No life. 'Sweetheart, what on earth happened?'

Addy didn't answer. She just lay limp in his arms, making a soft, sniffling sound.

Judd looked around to see Priscilla's reaction to all of this craziness, but she was gone. 'Jesus,' he said under his breath. 'Jesus Christ.'

With Emma trailing after, he carried Addy back to her room. Her bed had already been stripped and remade, and he lay her gently on the pillow. 'Get me a clean nightie, Emma,' he said. 'And a washcloth.'

Then as gently as he could, he sponged off his child and put on her fresh nightgown. She lay like a stone, as if she'd been drugged, and it wasn't until he was all finished and was tucking the covers up around her chin that she finally opened her eyes.

'Good night, Addy's Daddy,' she said. Her voice was sleepy but perfectly normal, and as if she hadn't a care in the world, she rolled over and fell into a deep, peaceful sleep.

Judd stood looking down at her, feeling an overwhelming urge to scream or cry or do something, anything that would explain, anything that would help his baby. Finally he turned away, and looked at Emma.

She seemed to be asleep but he bent over and kissed her anyway. Poor Emma, he thought. This isn't doing you any good, is it, what with all your fears about spooks and things that go bump in the night? And I guess I can't blame you. If I were ten years old, I'd be scared, too.

He was almost to the door when he heard her speak.

'Daddy,' she whispered softly. 'What's happening to us?' Quiet words but so full of fear that they exploded like bombs.

He went back and hugged her, trying to convey a confidence he didn't feel. 'Addy's just sad, sweetie,' he said. 'Just so sad.'

'About Mommy?'

'About Mommy.'

She lay her head against his shoulder, not speaking, but he could feel the tension in her. 'Is there something else, Emma?' he asked. 'Something you're not telling?'

She shook her head.

'You know if something's bothering you, you can talk to me, don't you?'

'Yes,' she said, but he had the most awful feeling that she didn't mean it.

125

He took a deep breath. 'Do you think you could talk to Doctor Roth?' he asked gently. 'Just in case there's something you can't talk to me about?'

She looked up at him with that same expression he had seen earlier. The one that said that he'd let her down. Somehow she'd been counting on him and he had failed her.

She was quiet for so long that he thought she had fallen asleep. He leaned over, kissed her, and was about to leave when she stopped him. 'Daddy, why did you think it wasn't Addy in there?'

Judd reflected for a minute. 'Well, I guess because I didn't think your sister would ever crawl into such a yucky place. Besides,' he said in a low voice, 'it didn't sound like Addy.'

'I know,' she said. 'But it was, all the same.'

'How did you know?' He didn't take his eyes off her face.

She stared up at him and he could see her battling with herself over something.

'Can't you tell me?' he asked.

She looked away. After a long pause she said, 'Do you like Doctor Roth?'

'Yes, Emma, I do.'

'Do you think he's smart?'

He nodded.

'Then maybe everything will be okay,' she said. 'Good-night, Daddy.'

'Good-night, Emma.' He kissed her and left the room, praying for all their sakes that the night would pass quickly. And without another incident.

Emma lay awake for a long time. There used to be a time when she loved to go to bed, to curl up snug as a

126

bug under her covers and make up stories that she was queen of all the animals, or that she could walk through mirrors. But no more. Now she felt as if she had to stand guard. But against what she wasn't sure.

Finally, in spite of her fears, she slept.

The night passed as night always does, and in the morning when Emma opened her eyes, she felt a great rush of relief to discover that it was daylight and nothing bad had happened. Not to her, not to Addy, not to any of them at all.

eleven

For the next four days, no one saw hide nor hair of
Priscilla Daimler except for Henry Adelford. She was
having one of her 'other times,' and when that happened
she would see no one, not even Rachel.

For Judd it came as a mixed blessing. He had wanted
to talk to his mother-in-law about Addy, to find out how
the hell she'd known where Addy had hidden that night,
but that was impossible, at least for now.

On the other hand, for four days now, life at Land's
End had been surprisingly pleasant. Almost normal
somehow.

The household staff was busy preparing for the annual
Summer Ball, traditionally held at Land's End on the
twenty-first of June. According to Elizabeth, however,
there had been no such gala for the past three years. Not
since Rachel had left. But last week, Priscilla had sent
down word that the custom was to be revived. Invitations
had been sent, extra staff put on, rooms opened and aired,
all kinds of people coming and going.

And in the face of all this chaos, Rachel was positively glowing. There was a reckless air about her, and an eagerness that Judd had never seen before. It was as if she had been waiting for this ball all her life and wasn't going to let one precious moment escape without wringing every drop of pleasure from it.

As for the children, these days had been halcyon. No episodes with Addy, no nightmares for Emma. After Addy's bed-wetting incident, Judd had been almost as concerned about Emma as he was about her little sister. But as each lazy, uneventful, summer day rolled by, he could see the pinched lines of tension fading from Emma's face and the purple smudges under her eyes disappearing.

Judd spent almost every minute with the two of them, taking walks, talking about things they liked and things they didn't, playing games. And Rachel seemed to understand how important this was to him because she left them alone, content to occupy herself with preparations for the ball.

He took careful notes for Dr Roth, but he didn't think anything he wrote was going to help diagnose Addy's problem. She talked a blue streak, but nothing she said seemed to be out of the normal range for a five-year-old. Although she got tearful when she talked about her mother, she seemed perfectly aware that Nicole was gone forever.

'I get sad sometimes,' she told him solemnly, 'because I can't see Mommy no matter how hard I try. But when I die and go to Heaven, then I'll see her. And she'll be so surprised because by then I'll know how to read.'

And later, when the three of them were sitting in the

sand at the edge of the surf, he asked her about Rachel. 'What do you think?' he said. 'Do you like her?'

'Sure I do,' Addy said, dribbling wet sand through her fingers onto her legs. 'She's so pretty that sometimes I could just marry her.'

'You can't marry her, silly,' Emma said, laughing.

'Why not?'

'Because she's a girl. Besides she's already married to Daddy.'

'Well then, I'll marry Elizabeth.'

'But she's a girl, too.'

Addy was not to be discouraged. 'Well then, I'll marry Daddy, and that's that.'

Emma rolled her eyes skyward. 'You can't marry him either, Addy. He's your own father. Besides you're too little to get married.'

Addy lost interest. She'd spied a sand crab scuttling along the beach. 'C'mere, crabby, crabby,' she said, and the two children followed it.

Judd watched them go, so unconcerned, so seemingly happy and free of anxiety, and he felt the tight coils of tension begin to loosen across the back of his neck. He looked down at his notebook and made an entry. 'Ten o'clock and all is well.' Then he gathered their things together and began to follow his children down the beach.

The next morning, Judd felt confident enough about his children's emotional stability to leave them at Land's End for a few hours while he and Rachel drove into Kennebunkport for lunch. She had begged him to take her, just to get away alone for a little while, and after much deliberation, he had agreed. He'd spent no time with her at all in the past few days, and neither of the children seemed to mind in the least when he mentioned

130

going. In fact they seemed surprised that he had even asked.

Besides, it wasn't as if he was leaving them alone. After all, Elizabeth and Priscilla were in the house, not to mention a full staff of servants.

'You can't be with them every minute of their lives,' Rachel had said. 'Besides, Addy finally seems to be adjusting. Not that I think she's any happier about me, but at least she's not performing.'

Judd had been surprised at Rachel's choice of words. Although he knew that Addy had been reacting to a combination of things, possibly Rachel among them, he thought 'performing' was a peculiar word to use. It suggested that Addy had known precisely what she was doing, and Judd didn't believe that for one minute. He'd been about to tell his wife just that when she tiptoed up and kissed him on the lips with breathtaking tenderness.

'I love you, Judd,' she said. 'You are the best husband anyone could ever have.'

At eleven o'clock that morning, Emma lay on her stomach in the game room, waiting for Addy to come back from the bathroom. They were in the middle of a game of Parcheesi and every time Addy started to lose she had to go to the toilet.

But Emma didn't mind. Not really. She had decided she could put up with almost anything her sister did as long as she did it like regular old Addy. And with each day that passed uneventfully, Emma, too, felt more and more like her old self. Her natural sense of optimism began to reassert itself, stifling her fears, and the reasoning part of her brain began to take control, forcing her imagination to grind to a halt. Nothing here was really wrong, she told herself. After all, if a ghost really did exist, it wouldn't simply come and go for no reason. It either was or it wasn't. Simple as that. Or so she told herself.

Last night she had even fallen asleep without the light on in the bathroom.

'Hurry up, Addy,' she called, then rolled over on her back and lay staring up at the ceiling. It was the strangest ceiling she had ever seen with fat little angels carved right into the plaster, some flying, others sitting around playing musical instruments.

She began to count, curious to see how many there were on this huge expanse.

Addy came in and flopped down on her knees. 'My turn,' she said, picking up the dice.

Emma didn't answer. She had counted forty-seven angels already and didn't want to lose track.

'Emma,' Addy said. 'I got a six and that puts me in the middle.'

'Hush. I'm up to fifty-four.'

'Fifty-four what?' Addy flipped over on her back next to her sister. 'What're you looking at?'

Emma pointed, making a mental note so she would remember where she had stopped counting. 'Look at that one,' she said, chuckling. 'It looks like Normy Barton.'

Addy giggled. 'Normy's fat.'

'He sure is,' Emma said.

'Is he having babies? Like Maude?'

'Boys don't have babies, silly,' Emma said, rolling over on her stomach, laughing hard. Addy really slayed her sometimes.

'How come?'

'Because boys don't have the right stomachs.'

Addy sat up and pulled up her shirt. 'I'm not having

132

a baby,' she said, then suddenly let out a squeal. 'There's Maude.' She pointed toward the door that led to the back of the house. She jumped up and headed in the same direction.

'Addy, where're you going?'

'Let's follow her,' Addy said, eyes wide. 'Maybe she's going to have her kittens.'

Emma scrambled to her feet. That *would* be exciting.

Together the two children made their way down the back hallway that led to the kitchen and the servants' quarters beyond in search of the cat. They had lost sight of her, but before they had a chance to despair, they turned a corner and there she was, sitting at the foot of the kitchen stairs, licking herself.

'Hi, Maude,' Addy whispered, approaching the cat on tiptoe. But just as she came within petting distance, Maude turned and waddled up the stairs. Normally she could easily have eluded them, but in her present condition the children had no trouble keeping up with her.

Maude took her own sweet time, sidling down the corridors, stopping every now and then to rub her head on a piece of molding or to lick herself. Once, Addy actually got close enough to pet her before she continued her slow stroll through the house.

Addy was keeping both eyes on Maude, but Emma was intrigued by what she was seeing along the way. Most of the bedroom doors were open, the rooms being aired out in anticipation of the arrival of the weekend guests, and for the first time since they had come to Land's End, Emma had a chance to really look around without feeling nervous. Having Addy and the cat meandering along just ahead of her gave her all the confidence she needed.

Suddenly she stopped short. 'Addy,' she breathed, looking in one of the open doors. 'Look at this!'

Addy was reluctant to let Maude out of her sight, but at this point the cat sprawled out on the hall runner, warming herself in a spot of sunshine streaming in from the window at the end of the corridor.

Addy turned back and looked. 'Wow,' she said.

Taking very small, hesitant steps, the two children inched their way into the room. It was a large room and dark, with a huge four-poster bed and bookcases all along the walls. But what had attracted Emma's attention, and now held the two spellbound, was the massive case on one side of the fireplace, displaying the head of what once had been a real, live horse.

Neither of them spoke for a minute. Then Addy wrinkled up her nose. 'Ugh. Who do you suppose did that?'

Emma was speechless. She'd never seen such a sight in all her life. The horse was looking right at her and he seemed so sad that Emma almost felt like crying. 'Maybe he just died,' she said. 'And somebody loved him so much that they stuffed his head.'

'Who would ever want to do something like that?' Addy said, shaking her head slowly back and forth. 'We loved Mommy but we didn't stuff her head.'

'That's different, Addy,' Emma said, although to tell the truth she wasn't sure why. If she had a horse and he died, she'd never stuff him no matter how much she loved him. She put one timid hand out as if to scratch the horse's nose, then jerked it back and turned away. 'Let's go,' she said, taking Addy by the hand, anxious to be out of here. She'd been feeling very confident up until now and she didn't want to ruin things.

Maude was still lying in the sun, but as if she'd only been biding her time waiting for the girls, she got up as soon as they appeared and continued on her way.

The three passed down one long corridor and stopped at a little alcove at the end to inspect a small china cabinet filled with antique bells of every description.

'I'd love to play with them, wouldn't you?' Addy whispered, breathless. Never had she seen such a collection. 'I'd be so careful I'd never break a single one.' She reached out to open the glass doors but Emma pulled her back.

'We can't Addy,' she said sternly. 'Not without permission.'

Addy stuck out her lower lip and crossed her arms in front of her, pouting, clearly intending to stay right where she was until Emma weakened.

'There goes Maude,' Emma said, pointing as the cat disappeared around the corner.

Instantly Addy forgot about the bells and darted after her. They followed the cat to a broad landing with wide stairs going up on one side, another corridor continuing on the other. This wasn't the place where Emma had lost her glasses, but she knew it led to the third floor, and in spite of her renewed feeling of self-confidence she prayed that Maude wouldn't go up the stairs.

But Maude didn't hear Emma's prayer, or if she did she paid no attention. She waddled up one step at a time, with Addy and a reluctant Emma bringing up the rear.

At the top the children found themselves in a long, dark hallway. The doors on this floor were all closed, the only light coming from the clerestory windows at either end of the house.

Maude went halfway down the corridor, then stopped outside a closed door and meowed.

'What do you think she wants in there?' Addy asked.

Emma shrugged. Up here, away from the bright sunlight and open, airy rooms, she was rapidly losing her desire to explore. 'Let's go back down,' she said. 'This is boring.'

'How do you know it is if we haven't even looked? Besides, if we go back downstairs you won't let me touch anything, so what's the fun of it?'

Clearly Addy was being a brat, still pouting because Emma hadn't let her play with the bells. 'Okay,' Emma said, putting her hands on her hips. 'Let's look then.' She opened the nearest door a crack, then threw it open.

It was much lighter inside the room than it was outside in the hallway, but there wasn't much to see because most of the furniture was draped in sheets.

The children stepped in, and Addy wrinkled her nose. 'It stinks in here,' she said.

'It's just musty because it's been all closed up.'

'What's under all these covers?' Addy walked over to a large, draped object, pulled up one corner and peeked under.

'Just old furniture,' Emma said.

'Yep. You're right. It's just an old desk or something.' She crossed to the window and looked out. 'Wow. You can see everything from here, Emma. Come look.'

Still a little nervous, Emma threw a quick glance over her shoulder, then crossed to where Addy stood. Her sister was right. From this window the view was awesome. Facing in the same direction as their own room downstairs, they were up high enough here to see right over the tops of the trees, all the way to the ocean.

Emma shivered, suddenly remembering the dark spot moving on the lawn and the humming. She squinted through her glasses, but everything below seemed perfectly normal. Still, she had a weird feeling. 'Let's see if we can go down to the beach and dunk our feet,' she said, eager to be out of here. 'Maybe Elizabeth will take us.'

Addy clapped her hands. 'Good idea.'

They were halfway across the room, Addy peeking under sheets as she went, when all at once the little girl stopped and let out a squeal of delight. 'Holy cow, Emma! Look at this!'

Emma was already in the doorway. 'Come on, Ads,' she said. 'I thought we were going down to the ocean.'

Now Addy's whole body had disappeared under the sheet. 'But Emma,' she protested, struggling with the drapery. 'Wait till you see this. Help me get this thing off.'

Reluctantly Emma went back and together the two managed to pull the cover off.

When Emma saw what was under it, she was speechless.

It was a doll's house, but such a masterpiece as neither child had ever even imagined. 'It's Land's End,' Emma breathed, and she was right, a perfect replica of the main house in miniature, even to the room in which they now stood. Hinged in the middle, the front rooms were on one side, the back rooms on the other. Every detail was the same down to the carpets on the floors and the portraits hanging on the walls. 'Oh Emma,' Addy whispered. 'It even has a tiny dollhouse.'

'And doors and windows that really open,' Emma said, absolutely enchanted. 'And look, Addy. Look at the little tea set.' Never had she ever imagined such a treasure. She felt for all the world like Alice in Wonderland.

Addy reached in and picked up a tiny lamp, holding it in the palm of her hand, her face wreathed in smiles.

'Be careful, Ads,' Emma breathed. 'We'll get killed if we break anything.'

'I wonder whose it is?' Addy said, gingerly setting the lamp back on its tiny end table.

'Probably Elizabeth's and Rachel's,' Emma said, not really paying attention. She'd picked up the miniature dollhouse and was absolutely intrigued. As she looked inside, everything she saw was getting smaller and smaller and smaller with each progession, until finally there was nothing left.

It made her so dizzy that she closed her eyes for a minute, and when she opened them, the first thing she saw was a tiny, painted rocking horse.

Carefully she picked it up. 'Look at this, Ads,' she said. The horse was in a room that had probably been the nursery, and it was filled with every kind of toy imaginable: tiny stuffed animals, dolls, a train set, even a little slippery slide and a seesaw.

Addy's eyes popped open. 'Where do you suppose it is? The real room, I mean.'

Emma counted. 'Down two doors and across the hall.'

Addy began to jump up and down. 'Let's go see if it's still there. Can we? Oh, please, Emma. Can we?'

Emma hated to leave the dollhouse behind but if the real nursery was anything like the one they'd just looked at, it would be a fairy tale come true. 'Okay,' she said. 'But first we have to cover this up.'

'You do it,' Addy said, 'because I'm too little. I'll go find the nursery.'

Emma opened her mouth to protest but before she

138

could say a word, Addy had already skipped out of the room.

Emma managed to get the sheet back over the dollhouse by herself. 'I'll be back,' she whispered, and with one last glance at the shrouded treasure she followed her sister.

The hallway was much darker than it had been inside the room and it took a minute for Emma's eyes to adjust. She walked two doors down and stopped, frowning. This was odd. All the doors were still closed. 'Addy?' she said, suddenly nervous. 'Addy Pauling, where are you?'

No answer.

She stared at the closed door. 'Addy?' Her voice was high-pitched now and frantic, like the squeak of a mouse about to be eaten by the cat.

She reached out her hand and with trembling fingers she turned the knob. There's nothing here that can hurt you, she said to herself. There's nothing here that can hurt you.

Slowly the door swung inward, and Emma found herself in a room filled with dust and shadows. Here there was no sheet-shrouded furniture, but the layers of dust had almost the same effect. She couldn't see what anything was. She took one step, then jerked back because she broke a cobweb with her face. Shivering, she picked it off, then slowly scanned the room, looking for Addy.

The air around her was warm. Unpleasantly warm. And it smelled. Not musty like the other room, but a funny smell. Like a cellar. Like dark, damp earth.

And then with a rush of relief, Emma saw Addy, sitting astride the rocking horse. 'Ads, you silly,' she said, weak with relief, laughing at her own stupid fears. 'Why'd you close the door?'

139

But Addy didn't answer. She just kept rocking up and down, up and down.

And all at once through the tepid air, Emma heard the echo of something that brought all her suppressed fears crashing back with a vengeance. It was the echo of a melody, the same haunting lullaby she remembered all too well. And with it came a terrible, penetrating cold. Not the kind she felt when she'd been outside sledding too long and her fingers and toes froze. This was different. This was all over her body, as though she were being stabbed with a million tiny shards of ice. 'Addy,' she whispered, filled with such dread that she couldn't move. 'Addy, I'm scared.'

Slowly her little sister turned and stared at Emma, her face twisted into the most ghastly, dead expression Emma had ever seen. But what made Emma almost choke with terror was that the face was one she had never seen before. A face that didn't belong to anyone she knew.

'Addy!' she screamed.

And then, to her horror, the corpselike child opened her mouth. 'Why do you call me Addy?' she said in a voice that sounded like the glacial whispering of an arctic wind. 'My name isn't Addy. My name is Lilith.'

twelve

As they pulled up the long drive that led to Land's End, Judd was surprised to see that while they had been away it had rained. Little clouds of mist were drifting up from puddles in the road, and the azaleas and rhododendron along the way shimmered wet in the afternoon sun.

'How odd,' Rachel said, frowning. 'It must have stormed out here. But it was so beautiful in town.'

Judd reached across the seat and took her hand. 'It was, wasn't it?'

'Thank you for indulging me today,' she said softly. 'I know it was selfish of me, but I just had to be alone with you. If only for a little while.'

He squeezed her hand. 'I know, honey. But don't worry. I really think things with the kids are finally straightening out. If I don't miss my guess, Doctor Roth is going to be out one small patient before too much longer.'

Rachel pulled her hand away. 'I hope so,' she said.

'Being alone with you today made me realize how much I need you. I'm not very good at sharing.'

'How can you say that? You're the most generous person I've ever known.'

'With objects, maybe,' she said quietly, then paused and when she spoke again she almost sounded angry. 'But there are some things no one should ever have to share.'

Puzzled by her tone, he glanced over but her face was turned away. 'Like what, for instance?'

'Oh, never mind,' she said, sliding across the seat to snuggle close beside him. 'I love you. I just hope we can get away alone more often, that's all.'

He put his arm around her. 'Not to worry. We have all the time in the world.' He let his hand slip down over her shoulder to her breast. She wore no bra and under the silk of her blouse he could feel her nipple harden.

She made a soft sound. 'Do you think you could spend just a few more private minutes with me when we get home?' Her voice was husky.

'I do believe,' he said. 'I do, indeed.'

When they came around the last curve in the drive, several delivery trucks were parked in the yard so he pulled around behind the house. He couldn't think about anything but how much he wanted her, so he didn't bother to put the car away. He simply stopped it in the drive and pulled her against him, kissing her. 'Let's sneak in,' he whispered, 'before anyone knows we're back.'

Years later, when he thought about that moment, Judd still couldn't believe that in the flash of the next instant it was possible for him to plunge from the heights of euphoria to the depths of despair. It was as if his arm or leg had been severed so unexpectedly that at first he didn't realize it had happened at all.

One moment he was lost in his passion for Rachel, the next he was staring at Elizabeth, seeing her grim, pallid face, hearing her voice, but her words had no meaning, no effect on him whatsoever. He simply stared at her over Rachel's head, smiling a jackass smile, as if Elizabeth were telling him some dumb joke that he didn't get but he was determined to smile anyway.

'Judd!' she said sharply. 'Did you hear what I said? Emma has had some kind of . . . of attack or something. You'd better come quickly.'

Numb, still not fully comprehending, he followed Elizabeth, leaving Rachel sitting alone in the car.

Emma was lying on the couch in the library, eyes closed, a wet cloth pressed across her forehead. She looked so small, so helpless that it brought a lump into his throat. Addy was sitting beside her sister, quietly sucking her thumb.

When she saw her father, Addy jumped up and ran to him, throwing her arms around his legs, almost knocking him over. 'Oh, Daddy,' she choked, 'Emma fainted and I couldn't wake her up. I tried and tried and then I ran downstairs and got Elizabeth.'

'Henry's on his way,' Elizabeth said from the doorway.

Judd crossed the room in three giant strides and knelt beside his daughter. She lay like a corpse, motionless except for the shallow up-and-down movement of her chest. 'Emma,' he said softly, trying to keep his voice calm. 'Sweetheart, can you hear me? It's Daddy.'

There was no response.

'She's been like this since we found her,' Elizabeth said.

'Did she fall?'

'No one knows. She was up on the third floor. In the old nursery.'

Judd felt a million questions rush to the surface of his mind but he pushed them back. His first, his only concern right now was Emma. 'Sweetheart, can you hear me?' He took the cloth off her forehead and gently brushed the strands of damp hair back from her face.

'Why won't she wake up?' Addy asked, her voice quavering. 'She isn't dead like Mommy, is she?' She began to cry.

Judd pulled her close. 'No, Addy,' he said, his voice deceptively calm. 'She isn't dead. She's unconscious.' He turned to Elizabeth. 'Where the hell is Henry?' he said between clenched teeth.

'He should be here any minute,' she said.

'Daddy?' A weak, almost inaudible whimper.

Judd turned back. Emma's eyes flickered open. 'Emma. Thank God.' He ran his finger gently along her cheekbone. 'You really scared your old Dad good, you know that?'

She stared up at him, but her eyes were opaque, glazed-over, as if she weren't certain just who he was. 'Daddy?' she whispered again. And suddenly her eyes flew open. With a jerk she rocketed up and threw herself against him, crying hysterically, as if all the hounds of hell were after her.

He held her, trying to calm her, feeling her small, thin bones, all at once remembering how very young she was, how dependent. 'Hush, sweetheart, it's all right. You're going to be just fine. I'm here.' He put his hand

144

under her chin and tipped her face up so he could see her expression.

Her eyes were closed tight, the skin around them all red and blotchy from crying. But when she opened them, Judd gasped. There was only one word to describe what he saw there. Terror. Stark, unadulterated terror.

'I saw her,' Emma choked. 'Oh, Daddy, I saw her.'

'It's all right, Emma,' he said quietly. 'Just calm down and you can tell me all about it.'

She put her head back on his shoulder, gasping great gulps of air, hiccoughing in between. Addy snuggled up on his other side.

'What's going on?' Henry Adelford appeared in the doorway.

Christ only knows, Judd thought numbly. Christ only knows.

The doctor came and went without finding anything physically wrong with Emma. 'I think that caution is the best approach, at least for now,' he told Judd in private. 'Something frightened Emma. We know that. But we don't know what it was. You already have one very sensitive situation on your hands and that's Addy. Now you seem to have another.' He had paused, considering. 'But it's not unusual. When children are as close to each other as yours are, sometimes one problem can feed the other. I'd give Martin Roth a call. Tell him what's happened. He's the expert.'

After Henry left, Judd sat between Emma and Addy on the couch and looked from one child to the other, feeling absolutely helpless. What could he possibly say that would explain what had transpired to one without terrifying the other?

Addy had just finished her version of what had happened in the nursery. She was rocking up and down on the horse, she said, minding her own business, and the next thing she knew, Emma went clunk, right on the floor. Addy tried to make her get up but she wouldn't so Addy ran and got Elizabeth.

Emma listened in absolute silence, and Judd could feel the tension building in her thin frame.

'Now it's your turn, Emma,' he said, but from the stricken look on her face, he knew what she was thinking: that he wasn't going to believe her.

'Someone else was there, Daddy,' she stammered finally, then cringed in anticipation of his disbelief.

'In the nursery?' he said.

She nodded, never taking her eyes from his face, searching for some sign that he might believe her. 'But it wasn't a real live person,' she said miserably.

Judd waited in silence, not trusting himself to speak.

Her eyes grew round and shockingly blue against the ashen pallor of her skin. 'There was this little girl. Her name was Lilith,' she whispered. 'And she was . . . she was inside Addy.'

Judd suppressed a terrible urge to groan. This was worse than he had imagined. Addy must have had another episode, and Emma had reacted to it. But how could he explain it to her when he didn't understand it himself?

At that point Addy jumped off the couch, wriggled past Judd's legs and stood in front of her sister, hands on her hips, face flushed. 'That's the biggest fat lie you ever told, Emma Pauling,' she said. 'There isn't anybody inside me. Just look and see if you don't believe me.' She opened her mouth wide.

'Ads,' Judd said casually, 'I'm really thirsty. Do you

146

think you could get me a glass of water? Without spilling a drop?'

Addy hesitated, tipping her head to one side, considering. 'But how will I reach the faucet?'

'Go to the kitchen and ask Kate.'

That was all she needed. 'Okey-dokey, Addy's Daddy,' she said. She held up one hand, carefully counting her fingers. 'I'll be back in one, two, three seconds.' Without a backward glance she bounced out of the room.

Emma had dropped her gaze and was staring down at her hands. 'You don't believe me,' she said quietly. It wasn't a reproach. It was despair.

Judd took a deep breath and pulled her close. All he knew was that he had to help her. Any way he could. 'I sent Addy out of the room because I don't want her to hear this. I think it would really scare her. This has to be our secret.' He tipped her face up so he could look into her eyes. 'I do believe you when you say something awful is happening here. I don't understand it but I believe you.'

Emma stared at her father, incredulous, her face flushed, her mouth open. 'You do?' she choked. 'You really do?'

He nodded.

'Oh, Daddy,' she said, laughing and crying at the same time, unable to hide her enormous sense of relief. She threw her arms around his neck, almost choking him. 'Oh, Daddy, thank you, thank you, thank you.'

Then the floodgates opened. He listened with a sinking heart as she told him about the ghost-child who had watched them in the stable and then later in the gallery, and about the locked door on the third floor. And finally about the terrible visage she had seen in the nursery.

'You know what, Daddy?' she said, finally stopping for breath.

'What, sweetheart?'

She answered so quietly that he almost didn't hear. 'I think we should all get out of here.'

Judd felt as if he had suddenly stepped off a cliff and was plunging into a dark, bottomless pit. This was far worse than he had imagined. Emma wasn't simply reacting to Addy's emotional trauma. She was suffering one of her own.

But that wasn't the worst. Now she had poured out her deepest secrets. She had shared with him her most private terrors. Because she thought he believed in her ghost. And now as far as Emma was concerned, there was only one logical solution. Leave Land's End. Leave the ghost behind and get the hell out.

He closed his eyes. Please, dear God, he prayed, don't let me have made a terrible mistake. Don't let me have harmed her.

Emma took his hand, her face inches from his own. 'You know what, Daddy?' she said solemnly.

Again he shook his head.

'I'm not anywhere near as scared as I was before. And you know why?'

'Why?'

'Because I'm not alone anymore. Because I know, no matter what happens, you'll figure out what to do.'

This time Judd couldn't help it. He groaned.

thirteen

'So now, Emma thinks Addy is possessed,' Judd said wearily. He had talked nonstop for almost half an hour, filling Dr Roth in on what had happened since their last visit. His head was splitting.

Dr Roth nodded. 'I can see why, can't you? To Emma, it's an eminently reasonable explanation for what she sees as Addy's absolutely unreasonable behavior. After all, Emma is only ten and she's afraid.' He leaned back in his chair. 'But it's not ordinary fear that's driving her. It's dread. It's the expectation of what may happen, not what really is happening. You see, most children her age can deal very nicely with even the worst circumstances when they see cause and effect. The problem is that here, Emma sees only the effect. Addy's bizarre behavior. The cause is hidden. So she's making one up. I'm guessing that this ghost of hers is an elaborate justification for something she doesn't understand. And at this point we can't help her much because we don't understand what's causing Addy's problem either.'

'So where do we go from here?'

Dr Roth leaned forward and took a pack of gum from his desk drawer. 'Have a stick?'

Judd shook his head.

'Have you noticed I'm not smoking?'

'I have.'

'It's been two days. Two days, seven hours . . . ' He glanced at his watch. ' . . . and twenty-four minutes to be exact.' He took a deep breath and straightened up in his chair. 'Just thought you ought to know in case I begin to behave strangely. Anyway. Your question. Where do we go from here?' He picked up a pencil. 'I'm going to take this all down as I say it,' he said. 'Sort of think out loud, if you will. Helps me organize.' He glanced up. 'You might want to do the same. Jot down anything that strikes you. See what you come up with. Then we'll compare.'

He began to talk, writing at the same time. 'Clearly our problem is not with Emma. It's still with Addy. If we can find out what's troubling the little one, it's my thought that her sister will respond accordingly. The key is to give Emma some logical answers, something concrete to hang her hat on, and I think she'll let this ghost of hers go.'

'I sure as hell hope you're right.'

Dr Roth looked up. 'I do, too. Anyway, first things first. I'm going to keep this as simple as possible because I need your input and if you're lost in technical jargon you won't be much help.' He bridged his hands over his nose and was quiet for a minute. Judd could almost see him arranging his thoughts. Finally he said, 'Let's see what we know about Addy. First, she's had these sudden but brief changes in consciousness, and her memory of these changes is nonexistent. Externally we see a whole new identity. Someone who has a different voice, who does things Addy cannot or does not do as a matter of course. You've seen it. Emma has seen it. Correct?'

Judd nodded.

Dr Roth paused, setting his pencil down. 'Assuming that Emma did in fact see another of these "episodes" yesterday, where does that leave us?'

'Right where we were last Friday,' Judd said bleakly. 'Except that now Emma is freaking out, too.'

Dr Roth gave no indication that he had heard. He continued to follow his own train of thought, thinking out loud, now and then jotting something down on his pad, occasionally leaning far back in his chair and closing his eyes. 'Unfortunately we know more about what this isn't than what it is,' he said. 'It's not a fugue state, where we would see her forgetting her own personal identity for much longer periods of time. Addy shows no signs of being phobic. No fear symptoms. No sweats. No shortness of breath. You've said that when she's herself, there's no evidence of anger, no nervousness, no lack of energy, no loss of efficiency.'

He looked up. 'Any compulsiveness? Like a need to repeat things? Prayers, for instance? Ritualistic behavior, like wanting you to check the windows over and over to make sure they're all locked? Or does she want to get into bed only on the left side? Anything like that?'

Judd shook his head.

'Apart from the thumb sucking, any regression toward infancy? Excessive crying or whining? Baby talk? Wanting to be held?'

'No. Nothing.'

151

The psychiatrist frowned, put his pencil down. 'Has Addy ever had a head injury?'

Judd shook his head. 'No. Not as far as I know. Why?'

Dr Roth stood up, crossed to the window and stood looking out at Emma and Addy, playing on the glider. 'Well, at first I agreed with Henry Adelford that this was most probably a psychological problem. A reaction to her mother's death. But now, if I may, I'd like to back up a little.'

Judd waited.

'I'd like Addy to have an EEG. And some skull X rays. To rule out the possibility that this could be a psychomotor attack of some sort.'

'Which is?'

'An epileptic seizure, for one thing.'

'Jesus.'

The doctor turned around. 'Emma's notion of possession is what made me consider it.'

'Possession?'

'For thousands of years, some forms of epilepsy were explained in those terms. The person loses his identity. He continues to perform, but he is completely out of touch with his environment. He has no recollection of his actions, and he may do many uncharacteristic, even impossible things in the course of the attack.'

'Like playing the piano.'

'Possibly. And you mentioned a bed-wetting incident, after which she hid in a closet.'

Judd nodded.

'In some instances, seizures can be mixed. Grand mal and psychomotor at the same time.'

Judd was stunned into silence.

'It would explain why Addy is in a perfectly normal

state between episodes. Why she shows none of the symptoms of anxiety or depression.' He lowered his voice. 'And if that's the case, it will make things a lot easier to explain to Emma. Certainly a lot less frightening than what she's dealing with right now.'

'But what happens if it is epilepsy? To Addy, I mean.'

'Well, there is the possibility of a surgical cure, if she's had an injury.' He held up a hand. 'But we're getting way ahead of ourselves here, Mr Pauling. First, let's get the EEG done. And some X rays. Today.'

Judd nodded. Addy, he thought. Poor, plump, jolly little Addy. 'It isn't going to hurt her, is it?' he asked quietly.

'No.' Roth picked up the phone, spoke to someone in clipped tones, then hung up. 'You can take her over right now and they'll fit you in.' He wrote down an address and handed it to Judd. 'Second floor,' he said. 'Then I'd like you back here, so we can discuss our next step.'

Judd stood up.

'Do you think Emma would mind staying here with me while you're gone? It would give me a chance to talk to her.'

'I'll ask her.'

'Don't push,' Dr Roth said. 'If she's at all reluctant, don't push.'

'Don't worry, I won't.' He left the office, and for the first time since she died, he wished Nicole were there to help.

Emma sat in the big chair across from Dr Roth and stared. Addy was right. He did look sort of like a lizard. His cheeks were fat and they hung down on both sides of his neck, and his eyes were shiny black and bulgy.

'Your dad said you didn't mind waiting here while he and Addy went for tests,' he was saying. 'So we could get to know each other.'

'I don't mind,' she said. She was feeling much more confident than she had at their last visit. And all because her father knew about Lilith. Besides she liked Dr Roth's voice. It was deep and warm but very serious. It sounded as if he were talking to another grown-up.

'Tell me what you think is going on with Addy.'

'Like what do you mean?'

'Do you think she's sick?'

Emma shook her head. 'Addy's not sick,' she said. 'Addy's just fine.'

'I thought something happened yesterday with her that scared you?'

'It did,' Emma said, watching him closely, not sure yet just how much she dared to say. 'But it wasn't Addy's fault.'

'Who's fault was it? And while you're deciding what you want to tell me, have a stick of gum.' He handed her the pack.

'Hey, Juicy Fruit,' Emma said. 'It's my favorite flavor. Did you know that moles can't swallow Juicy Fruit?'

Dr Roth looked surprised. 'No, I didn't. Is that really true?'

Emma nodded. 'People use it to get rid of moles when they dig holes in the lawn.' She opened the wrapper and put the stick of gum in her mouth. 'Do you believe in ghosts?' She asked the question before she even realized she was going to.

Dr Roth didn't seem a bit startled. In fact his black eyes didn't even blink. 'Well, to tell you the truth, Emma,' he said, 'I'm not sure. Why do you ask?'

Emma considered for a minute. 'Because there's a ghost at Land's End,' she said quietly, sitting straight up in her chair. 'And if you don't believe me, you can even ask my father.'

'I don't see why I should have to ask him,' Dr Roth said evenly. 'You seem like a sensible person. What makes you think there's a ghost?'

'First I heard it. But then I saw it.'

'Yesterday?'

Emma nodded.

He didn't say anything for a minute. Then he frowned. 'I must confess, Emma, that I myself have never seen a ghost.' He narrowed his eyes. 'Where did you see it?'

'It was inside my sister.' Again she watched to catch a sign of a negative reaction but Dr Roth's expression remained unchanged.

'That's most unusual, don't you think?'

'I guess so. But once I read a story about it. About a dead boy who got inside his brother.'

'Hmmm,' Dr Roth said, and little frown lines appeared between his eyebrows. 'But how did you know that this was a ghost?'

'Because it didn't have any body of its own.'

At that, the doctor began to chew his gum a little faster and he was quiet for a long time. Finally he said, 'Have you ever seen this ghost when Addy wasn't around?'

Emma frowned, thinking hard. 'Well, I haven't seen her exactly. But she's been there all the same. Hiding.' She told him about the day in the stable. 'And once she was there when Addy was in town seeing Dr Adelford. I didn't see her but I heard her.'

Dr Roth looked thoughtful. 'How do you know it's a she?'

'Because she told me. Her name is Lilith.' She shuddered, remembering that ghastly, dead face.

'Lilith frightened you, didn't she?' Dr Roth asked softly.

'Yes, she did,' Emma said. 'I almost screamed.' Then she laughed at herself and slapped her knee. 'I mean I *did* scream. I screamed my head off.'

He smiled. 'I bet you did. I think I would have, too.' He paused. 'Did the ghost have anything else to say, besides telling you her name?'

Emma shook her head. 'That's when I fainted.'

The doctor got up from his chair and came around to sit on the corner of his desk. He lowered his voice, suddenly sounding much more serious. 'I want you to think about this next question very carefully, Emma,' he said, rubbing his chin. 'What exactly do you think this ghost-child wants?'

Emma shivered. 'I don't know.'

'Do you think she wants to hurt you? Or Addy?'

Emma frowned. 'Maybe she does. Maybe she doesn't. But it doesn't matter what she wants, does it? Because she's hurting us anyway.'

'That's certainly true,' he agreed. He got up and went back to his chair. 'Another question. Do you think there's anything your father can do about all this?'

Emma hesitated. She had stayed awake most of last night thinking about this very thing. Finally she answered in a very small voice. 'I think he ought to take us away from Land's End.'

Dr Roth looked thoughtful. 'Considering what you've told me, that would seem like a logical move.' He paused.

'And do you think that Addy would be back to her good old self if you all went back to New York?'

For the first time, Emma was surprised by one of his questions. Clearly Dr Roth wasn't as smart as she had thought. 'Of course she would,' she said patiently. 'You see, this ghost is getting into Addy's body and that's what's making her do all these weird things. It hasn't anything to do with Addy at all.'

'Hmmmm,' Dr Roth said, 'you're a very perceptive young lady, Emma, so I want to ask you something you may not have thought about before. And this time it's a very difficult question.'

Emma waited.

'Why do you think this ghost is getting inside Addy, and not inside you?'

Emma narrowed her eyes, considering. She could see that Dr Roth was watching, waiting for a thoughtful answer. She sat up very straight in her chair, crossed one ankle carefully over the other, and smoothed out her skirt. 'Maybe it's because Addy is littler. She's only five. She's not as strong as I am.'

He tipped his head to one side, and his eyes got very round. 'Have you ever considered the possibility that maybe Addy wants her there?'

Emma gasped. 'Why the heck would Addy want that?'

'Because maybe when the ghost is inside her,' the doctor said quietly, 'Addy can pretend she's someone else. She can forget about your mother. She can forget about how very sad she is.'

Emma considered that possibility very carefully. 'There're two problems with that,' she said finally.

He waited.

'First of all, Addy doesn't even know the ghost is

157

there. And second of all, Addy isn't sad. Except for when Lilith is inside her, Addy is so happy that it almost gives me a headache.' She looked the doctor straight in the eye. 'I don't know why this ghost is bothering us, Doctor Roth,' she said, 'but I know one thing for sure. It doesn't have one single solitary thing to do with Addy.' She paused. 'And I know another thing.'

Dr Roth waited.

'If we stay at Land's End, more bad things are going to happen. You just wait and see.'

Emma was dreaming. She was on the school playground and everyone was watching her because she had suddenly learned how to fly. Well, not fly exactly. She wasn't flapping her arms or anything. It was more like bouncing. Only real high, way over everyone's heads. And once she was up in the air, she could make herself stay up by holding her breath. Like she was a balloon.

She floated across the playground and down Perkins Street, and over the big fountain in the park. It was making cool, splashing sounds as she passed and she decided to drift down and wet her feet.

She was almost in the water when she woke up, but oddly enough she could still hear the splashing.

She opened her eyes, then sat straight up.

Addy wasn't in her bed.

'Ads?' Emma whispered, feeling the all-too-familiar chill of dread clamp around her heart. 'Addy?'

No sound except for the water splashing.

Shivering, her skin crawling, she slid out of bed and inch by terrified inch she tiptoed to the bathroom door.

Addy was standing on a stool beside the sink with her back to Emma, washing her hands.

'Ads?' Emma stuttered. 'What are you doing?'

Addy didn't answer.

'Addy!' Emma wailed, frantic with fear that it might not be Addy, wanting to run but not knowing where to run to.

Slowly her sister turned, and to Emma's immense relief she saw Addy. No one else. Just good old Addy.

'I'm just washing my hands,' Addy mumbled, half-asleep.

'What're you doing that for at this hour?' Emma said. 'Come on back to bed right this minute before you wake Daddy.'

Addy looked sort of dazed. 'I got something on my hands,' she said. 'Something wet and yucky. And it's all over my nightie.'

Emma looked at Addy's hands, then at the water gurgling down the drain. Everything looked clean enough to her, but then she saw Addy's nightgown. Addy was right. It was yucky. 'Did you have a bloody nose?' she asked, tipping Addy's head back so she could look up her nostrils.

'No,' Addy said, wiggling away. 'But my nightie is sick.'

'It sure is. You must have had a nosebleed.'

Addy began to whimper.

'There's no need to get cranky,' Emma said. 'Dry your hands, we'll get a clean nightie, and then maybe we can get some sleep.'

Within minutes the two children were back in their beds, snug under the covers. Addy fell instantly asleep, but Emma lay awake for a long time. She was truly grateful that nothing bad had happened in the bathroom, but she still couldn't shake the terrible feeling of dread.

Please God, she prayed, make Daddy take us away from here. If you do, I promise I'll never call anyone a faggot again as long as I live.

In the morning, Rachel was the first to see it. Huge, shaky, blood-red letters. Scrawled all up and down the hall outside their bedroom. Shrieking a single word over and over and over. Momma. Momma. Momma.

Rachel collapsed.

fourteen

'What does it say?' Addy asked.

'It says "Momma,"' Emma said in a shaky voice.

'Someone's going to be in bad trouble, aren't they, Daddy?' Addy said. 'Boy, I'm glad it's not me. I can't even write all my letters yet, can I, Emma? Except for my name. A-D-D-Y.'

Judd said nothing, painfully aware that Emma was walking just behind them, staring with unabashed horror at the mess on the walls. Earlier, when he had questioned her about it she had pulled him aside and had told him in a trembling voice that she knew who had done it.

'Who?' Judd asked, not really wanting to hear.

'Lilith. She made Addy do it.'

'How do you know?' He had a sick lump in his chest.

Emma told him about Addy and the hand-washing and the sticky red stuff on her nightgown. 'I put it in the hamper,' she said, 'but you can still see it.'

Reluctant, fearful of what he might find, he looked.

Emma was right. Addy's nightgown was still damp. 'She must have had a nosebleed,' Judd said calmly.

'No, Daddy, she didn't,' Emma said with a fierceness that left no room for contradiction. Then she flushed, looked down at her feet, and turned away. She didn't say any more but Judd could feel the change in her attitude. All the self-confidence she had gained yesterday vanished, leaving her more anxious and frightened than ever. But clearly expectant, clearly waiting for him to make the next move.

'Let's get some breakfast,' Judd said, even though he couldn't imagine eating a thing. Hand in hand, the three of them made their way down the hall where the servants were busy scouring the walls.

Rachel had been the first to see the writing and then all hell had broken loose. Servants running from every direction, gaping, Elizabeth in a frenzy, and all the while a conscious but stunned Rachel staring, white-faced and silent. The only thing she said to him just before she disappeared downstairs was a whispered plea. 'She's got to stop, Judd. Please. Make her stop.'

No one seemed to know exactly what the stuff was on the walls, but it was something dark and red and sticky. And it had left a sickeningly sweet odor lingering in the air. If Judd hadn't known it was impossible, he would have sworn it was blood. But who could have done such a thing? And how? To get that much blood someone would have had to slaughter an ox. Addy? Impossible. He knew it couldn't be, but he kept thinking it anyway.

His headache was back now, redoubled, pounding his brain to a pulp, and as he walked toward the dining room with his children he wondered how the hell he was going to get through the day.

They were almost at the door when one of the maids stopped him. 'Telephone, Mr Pauling,' she said. 'You can take it in the library if you like.' She pointed.

'Thanks,' he said. He turned to Emma. 'Take your sister inside and make sure she asks for something sensible. I'll be right back.'

Emma hesitated, then took Addy by the hand.

'I don't want any of those funny eggs,' Addy whispered.

Emma didn't answer.

Judd crossed the hall, went into the library and picked up the phone. 'Judd Pauling,' he said.

It was Dr Roth. 'I just called to give you the EEG results.'

Judd waited, silently praying, without a clue as to what he was praying for.

'Everything is normal. Absolutely normal.'

Judd said nothing.

'Mr Pauling? Are you still there?'

'I'm here.'

'There are still a few additional tests I'd like to give Addy. To rule out all possibility that this might be a somatic condition. Can you bring her in this afternoon?'

'Yes. But first I'd better tell you the latest.'

After Judd finished, the psychiatrist was silent for a long time and when he spoke he sounded very tired. 'I don't mean to alarm you. Any more than you already are. But I need to ask you something. Is there anyone there at Land's End – anyone else, that is, besides Addy – who might have done this? Someone who might be willing to take advantage of two very vulnerable children? Someone who perhaps has his or her own motives for wanting to scare the hell out of everyone?'

163

Judd exhaled loudly. This was a possibility that he had not allowed himself to consider. It was too horrible. But now, hearing Dr Roth verbalize it, it seemed eminently more acceptable than the thought of Addy and insanity. 'Yes,' he said quietly. 'It's possible.'

'Consider it. It certainly won't hurt to discuss it,' Dr Roth said. 'We may be treating the wrong person. In the meantime bring the girls in.' Judd heard papers rustling. 'Let's see. Your original appointment was scheduled for two. Can you make it then?'

'We'll be there.'

Neither Judd nor Emma ate much breakfast but Addy finished a whole stack of waffles. She chattered on in between bites. 'What day do you like best, Emma?' She didn't wait for an answer. 'I like Monday because it comes after Sunday. Listen, Daddy. I can say all the days in order.' She began.

'Don't talk with your mouth full,' Emma said.

Addy bobbed her head back and forth. 'Dum, dum, dum, dum,' she sang.

'Addy!' Emma snapped. 'Didn't you hear me?'

'I'm not talking,' Addy said. 'I'm humming.'

'Finish your breakfast, Ads,' Judd said. 'Then we'll go down to the beach.' He watched his two children, completely confounded. Addy was clearly oblivious to what had gone on during the night, still content to take life just as it came. No problem at all that he could see. On the other hand, Emma was pale and nervous. She kept glancing over at him anxiously, still clearly expecting him to do something, say something that would fix things. And all the while, whirring around in the back

164

of his head, one question kept circling: If not Addy, then who?

He took a last sip of coffee and was about to leave the table when Elizabeth came in. She looked puzzled. 'Judd?' she said. 'I don't know why, but Mother wants to see you.'

Judd was stunned. No one but Henry had seen Priscilla for more than five days. 'Now?'

'Now. In fact she was emphatic. Right now.'

Judd frowned. 'She wants to put the screws to me about Addy.' He was surprised to find that he had said it out loud.

Elizabeth looked shocked. 'Why would she want to do that, for God's sake?'

Judd stood up and took Elizabeth aside. 'Rachel believes that Addy wants to get rid of her. And your mother does, too.'

'You told me that before, Judd,' Elizabeth said, 'and I told you to ask Mother about it. Now's your chance.'

'You're right. I hate to keep dumping this in your lap,' he said quietly, 'but would you keep an eye on these two? I don't dare leave them alone, and I haven't seen Rachel since she left this morning to meet with the kitchen staff. Something to do with the ball. Although to tell the truth, she was so unnerved by the graffiti in the hall that I'm really not really sure where she went.'

'I don't mind staying with the kids,' Elizabeth said. 'Go along. But Judd. A word of caution. When you talk to Mother, choose your words carefully. Like Rachel, she doesn't forgive easily.'

Judd took the steps two at a time. Ever since the night Addy had hidden under the stairs, he had been determined to find out how Priscilla Daimler had known where Addy was. He couldn't forget the terrified look on her face. If he didn't know better, he'd think that she and Emma were suffering from the same delusion about a ghost. And then there was Dr Roth's suggestion. Could Priscilla Daimler somehow have been responsible for the gruesome writing on the wall? To force his hand?

Just outside her room, he paused, took a deep breath, then knocked.

'Come in.'

Inside, the curtains were drawn, leaving the room in semidarkness. Priscilla was sitting in a wheelchair on the far side of the fireplace with her back to the door so he couldn't see her face, and there was something so still about her, so unmoving that for one shocked moment he thought she was dead. 'Priscilla?' he said. 'Are you all right?'

'I suppose it depends upon the definition of the term.' Her voice was little more than a rattle.

He walked around where he could see her and was instantly sorry he had. She looked ravaged.

'I'm sorry you have to see me like this,' she rasped. 'I realize that it's not very pleasant, but it couldn't wait. It's time we talked.' There was a note of resignation in her voice, as if she had finally accepted a loathsome task because she could no longer avoid it. 'Please sit.' She pointed to a chair directly opposite her own.

Judd did.

Priscilla stared at him for a moment without moving, a simple thing but there was something ominous in her immobility, and all at once Judd wasn't at all sure he wanted to hear what she had to say.

'First, I want your assurance that what I am about to

166

tell you will go no further,' she said, her eyes watchful, never leaving his face. 'Have I your word?'

He nodded.

'Then I'll get right to the point. I want you to leave Land's End.'

'I'm not surprised.'

'Rachel told you. Of course. I should have known she would. And did she tell you why?'

'She said it was because you think that my children are trying to hurt her. And that someday I will, too.'

She was silent for a minute, and when she spoke her voice seemed filled with regret. 'In the end, you will. I know it even if you don't.'

Judd felt a flash of anger. 'I'm not here to peer into your crystal ball. I'm here because Elizabeth said you had something to say. And by the way, before I leave I have a few questions of my own that need answering.'

His tone was harsh but Priscilla remained impassive. 'I didn't mean to offend you, Mr Pauling.' It came as no surprise that she had stopped calling him Judd. It simply meant that at least for the moment there were no polite pretenses between them. As far as she was concerned he was an unwelcome stranger. 'The truth of the matter is that I know my daughter. And you, I'm afraid, don't know her at all.'

He opened his mouth to protest, but she silenced him with a sweep of her hand. 'No. Don't say a word. Just listen.' She leaned her head back against the chair and closed her eyes as if gathering strength. 'Have you ever seen an owl parrot, Mr Pauling?' She didn't wait for an answer. 'Probably not. I should think they are extinct by now. But I saw one once. When I was a very young woman. Pathetic creatures. They can't fly, you see. Some-

167

where in the evolutionary process they lost the need. Until man introduced predators into their environment. Now it's too late for them. Now they sleep on the ground and climb trees to find food and wait to be devoured.' She opened her eyes and stared at him. 'My Rachel is like that. Somehow, somewhere along the line she lost her ability to fly. Or maybe she never really had it. But now she can only creep along the ground and wait for someone to come along and devour her.'

'A curious analogy,' Judd said flatly. 'But I'm afraid I don't see any connection between my wife and some wingless bird. Are you trying to suggest to me that Rachel is an emotional cripple?'

Her face grew hard. 'I'm trying to tell you that my daughter needs protecting. And there is only one person who knows her well enough to give her what she needs. Me.'

'Nonsense!' Judd snapped. 'If you're through talking in circles, why don't you give me some hard facts? Like why Rachel left you in the first place. And why she never wanted to come back here at all.' He paused. 'And while we're at it, how about telling me just why you are so terrified about what's happening to Addy. Where does it fit, Mrs Daimler, because somehow I'm sure it does. How did you know where she was hiding that night? And who made that mess on the walls? Because it sure as hell wasn't my daughter!'

In the face of his anger, Priscilla Daimler never blinked. It was as if she had expected this outburst and had steeled herself to defend against it. She watched him intently but she allowed no hint of emotion to cross her face. When he was finished she said, 'Rachel left Land's End because she had a nervous breakdown. She spent two years in a sanitarium. After her release she never came back.'

Judd heard the words but for some reason they had little effect on him. It was almost as if somewhere in the deep recesses of his mind he had always known that something like this had happened. 'But that doesn't explain why she never came home.'

'All of her life Rachel trusted me, and in the end I betrayed her. She never believed she was ill. But I sent her away. As far as Rachel was concerned, I betrayed her.'

'And did you?'

Something flickered behind her eyes, something so full of pain that Judd was caught off guard. 'In a way, I suppose I did,' she said softly. 'But at the time I felt I had no choice.'

'What caused her breakdown?'

For a minute her face took on the remote look of someone who has had a temporary mental lapse. Then she shrugged. 'Who knows what one can endure one day and not the next? It's a thin line, Mr Pauling. I know because I walk it every day of my life.'

A sudden hard suspicion came into his mind. 'What are you asking me to believe?' he said. 'That you of all people don't know why Rachel got sick?'

She gave no indication that she had heard. 'I think you love my daughter, and for that reason, I'm sure you want to do what is best for her.'

'And that is?'

When she answered it was as if she were picking her way through a minefield, choosing each word carefully, knowing that one misstep would blow them both into oblivion. 'You are perfectly aware that your Addy is creating a serious emotional problem for Rachel,' she said, and for a minute Judd saw real fear register across the sharp planes of her face. Then it was gone. 'Whether the child is doing it consciously or unconsciously, surely you've seen the effect it's having on your wife. First the piano incident, disrupting Rachel's welcome-home party. Then the scene in the car. And now this mess on my walls.' Her voice began to quaver and the fear came back into her eyes, but this time it didn't fade away. It overwhelmed her. 'I have never begged for anything in my life, Mr Pauling, but I'm begging now. Leave Land's End before . . . ' She was overcome by a sudden fit of coughing.

'Before what?'

She became angry. 'Are you so involved with your children that you haven't seen what's happening to your wife?'

'I know Rachel has been upset. But we'll work it out. Surely you don't think I'd abandon her just because you tell me to.'

'Rachel is more than upset. I know. I've seen it happen before, remember?'

Judd narrowed his eyes, trying to get a feel for her true motives. 'You think she's heading toward another breakdown?'

Priscilla nodded.

'What else, Mrs Daimler?' he said quietly. 'What else is happening here?'

She sighed. She looked beaten. 'Isn't this enough for you?'

He paused, measuring his words carefully. 'And exactly how do you think Rachel would react if I told her I was leaving her?'

Priscilla turned her face away, hiding it in shadow. 'She'd survive,' she said flatly.

Slowly, Judd got to his feet. 'Well, I'm afraid that I want more for my wife than just survival. I have no intention of abandoning her. If we leave Land's End, it will be as a family. Together. Which prospect, I might add, is becoming more and more appealing every day. Now if you'll excuse me, I have a great many things to do.'

He turned and was almost to the door when she stopped him with a single word. 'Never!'

He wasn't sure whether her next words were said more in anger or out of blind fear, but in either case they were explosive. 'You poor blind fool,' she snapped. 'Don't you realize that I can never allow you to take Rachel away.'

Judd lost control. He whirled around to face her. 'You can't allow? Who in the hell do you think you are that you have any say in the matter whatsoever? You call me a fool? Well, maybe so, but I know one thing. I'll never stand by and let you play God with our lives. And Rachel won't either. We're going to stay together in spite of you. If not here, then somewhere else.'

She went limp, as if someone had pulled a plug, draining all life from her. She looked dead. Except for her eyes. They were wide open, and something so cold, so dangerous moved behind them that for one minute Judd was chilled to the bone. 'I think we've said all there is to say,' she said in a voice that was as dead as her expression. 'I thought that you had some degree of concern for my daughter but now I can see I was wrong. You may stay in my home until after the ball tomorrow evening, only because I know it means a great deal to

Rachel. But then I expect you to take your two children and leave Land's End. Alone. Make no mistake, Mr Pauling. I am not begging you. I am not asking you. I am ordering you.' She wheeled the chair to a door at the far side of the room. She opened it. 'Since I don't expect that I will ever have anything further to say to you, I will say good-bye now. Good-bye, Mr Pauling.' Then she disappeared, leaving him as stunned as if he had just been punched in the face.

It wasn't until he was halfway down the stairs that he realized he hadn't gotten one single answer from Priscilla Daimler about Addy. But he guessed it really didn't matter. They were all going to leave Land's End the day after tomorrow, and for some unexplained reason he felt as though the weight of the world had been lifted from his shoulders. He actually found himself thinking about getting back to work. He had a sudden urge to create something alive and vibrant. Something that would have nothing to do with sickness and death.

fifteen

Judd found Rachel in the drawing room where furniture was being moved aside to make room for the buffet tables.

'Over there,' she was saying to the workmen. 'Along the wall. That's it. That's just perfect.'

'Rachel?'

She turned and his breath caught in his throat. She looked radiant. Clearly she had forgotten all about this morning's shock, at least for the moment. 'Oh, Judd,' she said, throwing her arms around him. 'I can't believe how wonderful I feel. It's as if . . . ' She flushed. 'It's as if I were a child again.'

Gently he pushed her away. 'Sweetheart, we have to talk.'

She frowned. 'Is it Addy again?'

He shook his head. 'No. But we have to talk.'

She waved her hand around the room. 'But I have so much to do.'

'It's important, Rachel,' he said.

A wary, animal look came into her eyes. 'What is it?'

He took her by the hand and led her across the hall into the library. Inside, it was cool and quiet, in startling contrast to the frenzied atmosphere in the rest of the house. They sat side by side on the sofa. 'I've just had quite a talk with your mother,' he said.

Rachel raised her eyebrows. 'With Mother? But how? She's still too ill to see anyone.'

'She saw me.'

'But why?'

'She wanted to ask me to leave Land's End.'

All color drained from her face. 'She doesn't give up easily, does she?'

Judd shook his head.

'Well, what is it this time? Still the same old theme? That you're going to hurt me and the only one who can protect me is the lady herself?'

He nodded. 'She says that this business with Addy has upset you far more than I realize.'

She narrowed her eyes. She seemed calm enough but he could see a tiny pulse beginning to pound in her temple. 'What else did my mother tell you?' There was something ominous in the way she asked.

For a minute he considered lying to her, but only for a minute. Rachel was his wife. She had a right to know. 'She told me you had had a nervous breakdown.' His words hung in the air, then settled like so much dust in some vast, empty space.

Rachel turned to stone. She sat silent, motionless. The only sound was the sound of Judd's own breathing.

His head began to ache again. 'Sweetheart?' he said. 'Are you okay? Look at me.'

She turned and her eyes were so full of pain that he had to look away. 'Jesus, Rachel, I'm so sorry.'

She smiled a bittersweet smile. 'For what?'

'I shouldn't have told you. I should have waited until you felt safe enough to tell me yourself.'

She shook her head, then took his hand. 'You mustn't blame yourself. It's my fault. I should have told you about it long ago, but when you've been hurt the way I have . . . ' She covered her face with her hands. 'I knew this would happen if I came back to Land's End. My mother . . . ' her lips moved, but no sound came out. It was as if she were trying to speak in a foreign language but didn't know any of the words that would make him understand.

'I gave her my word I wouldn't tell you,' he said.

She took a deep breath and when she spoke there was despair in her voice. 'My mother is a pathetic soul. I had hoped she'd changed but she hasn't.' She stood up, walked to the window and stood looking out across the gardens. 'You know I used to come here as a child. I'd look out this very window and imagine that if I was quiet enough and didn't peek, all the characters in all the books on these shelves would come to life. And I would never have to be alone again. I'd always have someone to play with.' She laughed bitterly. 'And *I* think *Mother* is a pathetic soul.'

She turned and came back to sit beside him. 'It's time we left Land's End. We should have gone days ago.' Her voice was strong now, determined. 'If it's all right with you, I'd like to stay until tomorrow night. For the ball. Some of these people I haven't seen for years. And I don't expect that I'll ever see any of them again.' There was genuine regret in her tone, but there was also strength. 'First thing Sunday morning we'll leave.'

Judd took her hand. He hadn't expected her to act so quickly, so decisively. 'Are you sure?'

She reached up and traced the line of his jaw with one finger. 'I love you, Judd. I will never let anyone destroy that. Not your children, not my mother, not anyone.' And then, as if there was nothing more in the world to worry about, she gave him a quick hug. 'Now,' she said, smiling, 'I'd better get back to work.'

The morning was warm and a light breeze blew in from the ocean. Golden squares of sunlight played across the flower beds and a thousand sounds of summer filled the air, but Emma didn't hear them. She was too preoccupied. She sat staring down at the book in her lap, trying to make some sense out of what she was reading but with little success.

Not far away under the trees, Elizabeth and Addy were sitting at a table, playing a game of slapjack. Every once in a while Addy would slam her hand down on the pile of cards so hard that Emma would jump, but Elizabeth only laughed. 'Are you sure you don't want to play, Emma?' she asked.

Emma shook her head and went back to the encyclopedia she had taken, along with a few other books, from one of the shelves in Mrs Daimler's library. 'For thousands of years,' she read, 'all forms of madness, of grossly abnormal behavior and, sometimes, of physical disease have been explained in terms of spirit possession.' And further on, 'Spirit possession, like hysteria, has two conditions: a basic condition due to the individual's intrapsychic tension and a precipitating condition due to an event or situation involving stress or emotion.'

Emma had read the same paragraphs over and over, feeling more and more depressed. Not only didn't she know half the words, but what sense she could make of the rest led her to only one conclusion: there was no such thing as ghostly possession.

She flipped a few more pages, then closed the book. She sat for a few minutes not looking at anything in particular, and all at once, she noticed her skirt. It was her favorite skirt, only somehow this morning it seemed different. Strange. Like it was too bright, making some of the squares stand out. It was so bright it hurt her eyes to look at it. She felt suddenly afraid, and she glanced across the garden to make sure that Addy and Elizabeth were still close by.

'Your deal,' Addy was saying.

Emma relaxed a little and looked back at her skirt. She blinked through her glasses and all at once the harsh brightness was gone. It was her good old skirt again. Nevertheless, she decided to move a little closer to Elizabeth and Addy. She picked up one of the other books from the pile and crossed the garden to sit next to Addy.

Elizabeth looked up from her cards. 'Changed your mind? It's not too late to get in on all this excitement.'

Emma shook her head. 'No, thanks. I'll just keep reading.' This book was called *Ghosts Are Ghosts*, and the first words on the first page made her heart pound. 'Are ghosts real?' she read. 'After all the data has been compiled, examined, sorted out, verified, and analyzed, the answer can be only one: yes.' Emma couldn't believe her eyes. Here in her hands was a book written by someone who really and truly believed in ghosts. 'Holy cow,' she said.

Elizabeth looked up. 'Is it that good?'

Emma smiled. It was the first real smile she had been able to muster all morning. Ever since she saw the mess on the walls. 'It sure is,' she said. She began to read.

She was so engrossed that she never noticed her father until he was right beside her. 'What're you reading, honey?' he asked.

Emma dropped the book in her lap, cover side down so he couldn't see the title. 'Oh, just some old book,' she said, without looking up.

He leaned over, curious, then frowned. 'A book about ghosts.' He didn't smile. 'Don't you think you've had enough of ghosts, Emma?' He sounded so tired.

She looked up. 'It's not a scary book, Daddy,' she said. 'It's about real ghosts.'

'And real ghosts aren't scary?'

'Not as scary as the ones people think you make up,' she said quietly.

'What's all this about ghosts?' Elizabeth said.

Emma flushed and shot her father a warning glance but it was too late because at that moment Addy said, 'Emma thinks there's a ghost living in the house.'

'Oh, Addy, I do not,' Emma mumbled, mortified now, because to hear Addy say it out loud made it sound so stupid that she wanted to die.

'You do so,' Addy said, shuffling her cards. 'You even told us her name is Lilith.'

What happened next was so unexpected that Emma forgot all about her own embarrassment. She had been sure that Elizabeth would laugh at her for being a silly baby, but instead, Elizabeth turned around and stared as if she had seen a ghost herself. 'Where did you hear that name?' she gasped.

Emma was too surprised to answer, but her father wasn't. 'Does the name mean something to you, Elizabeth?' he asked sharply.

Elizabeth seemed really flustered. 'No,' she said, shaking her head. 'It's just that it's an odd name, that's all.' She looked over at Judd. 'You wouldn't think she'd make up a name like that. I was just curious to find out where she'd heard it.'

'I didn't make it up,' Emma said quietly. 'I saw her. Her name is Lilith.'

Elizabeth laughed a funny, breathless kind of laugh, then she stood up. 'I think it's going to storm. We'd better go inside.' Without waiting for anyone else, she left the garden and disappeared up the path toward the house.

'That was odd,' Judd said, frowning. He had begun to rely on Elizabeth's calm support, but just now she had seemed truly disconcerted.

'And we didn't even get to finish our game,' Addy said.

'Later, sweetheart,' Judd said. 'Elizabeth's right. I think it's going to storm. Besides we have to get ready to go see Doctor Roth.' He turned to Emma, tipping her chin up so he could see her expression. 'Cheer up,' he said gently. 'I have some good news.'

She waited.

'Day after tomorrow, we're leaving Land's End.'

The color rushed into Emma's cheeks and she opened her eyes wide. 'We're leaving?' she gasped. 'We really truly are?'

'We really truly are.'

'Swear to Holy Bible?'

'Swear to Holy Bible.'

'Oh, Daddy.' She jumped up and threw her arms around him. 'Oh, Daddy, thank you, thank you, thank you.' Then she rushed over to Addy. 'Come on, Ads,' she said, grabbing her sister by the hand. 'Let's go inside and pack.'

'Whoa,' Judd said. 'You'll have all day tomorrow. Right now let's pick up these cards and get ready to visit Doctor Roth.'

Emma was shocked. 'But why do we have to see him? We're leaving Land's End, Daddy. Now everything's going to be just fine.'

Jesus Christ, he thought bleakly, I wish it were all that simple. 'Well, we probably won't have a chance to see the doctor again,' he said, 'so I want to thank him for all he's done for us. In person.'

Emma nodded. 'He's going to be surprised when he finds out that it's working out just the way I hoped it would.' She smiled. 'When we get back to New York I'm going to write him a nice, long letter.'

'He'll appreciate that, I'm sure,' Judd said. He picked up the deck of cards and together the three headed up the path toward the house.

They were almost up on the terrace when Emma stopped short. 'I forgot my books.'

'Well, run back and get them,' Judd said. 'We'll wait right here.'

Emma hesitated but only for a minute. She wasn't frightened anymore. They were leaving this place. They were going where they would all be safe. She flew down the steps and onto the path. Fine drops of rain had begun to fall and she prayed that the real storm would hold off until she got the books. She was sure that Mrs Daimler would have a fit if her books got wet, especially since Emma hadn't asked permission to take them out of the house.

Her feet skimmed over the ground, barely touching, and all at once, she had the weirdest feeling that she had run way past the garden. In fact, it seemed as if she had been running forever. Yet still, endlessly, the path rolled on ahead. She frowned. How could this be? The garden where they had been sitting was only steps away from the house.

She slowed down, glancing nervously over her shoulder, fearing for a moment that she had taken a wrong turn. Behind, she could see the roof of the house, with its huge chimneys soaring up into the darkening sky, at the same moment the air around her grew sharp and cold. The wind began to whistle, blowing stronger from the sea, but the sound was sad somehow, curiously mournful.

Emma stopped and listened. Now, above the wail of the wind, she could hear another sound. A soft rustling. Was there something coming up the path behind her?

Don't look back, she thought suddenly, wildly. Don't look back. Run.

She took off with a burst of speed, certain now that something was following. 'You can't hurt me!' she screamed. 'We're leaving here forever! Do you hear me? We're leaving!'

And to her horror, through the trees, she heard the echo of a child's voice, still behind her but coming closer and closer. And the words turned her blood to ice. *Too late. Too late.*

Stumbling, tripping over unseen obstacles, she raced

on, not knowing where she was heading, certain only that she was being chased. And then she fell.

She flew through the air and landed on her hands and knees in the grass right beside her pile of books. Panting, choking on her sobs, she grabbed them and, without bothering to look at her knees to see how badly they were scraped, she struggled to her feet and fled back up the path toward the house, the ghost-child, invisible, left behind in the garden. Whispering the same words over and over. *Too late. Too late.*

sixteen

The day of the great ball dawned gloriously warm and clear and the mood was infectious. Judd decided that he would make the most of these last hours at Land's End. Ever since the decision had been made to leave, he had felt amazingly relieved. Even their final visit with Dr Roth had ended on an optimistic note.

'I'm almost as eager as Emma is to have you all go back to New York,' the doctor said but he held up a cautionary finger. 'That doesn't mean I'm into ghosts, mind you. But the return to somewhat more familiar surroundings may be just what Addy needs to snap out of this.' He gave Judd the names of several therapists in the city. 'But to tell the truth, Mr Pauling, I don't expect you'll need them. I think from now on your little girls are going to be just fine.'

Afterward, on the way back to Land's End, the three of them stopped for ice cream and Judd couldn't help but smile at Emma. She was like an old-time movie, doing everything at top speed, as if the faster she moved the quicker Sunday would come. She was halfway through her ice-cream cone before Addy had even licked the sprinkles off the top.

'Slow down, Emma,' he teased, still smiling. 'Sunday will come even if you do slow down a little to catch your breath.'

She looked at him out of the corner of her eye and grinned sheepishly. 'I know,' she said. 'It just seems like it will come sooner if I hurry.'

Both children slept most of the way back to Land's End, and right after supper Emma asked if they could please, please pack.

'You have all day tomorrow,' Judd said, but Emma was insistent. She seemed afraid that if she didn't make all the preparations as quickly as possible, something might happen to change his mind.

Judd sat with them in their bedroom. He had thought he might do some sketching while Addy played with puzzles and Emma packed, but it was impossible. He watched in fascination as closets and bureaus were emptied, suitcases filled, toys packed, all with amazing speed, as if the contents had hands and feet of their own. When the last suitcase was slammed shut, Emma sat down hard on the edge of the bed, eyes bright, hands clasped tight in her lap. 'There,' she said, breathing a huge sigh. 'Now. We're all set.'

Judd crossed the room to sit beside her. 'Relax, sweetheart,' he said quietly. 'I know you're anxious to leave, but relax. The day after tomorrow will be here before you know it.'

She didn't look up. 'I don't suppose . . . I don't suppose we could go tomorrow,' she mumbled.

He hugged her. 'We can't sweetie. I promised Rachel

we'd stay for the ball. Besides, you'll love it. Tons of people will be arriving in the morning.' He paused. 'There won't be a quiet spot in this whole house, Emma. No place for even a friendly ghost.'

Emma nodded but she shot him a look that said she wasn't so sure.

He tucked them both in and just before he left the room Emma stopped him. 'Daddy?'

'Yes, Emma?'

'Is there any possible reason you can think of why we wouldn't be able to leave on Sunday?'

'Not a one.'

'Not even a tiny one?'

'Not even a tiny one.' He sensed her smile in the dark.

In the morning Rachel was up and gone from their bedroom before Judd was even fully awake, and he knew she was going to be busy all day, supervising last minute details, greeting old friends as they arrived. This was Rachel's ball, Rachel's day, and he was going to keep out of her way.

Last night he had decided that if the weather cooperated he would go up on the bluff where he had walked that day so long ago. He stopped, remembering. Could it possibly have been only ten days ago? It seemed like another century. Anyway, he'd do some sketches and he'd bring the kids along for a picnic. Even though their visit at Land's End had been a nightmare, there was no reason to end it on a sour note.

At breakfast he asked Elizabeth to join them. There wasn't much at Land's End he was going to miss but he would certainly miss Elizabeth.

'I'd love to go on a picnic,' she said smiling, giving his hand a quick, impulsive squeeze. But then almost instantly she drew back. 'I . . . I don't know what I was thinking of,' she stammered. 'I couldn't possibly do such a thing.' With that, she left the room.

'Darn,' Emma said.

'I know,' Judd said, frowning. He had really hoped Elizabeth would come with them. 'Oh well, it's still going to be a stupendous picnic. Right?'

'Right,' Addy said.

After a quick breakfast the three set out, passing as they went a battalion of gardeners bringing fresh cut flowers to the house: great baskets of blood-red roses and white lilies and purple lupine. Addy skipped along the path just ahead but Emma never left her father's side. First thing this morning she had piled all their belongings just inside the bedroom door, including the heaviest suitcases. He was amazed she could even lift them.

Now she walked quietly along beside him, carrying the picnic basket Kate had packed for their lunch, but she seemed nervous. She kept checking over her shoulder, as if watching for someone.

'Who're you looking for?'

She flushed. 'No one.'

'I'm right here beside you, sweetie. I'm not going to let you out of my sight,' he said. 'You don't have a thing to worry about.'

She gave a little sigh and smiled up at him. 'You're right, Daddy. I'm being stupid. We're going home tomorrow and today we're going to have a wonderful time.'

'Maybe we can even do some exploring,' he said.

Addy spun around. 'Maybe we can look for Maude,' she said, clapping her hands.

'Maybe we can,' Judd said. They had reached the top of the bluff where he had stood that other day, marveling at the landscape. 'Here's where we stop. You guys spread out the picnic things, I'll set up my equipment.'

Addy and Emma found a flat spot under a grove of trees where a few sheltered rhododendron were still in bloom. Emma opened the basket and took out a large linen tablecloth. 'Here, Ads,' she said. 'You take this corner and let's see if we can make it perfect.'

They had almost every wrinkle smoothed out when suddenly they heard their father call for them to come quick. 'It's Harold and Maude,' he yelled, pointing.

The two cats had appeared just below the top of the bluff and were meandering up the path toward him.

Harold stopped to rub against Addy's legs, but Maude continued on her way, barely pausing even to bestow a glance in their direction. 'Maybe she's on her way to have her babies!' Addy squealed and, at the sound of her high-pitched yell, both cats took off into the underbrush.

'Oh, no,' Addy said, flopping to her knees in the grass.

'I have a great idea,' Judd said.

Addy looked up, the corners of her mouth still turned down.

'Let's see where the old path takes us.' He pointed. 'That's where Maude went before. Remember?'

Addy's face lit up, Emma looked as though she were going to a funeral.

'I thought you loved to explore,' he said quietly, putting his hand on Emma's shoulder.

'Oh, I do,' she said hastily. 'But I'm just not in the mood.' He could feel her trembling.

He stooped down and pulled her close. 'Now listen, Miss Pauling,' he said. 'I know you've been having a terrible time lately. But you've got to try to be sensible. I can understand why you're afraid when you're all alone. But I'm right here now, and no ghost is going to bother you. I promise.'

She took a deep breath. 'I know, Daddy,' she said, looking down at her feet. 'It's just that . . . '

He waited.

She shrugged. 'Oh, never mind. I'm just being stupid. From now on I'm going to have a good time.'

'That's my girl.'

It wasn't easy going, particularly at the top of the bluff. There the hedges were thick and hopelessly tangled, and shrubs that had once been cultivated for their beauty now grew black and twisted, their blossoms meager and stunted. But once the three explorers made their way a short distance down the slope heading toward the ocean, the path opened up a little and they were able to follow it without too much difficulty. The only mishap occurred when Addy fell and scraped her leg, but to Judd's great relief she paid little attention, so intent was she on finding Maude.

The terrain wasn't quite so steep here, and as they came closer to the water the land leveled out into what once had been a terrace of sorts, laid with brick but cracked and crumbling now, overgrown with dune grass and nettles. Just beyond was a small, weatherworn cottage that Judd guessed was the place Elizabeth had called the summerhouse.

The windows were broken and the door, half-hanging from its hinges, moved slowly in the wind, banging intermittently against the battered siding.

'It looks like a witch's house,' Addy whispered, stick-

188

ing her thumb in her mouth, and close beside him, Judd felt Emma stiffen, then grab his hand.

'It's the old summerhouse Elizabeth told us about,' Judd said casually. 'Let's take a look.'

Inside the cottage the sunlight danced unimpeded through the broken windows, making it bright, almost cheerful. The one large room was fully furnished with chairs and tables and even a sofa, but, delightfully, everything was scaled down, child-sized. Layers of fine sand had sifted over the furnishings, giving silent testimony to the fact that the little cottage had been given up to the elements years earlier. Still, it was enchanting.

'Wow,' Addy said, taking a tentative step over the threshold.

'Wait a sec,' Judd said. 'Let me make sure the floor is still safe.' He walked carefully across the room, testing each floorboard, leaving a trail of footprints in the sand as he went. 'Walk where I walk,' he said, pointing.

Entranced, the children followed. 'It's a real playhouse, isn't it, Daddy?' Emma said, having left all of her fears at the door. Caught up now in the wonder of the place she crossed to the far side of the room. 'Oh, look, Ads,' she said, blowing the sand away. 'A little sink and stove. And I bet they really work.'

Judd nodded. 'They probably did once, but I doubt that they still do.'

'I wonder why Mrs Daimler let it get so yucky?' Addy said, wrinkling her nose.

'I can't imagine,' Judd said.

'I wish we weren't leaving Land's End. Then we could fix it up and play here all day long.' She opened the door to a small cupboard just her size. 'Holy moley, Emma, look at this!'

189

Emma crossed the room and stared. Inside the cupboard, protected from the sand that had sifted everywhere else, were pots, pans, china, even a set of real crystal. But not miniatures as in the dollhouse. These things were simply scaled down. All just the right size for a child.

Addy picked up a small crystal goblet. 'I wonder who belongs to all this stuff?'

'Probably Rachel and Elizabeth,' Emma said. 'Right, Daddy?'

'Right.' But even as he said it, a tiny alarm began to ring in the back of his head. Something was wrong here. Something didn't make sense. Frowning, he picked up a small, weather-beaten decoy from one of the tables, turned it over in his hand, then set it down again. He looked around. What is it, he wondered. What's not right? He could tell that most of the furnishings in the summer-house were at least twenty to thirty years old. But in spite of the damage done by the wind and the sand, he had the peculiar feeling that some of the things had been added much more recently.

Okay, Mr Private Eye, he said to himself. Like what, for instance? He began to look more carefully, taking time to brush the sand from each object, trying to figure out why he felt so uneasy.

And then Emma put it in his hand. A book. One of the first she had ever been able to read all by herself. 'Look, Daddy,' she said. '*The Magic Horses.*'

A small thing. A child's book. But one he knew had been published only five years ago. He remembered because he had bought it for Emma as a first-day-of-school present. So what? he thought. So some child had used the playhouse after Rachel and Elizabeth left Land's End. But it bothered him. For some reason it made him all the more eager to be away from here and back in New York City.

Only half paying attention, he opened the book, gasped, then slammed it shut before Emma could see what was written just inside the front cover. 'Let's go,' he said sharply, dropping the book on the floor.

'But Daddy,' Addy wailed. 'Can't we stay for just a few more minutes?'

'No. It's time to eat.' He tried to make it sound casual but inside his head his brain was exploding.

Emma stared up at him. 'What's wrong, Daddy?' She whispered and he could hear the fear in her voice.

'Nothing, honey,' he said, taking her by the hand. 'I just remembered that we left our picnic basket open, and you know what those rascal gulls can do if you give them half a chance.'

Emma nodded but she didn't seem reassured, and he cursed himself for not having done a better job hiding his shock.

It wasn't until they were almost to the top of the bluff that Judd finally caught his breath. He still couldn't believe what he had read inside the cover of that book. Printed in large, irregular, child's letters was the name of the owner. The name was Lilith.

Land's End came to life that evening, and so did Rachel. She wore white flowers in her hair and a gown of turquoise lace that matched her eyes, and she took his breath away.

'Will you love me forever?' She whispered as they came arm in arm down the grand staircase.

'Forever.'

'How about tomorrow?' She laughed, a delightful,

infectious sound, then tightened her grip on his arm and led him across the hall to meet some of the guests.

At the top of the stairs, Addy and Emma knelt on the carpet, peeking through the bannisters at the crowd gathered below. Judd had given them permission to stay up for awhile to see all the ladies in their beautiful gowns. Emma was grateful beyond words. It meant that on this last night at Land's End, she and Addy could sit outside their room in the brightly lit hall, with hundreds of people only steps away and happy music filling the air. Music that helped drown out the echo of those terrifying, ghostly words. *Too late. Too late.*

The orchestra was taking a break and for the first time all evening Judd found himself alone at the bar. He had been hoping to catch sight of Elizabeth so that he could question her about the name in the book, but thus far his sister-in-law had remained elusive. He ordered a Scotch, then realized with some surprise that he was actually having a good time. He hadn't seen hide nor hair of Priscilla, thank goodness. He was beginning to wonder if she had even come downstairs. He was enjoying the company of the other guests, he was madly in love with his wife, and they were all set to get the hell away from here and head back to New York first thing in the morning. What more, he wondered, could a man ask?

'Here you are, sir,' the bartender said.

'Thanks.' He picked up the drink and headed back across the room. He had just caught a glimpse of Henry Adelford through the doorway and he wanted to say goodbye, to thank him for his concern and for his help. He picked his way through the crowd and went out into the entrance hall where a small number of guests had gathered.

He was almost at Henry's side when, all at once, he stopped in his tracks. Above his head the crystal chandelier suddenly began to sway, making clear, tinkling sounds as it moved. It was as if someone had just opened a window or a door somewhere in the house and a cold sea wind was rushing through.

He looked around, curious to see if anyone else had noticed, and realized that they had. A hush had fallen over the company, people looking from one to the other with puzzled expressions on their faces, obviously wondering what was causing the sudden draft.

And then, over the sound of the wind, Judd heard the chiming of the doorbell and at the same time, from somewhere above, he heard a child cry out. A high-pitched voice, wild with desperation and unspeakable terror. 'Papa, save me! Oh, please! Papa!'

Addy! Judd thought, horror-stricken. But why was she calling him Papa? Before he could act the doorbell chimed again, and in the next instant the whole company froze. No one moved and time, as Judd had always known it, stopped.

He could see the butler, hand outstretched to open the door. Rachel, in midsentence, standing next to the Elliots at the foot of the stairs. Henry Adelford, arm suspended in midair about to bite down on a canapé, with Priscilla just behind him, a dark figure, motionless in shadow. And finally, on the stairs, Addy, open-mouthed, screaming a silent scream, her face so twisted that he didn't recognize her. His brain told him that it had to be Addy. His eyes said absolutely not.

The doorbell chimed again, and suddenly the company came back to life, staring, incredulous as Addy began her headlong flight down the stairs. 'Papa!' she shrieked again.

Judd stepped forward and held out his arms. 'Addy!' he said, but to his astonishment she brushed by him, knocking against people, pushing past their legs until she was almost to the front door. There she stopped and stood, staring.

The door opened and a man stepped in from the mist. A tall, handsome man with gray hair and gray eyes. 'Well, I can see I'm just in time,' he said in a voice that was faintly foreign. He handed his coat to the butler and moved into the hall.

Judd managed to reach Addy and grab her just as she crumpled to the floor, but the stranger walked around them without so much as a sidelong glance. He passed through the crowd, nodding, greeting each one, smiling at their stunned faces, until he reached the foot of the stairs where Rachel stood. Her back was to Judd and he couldn't see her face, but he heard her muffled cry.

And then the stranger put his arms around her. 'Rachel, my darling,' he said in a soft, teasing voice, 'is that any way to greet your husband?'

seventeen

Silence.

Judd sat in semidarkness in his children's bedroom. Through the gloom he could see the two small mounds that were Emma and Addy, huddled together in the middle of one bed. Judd had promised not to leave them and Emma had finally fallen asleep in spite of herself. As he sat numb, scenes from the night before flashed through his mind like a series of stop-action photos, each one totally separate yet somehow all inexplicably connected: Addy, shrieking mindlessly, her small face twisted into something unrecognizable; Rachel, pitching forward into the arms of the stranger who claimed to be her husband; a dozen voices whispering the name Peter; and watching it all from the shadows, Priscilla Daimler, motionless except for a little trickle of blood oozing from the spot on her lip where she had bitten down so fiercely. He felt sick, remembering her words as she came out of the shadow to stand in front of him. 'You left me no choice, Mr Pauling. Now you know.'

He had stood paralyzed, Addy limp in his arms. He had watched helplessly as Rachel was carried upstairs. He started to follow but Elizabeth held him back. 'I'm so sorry, Judd, ' she said, staring at him with stricken eyes. 'I kept begging her. She should have told you.'

Judd looked down at her, incredulous. 'Are you saying that it's true?' he rasped. 'That this man is Rachel's husband?'

She nodded.

He turned away and carried Addy to the stairs, walking slowly, deliberately as if a knife had been plunged into his back and he was afraid that any sudden movement might prove fatal. His only thought now was to find someplace solitary, invisible, where he could hide to think, to try to regain reason.

Emma met him at the top of the stairs, eyes wide with terror, filled with tears. 'Oh, Daddy,' she whispered, 'did you see her? Did you?'

Judd nodded and somehow managed a response. 'I saw, Emma,' he muttered. 'I saw.'

Together, the three made their way through the silent halls to the children's bedroom.

Now, in the darkness, Judd leaned his head back against the chair and closed his eyes. He tried to focus on what had happened to Addy but he couldn't. Right now he had to believe that Dr Roth was right. That taking Addy away from Land's End would save her. Beyond that, he was too stunned to concentrate.

'Rachel,' he groaned as if the saying of her name would wake him from this incomprehensible nightmare. 'Rachel.' And as the realization of what had happened took hold, he was overwhelmed with the enormity of what it meant. His Rachel, the darling of his life, was married to someone else. Bigamy. The word exploded in his brain and he began to shake, suddenly filled with blind rage. How could she have deceived him so treacherously? He wanted to curse her, beat her, kill her. But he couldn't sustain his anger. No matter what she had done, there was still that intangible quality of innocence about Rachel, as if no matter what, she couldn't possibly be to blame. Everyone who knew Rachel seemed guided by that same sentiment: Priscilla Daimler, Henry Adelford, even Elizabeth. But, above all, Judd loved her, and when the feeling of outrage finally drained away, he was left exhausted, filled only with a suffocating sense of loss.

He never heard Elizabeth until she was right beside him. 'Judd?' she whispered. 'Are you all right?'

'No.'

'Rachel wants to see you.'

He couldn't answer.

'Will you go to her?'

He shook his head.

Elizabeth sank down on her knees beside the chair. 'I know this has been a terrible shock for you,' she said. 'But she needs you. She . . . ' She paused and when she spoke again there was real urgency in her voice. 'She's in trouble, Judd. Real trouble.'

'So am I,' he said wearily. 'So am I.'

'I'll stay. I'll watch the girls,' she pleaded. 'Please, Judd. Please go to her.'

'Why didn't you tell me?'

For a moment she looked angry. 'It's not my place to tell you anything, Judd,' she said. 'Rachel is your wife. This is between the two of you. It always was. It still is.'

He exhaled. Slowly he stood up. 'Where is she?'

'In her old room. Next to Mother's.'

He started to the door, his feet like lead.

'Judd?' So quiet that he barely heard her.

He stopped.

'I know you have every reason to feel betrayed,' she choked. 'But please don't be unkind. She's still . . . she's still such a child.'

Rachel lay in her bed, her eyes closed, her hair a silver cloud against the white of the pillowcase. She looked so young, so defenseless that Judd's breath caught in his throat. He could see the dark shadows under her eyes, the tears sparkling on her eyelashes.

Suddenly she opened her eyes wide, and he could tell that she was frightened, confused, as if she had no idea where she was. But when she saw him, she broke into a radiant, spontaneous smile, the smile of a child who has been lost but is now found. She held out one hand. 'Oh, darling,' she breathed, 'thank goodness you've come.' She sat up, clasping her hands together, looking up toward the ceiling. 'Thank you, God. Thank you. I knew you'd help me.' In the next instant she flung herself out of the bed and across the room, throwing herself against him, kissing him, dampening his shirt with her tears.

Judd didn't move. He stood silent, his arms hanging limp at his side and suddenly she seemed to realize that something was wrong. She stopped kissing him and drew back, a tiny frown appearing between her eyebrows. Her face grew pale, her eyes opened wide. 'Judd?' she stammered. 'What is it? What's the matter? Surely you aren't still angry with me?' She was like a child who has misbehaved, been punished, and now assumes that everything is forgiven.

'Rachel,' he said as calmly as he could, 'I'm leaving

Land's End in the morning. Just as soon as I can pack the car.'

'I know that,' she said, smiling a tremulous smile. 'Isn't that what we'd planned?'

His head was beginning to pound. Could it be possible that she really believed nothing had changed? 'It doesn't matter what we'd planned, Rachel,' he said quietly, even though he felt like screaming. 'I'm going alone.'

Her head snapped back as if he had slapped her. 'What do you mean? I told you before that I'd go with you. I still will.'

At the sound of her words, a chill touched the back of his neck. What was wrong with her? He searched her face for some sign of awareness, some sign that in spite of what she was saying, she knew differently. But all he saw was disbelief.

Slowly she turned and sat down on the edge of the bed. 'Then Mother was right all along,' she said finally. 'She said you'd leave me one day and she was right. You're leaving me.' Incredibly, she made him feel guilty.

He crossed and sat beside her, taking her hand. It was ice-cold. 'Rachel, surely you understand what's happened here.'

She looked up at him, barely breathing, her eyes full of reproach, as if he had been the one who had been deceitful. Can this be possible, he wondered. Can she really not know what any of this means? But Jesus, how can she not know? This was no simple mistake. This was bigamy. How could she have been married to two men at the same time and not know that something was wrong?

'Is Peter Rostov your husband?' he asked quietly, trying to keep calm.

'He was.'

'Did you ever divorce him?'

Her next words were full of anger. 'Of course I did. At least I thought I did.' She looked at him out of the corner of her eye. 'Right after I was sent to that . . . that place, Mother told me that Peter wanted to be free of me. That he had filed for divorce. She said she had taken care of the details. That I wasn't to worry. I was to rest and get well.' She sighed. 'I was in no condition to question any of it.'

'Your mother told you you were divorced?' He was incredulous. No wonder Priscilla Daimler had been so shocked to discover that Rachel had remarried. 'But why?'

Rachel shook her head. 'I'm not sure.' She tipped her head to one side. 'Although it's not really surprising when you think about it. She wanted me to come home. She didn't want me to look for Peter after . . . after I got out.'

'But what about him? Didn't he ever try to see you?'

A cloud passed across her face. 'No. I'm sure Mother saw to that, too.'

Judd sat motionless, trying to make some sense out of this madness. Priscilla Daimler had deliberately deceived her daughter, had allowed her to think she was divorced. But why? Had she hated Peter Rostov that much? Or had she been motivated by the single selfish desire to keep Rachel all to herself? And if that were so, could it be possible that she was doing it again? Trying to drive him away from Rachel with lies and treachery? Somehow he knew it was all connected. But how? What was he missing?

Rachel must have misinterpreted his silence because

she began to talk quickly, her words tumbling one over the other. 'I know I should have told you about Peter, and I'm sorry. But I was so tired when I came out of that hospital. And so unsure. And I never wanted to think about any of it again. I didn't think I could bear it.' She shuddered. 'I don't love him. I love you. I'll get a divorce and then everything will be just as it was. We'll be together and we'll never have to see any of these people again.' She smiled the tight, confident smile of a child who thinks that just because she says something, it makes it so. She squeezed his hand. 'Don't you see? There's no reason for us to change our plans. We can still all leave in the morning.'

Judd took a weary breath. 'I wish it were that easy, Rachel.'

A look of alarm crossed her face. 'But surely you realize that it wasn't my fault. I didn't deliberately deceive you. I thought I was free of him, and I wanted to forget that I had ever known him. I know now that I should have told you about him.' She leaned forward, her voice suddenly soft, patient, as if she were trying to explain something that was all too obvious. 'I didn't tell you about Peter because I didn't want to speak his name ever again. I didn't think I'd ever have to. I thought we were finished.' She paused and her tone changed, became sharp, angry. 'Besides, I wanted to forget I ever knew him. He's the cruelest man I ever met. Oh, how I hate him.' She clenched her fists. 'If you only knew how much I hate him you would understand.'

He closed his eyes. He could still feel the pain in his head, and although it was a dull pain now, he still couldn't concentrate. All he wanted to do was sleep. He felt her move closer to him, cautiously, like a small puppy that wants desperately to be petted but hesitates, uncertain of its master's mood.

He put his arms around her and held her close for a minute, then gently pushed her away. 'I'm not angry, Rachel. But I have a lot to think about. The children and I will still have to leave in the morning,' he said softly. 'Alone.'

She searched his face, incredulous, as if somehow he hadn't understood. 'But . . . '

He put his finger against her lips. 'There's nothing more to be said, my darling. You've got to stay here until you get your life in order but I cannot stay with you. For one thing I have to think this through by myself . . . try to see if I can make some sense of it.'

She closed her eyes, pressing her lips together in a tight line. 'I don't know what you're saying. Don't you love me anymore?'

'You know I do,' he said.

'Then I don't understand,' she said, shaking her head. 'What's changed?'

He breathed deep. 'Everything's changed, Rachel. How can you not see it? Our marriage has been a lie. Whether you were aware of it or not, Peter Rostov is still your husband. Our lives are so bitched up that right now I'm not sure how we go about putting them back together. You are married to two men, for Christ sake, and until that's resolved we cannot even consider living together. Not here. Not in New York.' He paused. 'You must realize that we aren't the only ones involved in this mess. I have two children to consider.'

She sat motionless for a full minute, then suddenly slammed her hand against the side of her head as if understanding for the first time. 'Of course,' she said and

202

there was such a coldness in her voice that Judd shivered. 'I see now. Why am I always so stupid? It's not Peter at all, is it? It's your daughter. It's Addy. She's convinced you that I'm no good. She's convinced you to leave me.'

Judd reached for her hand but she pulled it away. 'I should have known,' she said, and the coldness gave way to angry tears. She stood up and backed away from him, her expression one of absolute betrayal. 'I should have listened to my mother. She warned me. She told me I'd never be happy with you as long as you had your children with you. She knew I'd never be able to compete with them. Especially Addy.'

Judd was incredulous. 'You don't believe that for one minute, Rachel,' he snapped. 'This has nothing whatever to do with Addy.'

She stared at him, her eyes blazing. 'It has everything to do with her! Leaving me is cruel enough. But how can you do it and try to pretend that it's all my fault?'

Judd felt something snap inside his head and he was filled with an overwhelming urge to grab her, to shake her until her teeth rattled. He took two quick steps toward her, then stopped dead in his tracks. She was looking at him with an expression so full of reproach that he was left speechless. Rachel truly seemed to believe what she was saying. She truly did. 'Jesus,' he said. 'Sweet Jesus.'

'Please don't go,' she cried suddenly, the anger gone as quickly as it had come. 'Please don't let her take you away from me.'

Beyond words, Judd spread his hands in a gesture of complete helplessness. Then he turned and without looking back he left the bedroom.

*

Priscilla Daimler walked through the passageway that led from her room to her daughter's. She had heard only the last words between Rachel and Judd but she knew that he and his children were leaving Land's End. Without Rachel. From her expression it was impossible to tell what she was thinking. She reached one hand out to steady herself and listened.

She heard the door to the hall open, then close.

Silence.

She did not move. Finally, when there was no more sound, she stepped through the doorway into Rachel's bedroom.

Rachel was sitting on the edge of the bed, her back to her mother.

'My dearest child,' Priscilla said softly. 'How are you?'

At the sound of her mother's voice Rachel turned. 'Why, Mother,' she said in a voice that expressed surprise but nothing more. 'What are you doing up at this hour?'

Priscilla stepped back, clearly startled, as if she had expected a different reaction from her daughter. Tears? Remonstrances? Perhaps. But not this.

'Surely you ought to be in bed,' Rachel said. She stood up and took her mother gently by the arm. 'Come now. This day has been a terrible strain on all of us.' She put her arm around her mother and led her back through the passageway to her own room.

With great care Rachel settled her into bed, then sat down on the edge. She was silent for a minute as if gathering her thoughts. Finally she spoke. 'Why did you send for Peter?' There was no anger, no reproach. Only simple curiosity.

'I was afraid you would be hurt again.'

Rachel's expression never changed. 'Judd would never hurt me,' she said quietly.

Exhausted, Priscilla lay motionless but she didn't close her eyes. She searched her daughter's face, as if trying to read her thoughts. 'But he *has* hurt you, hasn't he?' she said finally.

'Yes, he has,' Rachel said, still calm. 'Because you left him no choice. You brought Peter back.'

'I had no choice either. I had no choice. For once in my life I had to consider someone besides you.'

Rachel was silent for a minute, then she let out her breath in a long sigh. She tipped her head to one side, as if trying to puzzle something out. 'Why do you suppose it is, Mother, that in all my life I have never stood first in line with anyone? Not ever.'

Priscilla reached over and took her daughter's hand. 'Oh, my darling,' she said, 'how can you say that? You know that I have never cared about anyone but you.'

Rachel stiffened. 'Then why do you always manage to destroy everything that ever means anything to me?'

'Because I love you, Rachel. And because I'm frightened.'

Rachel tipped her head to one side again, a small, curious smile playing around the corners of her mouth. 'You? Frightened? Of what? What could there possibly be in this world that would frighten Priscilla Daimler?' The seconds ticked by without an answer. 'Mother?' Rachel's voice again, still calm but insistent now. 'What is it you're afraid of?'

'That it will happen again.' And then two short syllables barely whispered and yet they filled the room with sound. 'Lilith. I'm afraid of Lilith.'

Rachel's eyes opened wide, her mouth formed a round

'O' of shock. 'What are you saying?' Rachel said. 'What has she to do with this?'

'Everything.' Priscilla's voice was barely audible, as if all of her strength had left her. 'Lilith has come back.' She put her hand out to touch her daughter's arm. 'Think of it, Rachel. The piano playing. The hiding place under the stairs. And that ghastly writing in the hallway. I know it's unthinkable but it's true. Lilith has come back. She's come back . . . through Addy Pauling.'

Rachel was staring at her mother as if she didn't recognize her. 'Are you mad? None of those things had anything to do with Lilith. Lilith is dead.' She grabbed her mother's hand. 'Haven't you heard anything they've been saying about Addy Pauling? She's psychologically disturbed. Doctor Roth told Judd that she's suffering from the loss of her mother, that all this is her way of working through her grief.' She narrowed her eyes and for a moment it seemed as if she were thinking out loud. 'I'm not sure about Doctor Roth, but I do know one thing about Addy. She hates me and she wants to be rid of me. That's why she did all those things. She's a very sick child.'

'I know what the doctor said, Rachel. And I know what you think about your stepdaughter. But I don't believe any of it. Not for one minute. This has nothing to do with Addy Pauling's mental condition or her desire to be rid of you. It has to do with Lilith. Lilith is here. In this house. And that child is her medium.'

A look of anger crossed Rachel's face. 'You must take me for a fool, Mother. You brought Peter back to drive Judd away. That was what it was all about, wasn't it?'

Priscilla drew her lips tight. 'All right, Rachel. I did it to drive him away. Because if you went with them, I couldn't be sure what would happen. I am an old woman, Rachel, and I am dying. I cannot bear any more guilt.'

Rachel's expression changed. A small, sad smile began to play around the corners of her mouth. 'There is no reasoning with you, is there?' she said. 'No matter what anyone says, you always manage to manufacture your own lies to get what you want.'

'And what is it you think I want?'

'You want me here with you forever.' Rachel pressed her hands against her temples as if suddenly in terrible pain. 'I've known from the first that Addy Pauling wanted me out of her father's life. She's tried at every turn. First my welcome-home party. And then the terrible things she said to me that day in the car. And the mess she made on the walls. But I knew why she was doing it. And I was determined not to let her succeed.' She laughed a bitter laugh. 'And now she's won. And *you* did it for her, Mother. You. My own, my dearest mother.' Trembling, she dropped her hands into her lap. 'You've never let me live my own life in my own way, have you? It always had to be yours. I haven't forgotten. Just when Peter was finally coming home to me, you sent me away. To be locked up like an animal. And now you don't want me to have Judd either. You want me to stay here alone at Land's End until I die.'

Shuddering, the old woman turned away.

'No, Mother, don't look away. Look at me.' She spoke with a peculiar detachment, as if none of this really affected her. 'See what you've done. Not only have you tried to control my life but now the final absurdity. You want me to believe that it's all because of Lilith.'

Priscilla held out a trembling hand but her daughter ignored it.

Slowly Rachel stood up, her face devoid of all expression. 'I never start out wanting to leave you, Mother,' she said, 'but somehow you always manage to make it happen. Now it doesn't matter if Judd leaves Land's End. I'll follow him to the ends of the earth. And I'll do whatever I must to make him love me again. Whatever. And without you to interfere, maybe this time I'll win.'

'Rachel . . . please.' A strangled gasp.

'Good-bye, Mother. I won't be seeing you again.' Without a backward glance, Rachel left, closing the door quietly behind her. Had she looked back and seen her mother's face, seen the spasms that wracked her body, she might have called for help.

As it was, in her hour of greatest need, Priscilla Daimler was left alone.

As was the custom at Land's End and had been for almost half a century, each morning precisely at eight o'clock Priscilla Daimler would notify the staff as to where she would be taking her breakfast. It was not surprising therefore that there was some alarm in the kitchen when the hour came and went with no word from Mrs Daimler.

Her maid found her unconscious, barely breathing. Henry Adelford was summoned.

eighteen

It was Sunday morning, a clear, sparkling summer morning and in the distance Emma could hear church bells ringing. 'Hurry up, Daddy,' she called, then sat down on one suitcase beside the drive, watching as her father went back inside to bring out the last of their luggage. Across the terrace, Addy was busy inspecting a solitary ant dragging a dead beetle across the bricks.

Emma opened her book to page ninety-three and tried to read but her eyes wouldn't focus. She kept hearing echoes from the night before, especially Addy's terrible shrieking. She took a deep breath and looked over at her sister, and something so awful suddenly occurred to her that she almost fell off the suitcase. What if . . . what if Dr Roth was wrong? What if Addy didn't get better? What if the ghost followed them all the way to New York? 'Addy,' she yelled, 'come over here right now.'

Addy didn't even look up. 'I can't. I'm busy.'

Emma put her book down and walked across the terrace to the spot where her sister was squatting.

'Be careful, Emma,' Addy said, frowning. 'Don't step on him.'

'Step on who?' Emma looked down.

'Mr Ant.'

'What's he doing?'

'He's dragging a big bug.'

Emma forgot her momentary panic. 'I wonder where he's going?'

'Probably to his house.'

Emma watched the ant struggle. 'I wish we knew where he lived. Then we could help him.'

'How?'

'We could carry the bug for him.'

Addy jumped up. 'Good idea, Emma. You're the smartest sister in the world. Let's look for his anthill.'

'Oh, Addy, don't be goofy. We could look forever and not find the right one.'

Addy tipped her head to one side, considering, then held up one finger. 'First of all,' she said, 'we find an anthill. Then very carefully we pick him up with his bug and put them right next to the hole and see if he goes in. If he doesn't we'll look for another one. See?'

Emma looked doubtful but she guessed it was as good a way as any to kill time until they were ready to leave. It certainly beat sitting alone, getting scared worrying about Addy. Not to mention puzzling over why Rachel wasn't coming with them. Not to mention the sickening fear she still had in her stomach that somehow, something was going to keep them from leaving Land's End. 'Okay,' she said. 'Let's look.'

Together the two children began to walk slowly along the edge of the terrace, peering down between the bricks, searching for the small, telltale mounds of dirt that meant ants lived below.

'Here's one,' Addy said.

Emma bent over and watched until an ant came crawling out. 'Nope,' she said. 'He's too small. Not the same kind.'

'I wish we didn't have to leave,' Addy said without warning, shuffling along just ahead of her sister. 'I like it here.'

Emma rolled her eyes skyward. 'Not me,' she said fiercely. 'I hate it and I can't wait to go.'

'But we never got a chance to play with the dollhouse,' Addy protested. 'Or in the nursery with all those neat toys. Or even in the summerhouse.' She suddenly stopped and her face got all red and puckered up. 'And worst of all, Emma, I didn't even get a kitten.'

'Oh, Addy, shush. Daddy said he'll get you one in New York.'

'But I don't want one in New York,' Addy said. 'I want one of Maude's.' Her lower lip began to tremble and teary storm clouds started building.

'I wish Daddy would hurry up,' Emma said, glancing back anxiously toward the house. And suddenly she was scared. She stared wide-eyed, stricken with that all-too-familiar feeling that they were being watched. 'Addy,' she whispered. 'Do you see anyone up there?' She pointed to the window on the third floor that she knew was the nursery.

'I don't see anything,' Addy pouted, not even looking up.

'Stop being a baby and tell me.' The very real fright in Emma's voice snapped Addy out of her sulky mood.

'Oh, all right. Where?' She stepped over to stand close beside her sister.

'Up there.'

Addy looked up at the house, then nodded. 'Yep. Someone's up there all right.'

Emma jerked her head up. 'You see someone?'

'Yep. I think it's Rachel.'

Emma squinted through her glasses, then let out a long sigh of relief. It *was* Rachel. 'I wonder what she's doing up in that yucky room?'

'It isn't yucky at all,' Addy said. 'She's probably playing with all those neat toys.' Her eyes lit up. 'Hey, Emma, I've got the best idea in the world. Maybe while we're waiting for Daddy, we can go up and play with her.'

'We don't have time!' Emma snapped, giving silent thanks that they didn't. She couldn't imagine any place she'd rather not be than upstairs in that icy, terrifying room.

'Well, you don't have to yell about it. I don't know why you're always yelling at me. You never want to do anything fun anymore.' With that, Addy turned away and began to stomp across the terrace toward the garden path.

'Where are you going?'

'I'm just walking, that's all.'

'Well, don't walk too far because Daddy will be right out.'

Ignoring her sister, Addy continued to march away, then all at once, she stopped dead in her tracks. 'Emma, look!' she yelled. 'There goes Maude and, holy cow, she's skinny!' She clapped her hands and began to run up the path after the cat.

'Addy, you come back here!' Emma shouted. 'Right this minute!'

Addy paid no attention.

'Addy!' Emma wailed. 'Daddy's going to give you the worst spanking of your life!' But her threat fell on deaf ears. To her dismay, Addy kept right on running, finally disappearing up the path that led to the stables.

Emma stood frozen. She didn't want to go after her sister. She was too scared. In fact, she didn't want to step one foot off the terrace. But Daddy told her not to let Addy out of her sight. 'Not for a minute,' he had said. 'Not for a minute.'

She hesitated, looking anxiously over her shoulder toward the house. Please, Daddy, she prayed. Please come out. But the door remained closed. With a sinking heart, Emma took a few tentative steps, then driven by fear, she broke into a run, flying up the path where Addy had disappeared moments before. 'I'm going to smack you, Addy Pauling!' she yelled as she ran. 'When I catch up with you I'm going to smack you real hard!'

Once she reached the top of the bluff she could see her sister not too far ahead. She had just climbed over the fence and was running across the pasture where Clarissa was peacefully grazing. Panting, Emma followed.

Addy was almost to the stable door when Emma finally caught up with her. 'Addy Pauling, you're really going to get it! Daddy said not to go anywhere.' She was close to tears. She took Addy by the arm. 'Now, come on.' She started to pull her sister across the paddock, but Addy wiggled away.

'You're not the boss of me,' Addy pouted. 'I'm going to see Maude's babies even if you do get mad. And besides, I don't even like you anymore.' Before her sister had a chance to move, Addy was off.

Hot tears of anger and frustration rolled down Emma's

cheeks. 'Addy, you come back here!' she wailed, but Addy had already disappeared inside the stable door.

Suddenly all the anger went out of Emma, leaving only throbbing fear. She stood frozen. No way did she want to follow her sister inside. She remembered all too well what happened the last time she was in there. 'Addy!' she yelled.

No answer.

She wiped her eyes and took two tentative steps toward the door, then stopped. She listened.

Silence.

'Addy?'

No answer.

Reluctantly she inched her way as close as she could get without actually going in, and she peered through the door. Inside the stable, the sun filtered through in splotches, making weird, shadowy patterns on the walls. Suddenly, at the back of her neck Emma thought she felt something touch her. 'Too late, Emma,' it whispered. 'Too late.' She whirled around but nothing was there.

'Don't be a baby,' she told herself fiercely. 'You're just imagining things. We're leaving today and then everything is going to be fine.' She took one step forward. 'Addy,' she said loudly, 'come on out of there. Daddy says.'

Still no answer.

In spite of her resolve to be brave, the thick silence was too much for her and she began to cry. 'Addy, I'm scared!' she shouted into the gloom. 'I really mean it, and if you don't come out here right now I'm never going to speak to you again!'

The only reply was the faint whicker of a horse somewhere down the line, but it gave her just enough courage to step through the doorway.

In the dim light she thought she could see something over in the corner by one of the open stalls. She squinted. 'Ads?' she whispered. 'Is that you?'

The only answer was the sound of her own breathing.

And then she saw Maude. The white cat was crouching in the shadow not far from where she stood and she could see how skinny she was. 'Oh, Maude,' she said, feeling a rush of relief. 'Addy was right. You did have your babies.'

She took two steps toward the cat, then stopped. She could see now that Maude was backed up against the wall, arched up like a witch's cat, ears flat against her head. 'What's the matter, Maude?' Emma whispered, but the cat only bared her teeth and began to growl a terrible, savage growl that began way down in her throat.

'It's okay,' Emma said soothingly. 'I won't hurt your kittens.' She took one more step toward the cat, then stopped again, realizing suddenly that Maude wasn't looking at her at all. She was staring past Emma, green eyes wild, tail lashing.

Unnerved, Emma threw a frightened glance over her shoulder, then with a tremendous sigh of relief she exhaled. Near the stable door she saw Addy step out from behind a bale of hay. 'Boy, are you going to get it when I tell Daddy,' Emma said, her relief now replaced with anger. She reached with one hand to grab her sister, then froze, her mouth opening and closing without a sound.

It wasn't the sight of Addy that paralyzed her. It was the smell. The smell in the nursery. The damp, dark smell of digging down where rotting things lie buried.

215

And with the smell came the bitter arctic cold, piercing to the bone.

Then Addy stepped out of the shadow. Only it wasn't Addy. It was a child whose face seemed carved out of ice, whose eyes reflected nothing but eternal coldness, a frigid, lifeless creature out of Emma's worst nightmare.

Emma's hands curled into tight fists and in spite of her terror, she stood her ground. 'Go away!' she shrieked. 'We're leaving this awful place so go away and leave us alone!'

The child that was Addy didn't answer. She just shook her head back and forth, back and forth.

Emma stared, mute now with fright, as the child opened her mouth. In a voice that came from some desolate, distant galaxy, Lilith spoke. 'Too late, Emma,' she keened. 'I can't let you leave. I've waited too long for you to come.'

Shaking uncontrollably, Emma shrank back against the wall; at the same moment from behind, she heard a terrible growling. Her eyes darted back and forth from the corpselike child that was her own sister to the snarling, wild-eyed cat, crouched, ready to spring.

Suddenly something inside Emma snapped and she could bear no more. 'Daddy!' she shrieked and flung herself through the open door. 'Daddy, save us!' With feet flying she raced across the paddock, shot over the fence and headed out into the open pasture.

Half out of her mind with fear, she knew only one thing. She had to get to her father before . . . before what she didn't know. She was almost across the clearing when she tripped over something and pitched forward, landing facedown, scraping both knees and the palms of her hands. A million needles of pain stung her but, frantic

216

to get help, she leaped to her feet, at the same time glancing over her shoulder. It was then that she saw Addy come out of the stable and walk slowly across to the fence.

Emma stared, part of her wanting desperately to escape, the other part telling her not to leave her little sister behind, that somewhere beneath that frozen, lifeless face, Addy was trapped. 'Addy!' she screamed as loud as she could. 'Make her let you go! Make her go away!'

There was no answer, and then to Emma's horror, she saw the child climb over the top of the fence and begin to walk slowly toward her, one small arm rising and falling, hypnotically beckoning Emma to come back.

Emma stood mesmerized, trembling with fear, wanting to turn and flee but, as in her worst nightmare, powerless to make her legs move. Tears stung her eyes and everything blurred. She's going to catch me! she thought wildly. She is! There was a monstrous roaring in her head, but suddenly through the din she heard Clarissa whinny, a high-pitched, nervous sound. She whirled around just in time to see someone coming down the path. 'Daddy!' she screamed, her legs coming back to life. She raced toward him, arms outstretched. 'Daddy, hurry! Something awful's happening to Addy!'

Without breaking his stride, Judd veered off the path, jumped the fence and ran toward his daughter. Even at this distance he could see the look of stark terror on Emma's face. But what filled him with a dread unlike any he had ever experienced before was what he saw beyond: it was the small figure of a child walking toward them across the pasture. She was the same size as Addy, she was wearing Addy's clothes. But it wasn't Addy.

'Jesus Christ!' he gasped. 'What in the sweet hell?' He was aghast. So aghast that he never saw the horse.

But Emma did. For a moment she was so stunned she couldn't find the breath to scream. As Emma stood gasping, Clarissa threw her head back and snorted. Just once. Then for no reason except that something terrified her to madness, she reared up and came thundering across the clearing toward Judd.

'Daddy!' Emma shrieked, but it was too late. Eyes rolling, muzzle flecked with foam, the horse, gone berserk, passed within inches of Emma's trembling body, then rose up in blind fear to strike at the one thing in her path: Judd Pauling.

nineteen

The grandfather clock in the lower hall struck four and a swollen-eyed Elizabeth glanced at her watch. 'Damn,' she said. 'Goddamn thing keeps losing time.' Her voice shook.

Henry Adelford put a hand on her shoulder. 'Calm down, Elizabeth. There are worse things in this world than malfunctioning timepieces. Besides, I can't have *you* breaking down now, can I?'

Elizabeth sighed. 'Don't worry. I'll be all right.' She sank down on the couch and stared across the room at the bed where Emma lay motionless. 'Any change?'

Dr Adelford shook his head.

'What next?' Elizabeth said. 'First that monster Peter appears out of nowhere. Then we find Mother in some kind of a coma. Now this.' She shook her head. 'I'm not an hysterical person, Henry, but right now I would love to go somewhere dark and cry until I couldn't think anymore.'

Henry sat down next to her. 'I don't blame you. I feel

like crying myself. I just wish I knew what happened here last night. If only I had stayed. But someone had to get Peter out of here as quickly as possible and I seemed to be the only one available.'

'Not that I care, but where is the bastard?'

'On his way to Boston.'

'Is it true? Did Mother really send for him?'

Henry sighed. 'I'm afraid so. Though you know this had to happen sooner or later. It was madness to think that Judd wouldn't find out.'

'I know. But we'd all agreed that it was Rachel's place to tell him about Peter. And she'd promised she would. So why did Mother bring him back?'

'Your mother has had only one goal in her life,' Henry said quietly, 'and that has been to protect Rachel.'

'I know that. That's why I find this so impossible to understand.'

'Didn't you talk to her after I left?'

Elizabeth shook her head. 'Mother went straight to her room and refused to see anyone.'

'Not even Rachel?'

'Rachel didn't want to see her.'

Henry sighed. 'So it begins again. Again the person who Priscilla treasures most in the world is lost to her.' He said it almost to himself.

Elizabeth was silent for a minute, then she said, 'That's not all. When I told Rachel that Mother had had a seizure during the night she didn't even ask to see her. She simply said she hoped I could stay on for a few more weeks because she would be leaving this morning with Judd.'

Henry raised an eyebrow. 'You mean he was going to take her with him in spite of this bigamy business?'

Elizabeth nodded. 'He loves her.' There was a wistfulness in her voice.

'Poor Elizabeth,' he said gently. 'If things had only been different . . . '

'But they aren't,' she said quickly, stopping him before he could say any more. 'And that's that.'

Henry nodded. 'Well, at least my poor Priscilla doesn't know that Rachel is leaving her,' he said.

Elizabeth looked over at him. 'You really love her, don't you.'

'Yes. I do.'

'How sad that you never told her.'

He smiled, considering, then shook his head. 'It would have ruined us, you know. She would never have trusted me again.'

Elizabeth nodded. 'You're right. She wouldn't have.' She took a breath. 'She would have thought you a terrible fool.'

He smiled. 'She would indeed.'

They sat, not speaking, each trying to adjust to the tragedies that had befallen them so unexpectedly. 'Do you think anyone can help my mother?' Elizabeth asked, finally breaking the silence.

Henry shook his head. 'Not unless you're willing to rip her out of her home, send her away. To Boston. Or New York. Where they'll do Lord knows what to her. Torture her a little, or a lot.' He took a deep breath. 'And then if they're successful and bring her back, you have to ask yourself what for? What's the point? Bring her back from wherever she is now so she can watch herself die?' He sounded angry. 'It's not my decision to make, Elizabeth, but if it were, I'd leave her alone.' He sighed.

'Right now I almost feel relieved. I was dreading it, you know.'

'What?'

'The end of her. Knowing the agony she had in store. She's a tough, tough lady but there are some things that break even the strongest of spirits. At least the way she is now she won't suffer.'

'How do you know that wherever she is, she isn't suffering?' A tear came out of the corner of her eye and ran down her cheek. 'I love her too, Henry,' she said quietly. 'Even though she never really cared.'

He took her hands. 'She cared, Elizabeth. She was just never very good at showing it.'

'Except with Rachel.' There was no bitterness in her voice. Only regret.

'Except with Rachel.' He reached up and touched her gently on the cheek. 'Do you want my advice, Elizabeth?'

'You know I do.'

'Wherever your mother is right now, she's peaceful. And she hasn't been that for a long, long time. I'm sure of it. So let her be. Don't try to bring her back.' It was a plea.

Elizabeth didn't have a chance to respond, because at that moment a sudden movement across the room brought them both to their feet. 'Emma?' Dr Adelford said.

No further response from the child. She lay as if dead.

'Where's Addy?' he asked.

'Across the hall in Rachel's room.'

'Maybe you ought to bring her here. It might help.'

Elizabeth was gone only a minute. When she came back she had a tearful Addy by the hand.

'What's the matter with my sister?' Addy choked. 'Why can't she wake up?'

'She's had a bad scare, Addy,' Henry said quietly.

'Did Clarissa tromp on her, too?'

'We don't think so. But we know she must have seen what happened to your father.'

Addy nodded, then climbed up on the bed next to her sister. 'Emma?' she whispered. 'Why can't you hear me? Are you still mad at me? Are you? Emma? Answer me.'

From a long way off Emma heard Addy's voice calling her but she didn't want to answer. She lay on her back, eyes shut tight and tried to make herself stay unconscious. Something so horrible had happened that she couldn't cope with it. Something so horrible. She moaned.

'Emma?' Addy's voice close by her ear, stuffy-nosed from crying. 'Emma, can you hear me?'

No answer. Then Emma heard a man's voice. Daddy?

She opened her eyes a crack but it wasn't her father. It was Dr Adelford leaning over her, his face looking old and very grim. And then with a rush of horror she remembered. 'Daddy!' she cried. 'Oh, my poor Daddy!'

'It's all right, Emma,' Dr Adelford said gently. 'Your father's all right.'

Emma heard the words but they didn't fit with what she knew to be true. Daddy was dead. Just like Mommy. That was the truth. She covered her face with her hands.

'Daddy's going to be just fine,' Addy said. 'I even saw him.'

'What?'

'Your father is fine, Emma,' Dr Adelford said.

Emma sat straight up. She couldn't believe her ears. The last thing she remembered was the thunderous rush-

223

ing of Clarissa's hooves and her father falling. 'He's all right?' she breathed, disbelieving. 'He's not dead?'

'He's all right, Emma,' Dr Adelford said. 'He's in the hospital. He's got a few broken ribs and a big lump on his head but other than that he's fit as a fiddle. Rachel's with him.'

Emma hugged herself tight. 'Thank you, God,' she whispered. 'Thank you, thank you, thank you. I'll never say kiss my ass again only this time I really mean it. And I won't ever laugh even if Mary Mongitori wets her pants in school.'

'It's you we're worried about.' Elizabeth came into her line of vision. 'You poor child, what happened?'

Emma opened her eyes and looked around. She was in her own bed and Addy was propped up on the pillow next to her, eyes red-rimmed, sucking her thumb. 'Ads?' Emma whispered. 'Is it you?'

'Of course it is,' Addy said. She sat up and put her hands on her hips. 'And I'm really mad at you, Emma. You scared Maude away so I couldn't find her.'

Emma let out a weak, exasperated sigh. At least Addy was Addy. But for how long? she wondered bleakly. She looked up at Dr Adelford. 'Are you sure my father's all right? You aren't just saying it?'

He smiled. 'He's in the hospital, Emma. Clarissa gave him quite a going over.' He took her hand. 'But he's going to be okay.'

Elizabeth sat down on the edge of the bed. 'What happened, Emma? Do you remember?'

Emma threw a nervous glance over at her sister, wondering how much Addy had told them. If anything. Oh, Daddy, she said to herself. What should I tell them? What should I say? 'I don't remember very much,' she lied.

Elizabeth shook her head. 'All we know is that one of the gardeners found Addy up on the bluff crying her eyes out. She said that Clarissa had jumped on her father. And that he told her to get help.'

Emma looked over at her sister. 'Did Daddy really talk to you?'

Addy nodded. 'He told me to run get someone and he had all this blood coming out of his nose. And I tried to wake you up but you wouldn't answer me.'

Emma nodded.

'What happened to spook Clarissa, Emma?' Elizabeth asked. 'Do you know?'

Emma felt the tears coming in spite of her resolve not to cry. 'Something . . . something scared her. I'm not sure. I tried to yell to Daddy to watch out but it was too late. Clarissa just came galloping over and . . . ' She covered her face with her hands, unable to go on.

Elizabeth pulled her close. 'Hush, sweetie. Everything's going to work out. Your dad will be out of the hospital in a few days and then . . . well, you can talk to him about it.'

Emma sat straight up. 'Can I see him? Can I?'

Elizabeth looked over at Henry and he nodded. 'I'm going to check on Priscilla,' he said. 'Then I'll take the girls to the hospital.' He left the room.

'Will you come with us, Elizabeth?' Emma said uneasily.

'I'd just be in the way,' she said, shaking her head. 'But don't worry. You'll be just fine once you see your father. And then Rachel will bring you back.'

Emma looked uncertain but Addy jumped off the bed and ran around to stand in front of Elizabeth, her eyes like saucers. 'Guess what, Elizabeth?'

225

'What?'

'Maude had her babies.'

'She did? Well, that is exciting news. Where are they?'

Addy threw a devastating look of reproach at her sister. 'I don't know because Emma wouldn't let me stay in the stable to look for them.' A frown creased her forehead. 'I don't remember exactly what happened but I never got to see the kittens.' She turned to Emma. 'I bet you spanked me and I'm going to tell Daddy.'

'I didn't,' Emma protested.

'Well then, how come I came with you?'

'You didn't.'

Addy tipped her head to one side. 'Well then, how come I came out before I found Maude's kittens?' She threw Emma a dark look. 'I remember that you yelled at me. And I bet you spanked me, too.'

'I did not!' Emma shouted. 'I don't know why you came outside.'

Addy turned away, clearly sick of the argument. She grabbed Elizabeth by the hand. 'Will you come with me to look for Maude's kittens? Will you?'

Elizabeth smiled. 'As soon as you get back from the hospital we'll see what we can do.'

'Goody.' Addy clapped her hands. 'Right, Emma?'

A sick lump came up into Emma's throat. She nodded but she didn't answer her sister. She couldn't. Something had just occurred to her. A prospect so frightening that it left her speechless. Daddy wasn't dead, and that was good. So good she couldn't believe how grateful she was. But he was in the hospital and that meant they'd have to stay here at Land's End until he was well. Alone. She shuddered. She knew what had scared Clarissa. She was sure of it, and now they wouldn't be leaving. Lilith had

226

seen to that. But why? What did she want from them? She had hurt Daddy. Emma wondered if she'd be next? Or would it be Addy? A suffocating feeling of dread crept over her.

'Why, Emma,' Elizabeth said, alarmed. 'You're shaking like a leaf. Are you cold?'

Emma shook her head and slid off the bed. 'I just want to see my father,' she said, grabbing her glasses off the night stand. 'I'll be good as new once I see my father.'

Judd drifted in and out of consciousness with a dim sense that time was passing and he had something critical to do before it was too late. But what? Fragments of memory kept sifting through his mind but he was unable to keep them from falling away. Sleep. The thought of it was narcotic. Sleep. Then you'll feel better.

And suddenly he remembered. 'Addy,' he groaned and tried to sit up. Pain exploded inside his chest and he fell back against the pillows, gasping for breath.

'It's all right, darling.' A gentle touch on his forehead. 'It's all right.'

He opened his eyes a crack. 'Rachel?' His tongue felt thick, too big for his mouth.

'Yes, darling. I'm here.' A soft, sweet voice.

'What happened?'

'You were trampled. Clarissa trampled you.'

Full memory came rushing back and with it full pain. The ground trembling, the horse thundering down on him, Emma shrieking. And the pain. The incredible crushing pain. He frowned. But what else? There was something more to be remembered. Something so much worse than all the rest. His mind grappled with it. What was it? What was it?

'You're going to be just fine, darling.' Rachel's voice again, sweet, soothing.

'Where are the kids?' The kids. Something about the kids. Through the haze he felt a terrible sense of urgency.

'They're at home. Don't worry. They're perfectly all right.'

Perfectly all right. No, they're not! He wanted to scream his fear to her without even knowing what it was, but he couldn't. His head was pounding. Emma. Addy. Emma. Addy. And then the way a dream slides into conscious thought, it came to him. The mind-boggling, ghastly image of a child who was supposed to be his precious five-year-old Addy but wasn't. 'That wasn't my daughter,' he whispered. 'It wasn't.'

'What's the matter, Judd?' Alarm in her voice. 'Are you in pain?'

He shook his head, unable to speak, not knowing the words to describe his horror.

She took his hand and pressed it to her lips. He could feel her tears. 'Oh, Judd,' she sobbed, 'I can't bear to see you hurt like this.'

He tried to open his eyes but the lids were heavy, pushing him back into semiconsciousness. 'The kids,' he whispered, struggling. 'I have to see the kids. Now.'

He heard the sharp intake of her breath. She dropped his hand and drew back. 'I had hoped you'd want to be with me. I guess I was wrong.' It was the last thing he heard. He didn't see the look on Rachel's face. If he had, he would never have let her go.

Emma stood in the elevator, holding tight to her sister's hand. Dr Adelford pressed the button and the elevator began to rise, but so slowly that Emma felt like screaming.

'Emma!' Addy squawked, pulling her hand away. 'You're squeezing too hard.'

'I'm sorry, Ads. It's just that I can't wait to see Daddy.' It was true. She couldn't. She had to know if her father had seen what she saw. Lilith inside Addy's face. If he had, he would know for sure that Emma had been right all along. That there really was a ghost.

He'll never make us go back to Land's End now, she thought. No way. If there was one thing she knew she could still count on, it was her father.

She frowned. But if they didn't go back, then where could they go? And who would take care of them? Oh, you silly jerk, she thought suddenly. Rachel will stay with you. Of course. Probably in some hotel until Daddy's better. She began to breathe a little easier.

The elevator came to a stop on the fifth floor and the door slid open. The two children stepped out behind Dr Adelford.

Emma had never been in a hospital before and she decided she didn't like it one bit. It smelled. And as they passed down the hall she could see people in beds with tubes in their noses and other gross things.

'I don't like it here,' Addy whispered.

Emma found Addy's hand. 'Me neither.'

They were almost at the end of the corridor when they saw Rachel coming around the corner just ahead. She looked right at them but for some weird reason she acted as if she didn't even see them.

'Rachel?' Dr Adelford said.

For a minute she looked confused. Then she said, 'Henry. How good of you to come.'

'How's Judd?'

'He's . . . he's in a lot of pain.'

'That's to be expected, Rachel,' he said gently. 'He's had a bad accident. But his children would like to see him if only for a minute.'

Rachel looked down at Emma as if realizing for the first time that she was standing there. She never even looked at Addy. 'Oh. Yes. Of course.'

'Can we see him now?' Emma asked, uneasy. Something was so strange about Rachel. 'Is Daddy all right?' she whispered.

Rachel didn't answer and Emma felt her stomach turn. Something was wrong. She just knew it. But what?

'Rachel?' Dr Adelford said. 'There hasn't been a change, has there?'

She shook her head. 'No. No change. He's just very tired, that's all.' With that, she turned away and took a few steps down the hall toward the elevators.

Dr Adelford seemed concerned. 'Rachel?' he called.

She stopped but didn't turn.

'Are you all right?'

She nodded.

'Will you wait? So the children can go back to Land's End with you?'

Emma saw her shudder but she nodded. 'I'll be just outside. I . . . I have to get some air.' Then she was gone.

Dr Adelford stared after her, his frown deepening, then he sighed. 'Well, come on, you two. Let's go see your dad.'

Emma couldn't believe how small her father looked. How very small. And helpless. She and Addy stood beside the bed and watched silently as a nurse did something with his arm.

'There,' she said. 'Now he should rest comfortably.' She turned to Emma. 'Don't worry. He looks a lot worse than he really is. We've given him something to make him sleep, but tomorrow he should feel much better.' Then she said a few words to Dr Adelford and left the room.

Emma moved closer. 'Daddy?' she whispered. 'Daddy, it's me. Emma.'

At first he showed no sign of awareness, then slowly his eyes fluttered open. 'Emma,' he muttered. His mouth looked funny, all puffy like he'd been to the dentist.

'Are you okay?' she asked.

He nodded and took her hand. 'Where's your sister?'

Addy squeezed in beside Emma. 'I'm right here, Daddy. You look gross. Your face is all purple.'

'I'm sure,' he said, grimacing. 'It feels purple. You two okay?'

Emma nodded, but suddenly she felt sick. How could she talk to her father about what had happened when he looked so terrible? Besides, Addy and Dr Adelford were standing right beside her. How could she beg him not to send them back to Land's End?

Desperate, she moved as close as she could and put her lips right next to his ear. 'Daddy,' she whispered, 'did you see? Did you?'

Judd heard the whisper but waves of unconsciousness kept sweeping him away. He closed his eyes, then forced them open again to see Emma's face inches from his own, and behind her glasses he could see her eyes so frightened, waiting for his answer.

He nodded. 'I saw,' he said.

'Oh, Daddy,' she whispered, 'then you know we can't go back there.'

'Why are you whispering?' Addy said loudly. 'Are you telling something bad about me?'

Emma ignored her sister. 'Daddy?' she said, grabbing his hand. Her father's eyes had closed again and she felt the panic mounting. 'Tell me what to do.'

With supreme effort he fought his way back. 'Take care of Addy,' he mumbled. It wasn't all he wanted to say but it was all he could manage.

'What?'

'Don't let Addy out of your sight.'

Emma stared. 'But where should we go?'

'Stay with Rachel.' He felt giddy. Now nothing seemed within his grasp but sleep. Warm. Painless. Healing.

'Daddy!' There was a note of hysteria in Emma's voice but Judd didn't hear it. Unable to fight the drug any longer, he slipped away into dark, heavy sleep.

Emma's heart stopped. 'But we can't go back,' she sobbed. 'We can't.'

She felt Dr Adelford touch her gently on the shoulder. 'Don't worry, Emma. Everything's going to work out. You'll see. And tomorrow you'll be astonished at how much better your father is.'

But what about tonight? Emma thought wildly. What happens to us tonight?

'Oh, boy, we get to ride in Rachel's sports car,' Addy whispered as the two children hurried along behind their silent, white-faced stepmother. At the corner, Rachel didn't even break stride. Without a backward glance she stepped off the curb and, ignoring the traffic, made her way across to the parking lot on the other side.

Without hesitation, Addy stepped off the curb to follow but Emma jerked her back. 'No, Addy!' she yelled. 'Hold my hand and don't you dare move until I tell you to go.' She stared after her stepmother, unable to imagine that Rachel had actually left them to cross by themselves. But she had, so at the first lull in the flow of traffic, Emma yanked Addy by the hand. 'Run!' she said and the two children sprinted across the street.

They finally caught up with Rachel just as she was backing her car out of the parking space, and for a minute Emma thought she was going to leave without them. 'Rachel!' she cried. 'Wait for us!'

Her stepmother jammed on the brakes and, still without speaking, motioned for them to get in.

'Oh, boy,' Addy said, pushing ahead. 'The top's down. This is going to be fun.'

'You sit on my lap,' Emma told her sister, but almost before she could close the door, Rachel threw the car into gear and with tires squealing, they roared out of the lot and into the stream of traffic.

Rachel didn't follow the main highway. Instead she turned off and, still at breakneck speed, headed north over the back roads. At one point they almost flew off the road, and Emma threw a frightened glance at her stepmother. But she didn't dare speak. Rachel looked too grim. Her face was chalky white and her lips were pulled tight across her teeth. Emma shivered.

'Isn't this fun?' Addy shouted as the car hit a rut in the road and she bounced almost a foot in the air, coming down hard on Emma's knees.

'Ouch!' Emma cried. 'That hurts. Besides, you'll fly

right out of this car if you're not careful!' She turned to Rachel for support but her stepmother still seemed unaware that they were even there.

Suddenly they hit a huge dip in the road and the car was airborne. Addy flew out of Emma's grasp and banged her knee on the dashboard. She let out a yelp and began to cry.

'It's okay, Ads,' Emma said, pulling her sister back onto her lap, trying to soothe her and at the same time trying to keep calm herself. It seemed as if Rachel were driving faster and faster, and now, each time the car hit a rut, the two children were thrown violently forward. But it was Addy who was taking the brunt of it. Emma wasn't strong enough to hold her firmly in her lap.

Addy was crying with a vengeance now and Emma was certain they were all going to be killed, when all at once, Rachel slammed on the brakes and the car screeched to a stop.

The three sat paralyzed for a minute, Emma and Rachel both breathing hard, Addy crying her eyes out.

'I think I'd better slow down a little,' Rachel said quietly. 'I guess I wasn't paying attention. Are you two okay?'

Neither of the children could answer. Addy's sobs had slowed to erratic hiccoughs but she was still shaking.

As for herself, Emma was filled with dread. Her father had told them to stay with Rachel. That she would take care of them. Now Emma wondered if that was going to do them any good at all. In fact, Rachel didn't seem to be able to take care of herself, never mind two frightened children. Emma shuddered. The worst thing she could have imagined was really happening. They were heading back to Land's End. Alone.

This morning she had thought her nightmare was about to end. Now she realized that it was only just beginning.

twenty

Emma sat across from Addy at the supper table set up by the servants in one of the small sitting rooms, watching her sister trying to wind strands of spaghetti around her fork. She would get a batch all rolled up, lift it to her mouth and just as she was about to eat it, it would slide off, *plop*, back onto her plate. 'Why don't you cut it?' Emma said, finally losing patience.

'Because it doesn't taste as good cut.'

Emma leaned over and wiped Addy's mouth. 'You're making a real mess.'

Addy ignored her and continued to twirl her spaghetti with intense concentration.

'You'll starve to death before you finish that,' Emma said.

'Well, how about you? You aren't even eating.'

Emma looked down at her own plate and shuddered. She knew if she took one bite she would get sick.

The door opened and Elizabeth stuck her head in. 'Everything okay?'

Emma nodded.

'I just have to check on my mother and then I'll be back for dessert. And afterward if you're not too tired, maybe we can play cards or something. Get our minds off our troubles.'

'Goody,' Addy said.

Emma put her napkin on the table, leaned back in her chair and shivered. Sitting here in this cozy room with Addy acting normal as pie, she had begun to relax a little. But now as the shadows outside lengthened, they served as a grim reminder to Emma that night wasn't far off. The mere thought of it made her tremble. Land's End was frightening enough now in broad daylight, but once the sun slipped quietly behind the hills, the household staff disappeared behind closed doors, and then Emma felt truly alone.

Not that daylight saves us, Emma thought despairingly. The ghost comes day or night. She threw a quick glance over at Addy who was still waging war with her spaghetti. I hope Elizabeth hurries back, she thought.

Almost as if she had heard, Elizabeth came in. She looked worried. 'Emma, did something happen at the hospital?'

'What do you mean?' Emma said.

'Did you see your father?'

Emma nodded. 'But he was too tired to talk.'

'Was Rachel with him?'

'No. She left when we came in.' She paused. 'Is something the matter?'

'She seems upset, that's all.'

'Why does Rachel hate me?' Addy asked suddenly, pushing her plate away.

Elizabeth's eyes widened. 'Rachel doesn't hate you, Addy. Whatever would make you say a thing like that?'

'Because she hates me. She really does.' Addy's lower lip began to quiver.

'Aren't you going to finish your spaghetti?' Emma said, changing the subject before Addy had a chance to tell Elizabeth about their wild ride home.

Addy shook her head. 'It's cold.'

'I'm not surprised,' Emma said.

Elizabeth picked up a bell and rang. 'As soon as they clear these dishes away, we can have dessert. And then what do you say we make some get-well cards for your dad?'

That notion appealed even to Emma. 'That's a wonderful idea, Elizabeth,' she said. 'And I'm going to make the most beautiful one ever.'

'I'm going to draw Maude and her babies on mine,' Addy said. She held up four fingers. 'I'm going to pretend she had four kittens.' She jumped up and came around the table to stand beside Elizabeth. 'How many do you think she has really?'

Elizabeth shook her head. 'I've no idea, Addy. But tomorrow if it's a nice day, we'll go and look for them.'

Addy clapped her hands. 'Oh, I'm so glad we didn't leave here.'

Emma groaned.

Elizabeth looked over. 'Emma? Are you all right?'

Emma flushed. She hadn't meant for Elizabeth to hear. 'I was just thinking about my father,' she lied.

The table was cleared and dessert served. It was lemon meringue pie and, in spite of her queasy stomach, Emma couldn't resist. It was her favorite. Besides, sitting in this small, cheery room with Elizabeth and Addy, she began to think that they might survive until tomorrow after all.

'That was the best pie I ever ate,' Addy said.

'Me, too,' said Emma, wiping her mouth. She felt much better. After all, they had to sleep here only one more night. Then she could talk to her father and he'd find somewhere else for them to stay until he was well, she just knew it.

'Now let's see,' Elizabeth said. She got up and began to rummage through the drawers in a small desk that stood along one wall. 'Aha. Here's some very fine paper that I think will make lovely cards.' She continued her search. 'But it appears we have one small problem. No crayons.'

'Oh, no,' Addy said, her face falling a mile. 'You can't draw good without crayons. Especially me.'

'I know,' Elizabeth said, snapping her fingers. 'Upstairs in the nursery there used to be a whole trunkload of crayons. Let's go look.'

'Hooray,' Addy said, hopping off her chair. 'We get to see the nursery again. And I'm going to rock on the horse.'

Emma froze. She felt all her blood drain from her face. 'The n . . . n . . . nursery?'

Elizabeth and Addy were already at the door. 'Come on, Emma,' Addy said.

Emma had no choice but to follow even though the idea of going up to that room on the third floor filled her with profound terror. But worse was the prospect of being left behind. Alone. Besides, her father had told her only one thing. Not to let Addy out of her sight.

Miserable, she plodded after, her feet reluctantly taking her toward the place she feared the most. Each step was a supreme effort bringing her closer and closer to that shadowy stairway and that icy horror lurking above.

Twenty-two steps to the second floor. She counted each one, her pulse pounding in her throat.

Down the hall, her feet soundless on the thick, oriental carpets, around the corner, through the passageway, hurrying to keep up, all the while dreading what lay ahead.

'Come on, slowpoke,' Addy called over her shoulder and the sound of her voice made Emma jump.

'I am.' She looked neither right nor left, sensing where she was going, not seeing.

And then the last flight of stairs.

The grandfather clock in the lower hall struck seven and tears of fright began to sting Emma's eyes, fogging her glasses. She stopped to wipe them on her skirt, but in that short time, Elizabeth and Addy were already at the top of the stairs and through the door.

'Wait for me!' Emma yelled and flew up the steps, but when she got to the top they had disappeared.

The hallway was even darker and colder than she had remembered and she threw a frightened glance back over her shoulder, praying that she wouldn't see anything coming up the dark stairway after her. Behind, there was no sign of life; ahead, the corridor stretched black and deserted.

'Addy!' she yelled. 'Elizabeth! Where are you?'

Silence.

She inched her way along the hall and suddenly, just ahead and to her left, the door to the nursery swung inward.

Emma took two halting steps forward, hands clamped tight over her mouth in utter panic, and looked in.

'Boy, you sure are a turtle,' Addy said, hopping off the rocking horse. 'Do you want to take a turn?'

Emma stepped inside the room and blinked hard. The nursery was flooded with light. The dust and cobwebs were still there, but for some reason it didn't look a bit scary. It just seemed like an old forgotten place that hadn't been used in a long, long time.

Across the room Elizabeth was going through the cupboards, looking for crayons. 'I found them,' she said, pulling a box from one of the shelves. 'Let's go.'

'Can't we stay and play?' Addy said.

'Not if you want to make a card for your father.' She glanced down at her watch. 'It's already after seven.'

'Okey-dokey,' Addy said, taking Elizabeth by the hand. 'Come on, Emma.'

All of a sudden Emma had to ask. She wasn't sure how she dared but she just knew she had to. 'Elizabeth?'

'Yes?'

'Do you know someone named Lilith?'

This time Elizabeth didn't get quite as pale as she had that day in the garden, but she looked at Emma for a long minute without answering. Finally she said, 'That's still bothering you, isn't it.'

Emma nodded.

'Where did you hear about Lilith?'

'Don't you remember? I told you that day in the garden. I saw her.'

Elizabeth smiled a nervous smile. 'What does your dad say about all this?'

Embarrassed, Emma dropped her gaze to stare at her feet. 'He doesn't really believe me.'

'Well, I must admit that it *is* a little hard to believe. But just because grown-ups don't believe something doesn't mean it can't be so.' She put her hand on Emma's shoulder. 'I can tell you this much. Once upon a time there was a little girl who lived here and her name was Lilith. But it would be just as well if you forgot all about her. It makes everyone too sad to think about her. We even took her portrait down because it made us cry.' That said, she and Addy left the room.

Emma didn't waste any time following. With a last, furtive glance over her shoulder she closed the door and hurried after them down the hall, the same wild thought racing over and over in her mind. Lilith was real. Lilith was real. She wasn't sure what it meant, or even if it made her feel more or less frightened. All she knew was that there used to be a little girl named Lilith and she had once lived here in this very house.

Emma sat at the table and with meticulous care she edged her paper with a delicate pink-and-white floral border. 'How's this?' She held it up for Elizabeth's approval.

Elizabeth looked up from her book. 'That's great, Emma. You really are a very good artist. Must take after your father.'

Emma flushed and leaned back in her chair, very pleased with what she had accomplished so far.

Across the room Addy lay on her stomach on the floor, a pile of crumpled papers beside her. She had made several attempts to draw a cat with kittens but thus far nothing had worked out to her satisfaction. She had been providing steady commentary as she scribbled, not really caring if anyone was listening, happy to hear the sound of her own voice.

Now suddenly, she was quiet.

'How're you doing, Ads?' Emma asked, glancing over.

Addy didn't answer. She just kept on drawing.

Emma felt a faint touch of uneasiness. Something about Addy's unnatural silence struck a chord. She looked over at Elizabeth to see if she had noticed anything, but she was still buried in her book.

Emma took a deep breath. 'Ads? Are you almost done?'

Silence.

Reluctantly, Emma slid off her chair and stood watching her sister but she didn't go any closer. She was afraid to. In desperation she turned to Elizabeth. 'Let's see what Addy's doing,' she said, trying to sound casual.

Elizabeth looked up. 'Looks like she's creating a real masterpiece. Can we have a peek, Addy?'

Addy didn't even look up.

For a minute there was no sound in the room but the scritch-scratch of Addy's crayon on the paper.

Elizabeth frowned. She stood up, walked across the room and stooped down beside the little girl. 'Can't we see what you've been so busy doing?' She might as well have been talking to one of the chairs for all the response she got from Addy.

Emma took a few fainthearted steps forward, then stopped, the old familiar feeling of dread grabbing her by the throat.

'Addy?' Now there was a note of alarm in Elizabeth's voice. She put her hand on Addy's arm. 'What's wrong?'

No answer. Then as if she were waking from a deep sleep, Addy sat up, rubbed her eyes, and began to cry.

'I'm too tired to do any more,' she sobbed. 'Please don't make me.'

Elizabeth picked her up. 'It's all right, sweetie,' she said. 'Of course you don't have to do any more if you don't want to. We'll take you to bed, won't we, Emma?'

Emma had finally worked up enough courage to cross the room. She stood just behind Elizabeth, trying to see Addy's face but it was hidden in the curve of Elizabeth's shoulder. She bent down and picked up the get-well card her sister had been working on so diligently.

'Elizabeth,' she said, barely able to speak. 'Oh, Elizabeth, look at this.'

They both stared. There were no pictures of cats on the paper and no kittens. Instead, printed across the top of the paper in shaky, irregular letters were two words: *HELP ME!* And across the bottom of the page was scrawled a single name. *Lilith*.

twenty-one

From far off Judd heard her call his name, and for a minute he forgot everything but how happy he was to hear her voice. So sweet, so familiar. 'Rachel,' he breathed, then opened his eyes to find her sitting close beside him on the bed.

'Oh, darling,' she said, seeing him smile. 'I knew as soon as you had a chance to think it over that you'd want me with you. I just knew it.' She took his hand and held it against her cheek.

For a minute Judd didn't move. Then as gently as he could he pulled his hand away. 'Why are you here, Rachel?' he asked.

He saw the light go out of her eyes. 'Then you haven't forgiven me.'

'It's not a case of forgiving, Rachel,' he said as calmly as he could. 'I told you before. I need time to think. To try to sort it out.' He softened his tone. 'And you, my darling, need time to get your life in order. Right now, like it or not, you are married to two men. You need a lawyer.'

'The only thing I need is you.' There was a look of obstinacy in her face, a fierce resolve. She was still trying to make things right by refusing to accept reality. 'All you have to do is tell me you want me with you. That we can be together again.'

Exhausted, he closed his eyes. 'I can't talk about this anymore,' he said.

All color drained from her face as she sat beside him, silent, expressionless. Once she held out her hands to him in a kind of pleading gesture, like a child who in perfect faith implores a grown-up to fix what is broken. Then she let them drop lifeless into her lap. 'You tell me just one thing and then I'll leave. If you had no children, would you take me with you?'

He sat straight up in bed, wincing in pain. He reached over and took her face between his hands. 'Listen to me, Rachel,' he said between clenched teeth. 'For the love of Christ, listen. My children are real and I have to consider them. But this is between you and me. I'm not saying that we can't work things out. But for now *we cannot live together!*' He pulled his hands away and was shocked to see his fingerprints, angry red against the pallor of her skin. 'Oh my God, Rachel, I didn't mean . . . ' He reached out but she drew back.

'There is only one place you have hurt me, Judd,' she whispered, 'and that is in my soul. You can say what you like about lawyers and lies and all the rest, but no one has been more faithless than you.' She paused and something so cold, so uncompromising came into her eyes that Judd was caught off guard. 'I loved you more than anything in this world and I trusted you to love me in kind. Now I know you don't. You love your children more.'

He opened his mouth to speak but she silenced him with a gesture. 'It's not Peter who's the issue here. It's Addy. It's your daughter Addy.' She closed her eyes. 'I tried so hard to fight her but now, if you go away without me, she will have won. And you're too blind to see it.' She stood up. 'Say what you will, but don't ever tell me that if it weren't for Addy you would leave me. Because you wouldn't. I know you wouldn't.' She turned and walked to the door. 'I have to go now.'

Speechless, Judd could only stare after her.

She stopped at the door and when she turned it was his own sweet Rachel looking back at him across the room. Her eyes were full of tears but she smiled a hopeful smile. 'You won't leave me, Judd,' she said. 'You just wait and see. I'll fix everything and then you'll love me all over again.'

By noon Judd had made up his mind. He had to leave, get back to Land's End no matter how much pain, both physical and psychic, it caused him. He took a few tentative steps toward the closet, then stopped to catch his breath. When he moved, the pain was intense but he was driven by something far more painful. It was a deep, ominous feeling of foreboding, of sensing that something disastrous was about to happen at Land's End. Not sure what, or to whom, but knowing it all the same. He was almost dressed when Dr Roth came into the room.

'What are you doing up?' the doctor said, surprise registering on his face. 'Henry told me this morning that you would be here at least two more days.'

Judd backed up and sat down gingerly on the edge of

the bed, his breath coming in short, shallow gasps. The pain in his chest had eased a little but it still felt as if all of his ribs had been ripped loose and were rattling around inside his rib cage. 'I'm leaving,' he said.

'You can't be serious. You're in no shape to do anything of the sort.' He sat down next to Judd. 'Why the hurry? What's happened? Not more trouble with the children, I hope.'

Judd pushed the thought of Rachel out of his mind and tried to concentrate on what had happened to Addy the day before. He began to talk, watching the doctor closely for his reaction. 'That thing wasn't Addy,' he said finally. 'Jesus Christ, it wasn't my child.' He paused, not really able to believe what he was about to say. 'To tell you the truth, Doctor Roth, I'm not even sure it was human.'

Dr Roth listened without expression, not speaking until Judd had finished. Then he said, 'Have you ever heard of a disorder of excess?'

Judd shook his head.

'In simplest terms, it's what happens when physiology goes wild. Too much of a muchness, if you will.'

Judd looked blank.

'It means that in a state of high anxiety Addy has displayed paranormal activity. She played the piano without the ability to do so. You accepted that as mind-directed. Why not this?'

Judd groaned. 'Because it's unbelievable, that's why.'

Dr Roth smiled. 'And a supernatural explanation isn't?'

'Emma doesn't think so,' Judd said lamely.

'Emma is a very bright little girl. But she's only ten

years old. I would expect a more reasonable approach from you.'

'Nothing about this is reasonable,' Judd snapped.

'I know it doesn't seem so, but once we dig deep enough it will all begin to make sense. Even if we're not happy with what we find.'

Judd sighed and threw up his hands. 'What do you think I should do?'

'Where are the children now?'

'At Land's End.'

'And that's where you were headed?'

Judd nodded.

'Well, I do think you were on the right track. Personally I don't think they ought to stay out there alone. Obviously the place scares the devil out of Emma.'

'That's putting it mildly.'

Dr Roth put his finger to one side of his nose, considering. 'Why don't you let them come with me to the clinic? They'll be safe there, comfortable, and it will give me a chance to observe the two of them closely in a controlled, clinical environment. With luck we may trigger a response in Addy.' He paused. 'Have you ever heard of release therapy?'

Judd shook his head.

'Well, in simple terms we try to encourage the child to work through his or her anxieties by playing with toys. Although I don't always recommend it, Addy is a good candidate because her problem seems to have one specific cause: namely the loss of her mother. In addition, she's been experiencing symptoms for only a very short time. And third, maybe if Emma sees that the problem is inside Addy's head and not hovering around in some room in her step-grandmother's house she might relax a little.'

'There's nothing Emma would like better than to leave Land's End.'

'Do you think they'd come with me?'

'If they know I want them to they will. I'm sure you'll have no trouble with Emma. Addy may be a little reluctant but in the final analysis, she'll go anywhere Emma goes.'

'Shall I go out and get them, then?'

'I would be forever in your debt.'

Dr Roth smiled. 'When you get the bill you may not be quite so enthusiastic.' He headed for the door. 'I just have to stop by my office and make a few phone calls, and then I'll head out to Land's End. You stay here and relax. Give yourself some time to heal. The last thing those little girls need is an invalid father.'

Judd tried to sleep. He was exhausted but something kept gnawing at his insides. He felt much better knowing that Dr Roth was going to take charge of Addy and Emma, but what about Rachel? Deep down inside he had a gut feeling that someone ought to be taking charge of her. But who? Yesterday morning, just before he left the house, Elizabeth had told him that Priscilla Daimler had suffered a stroke, so if Rachel's bizarre behavior this morning meant she was heading toward another breakdown, who was going to take care of her? So intent was he on thinking it through, he didn't see Elizabeth until she was right in front of him.

'Judd? How are you feeling?'

'Not so great. But I'm glad you're here. Have you seen Rachel today?'

Elizabeth nodded. 'Just for a minute. This morning. Before she came in to see you. Why do you ask?'

'How did she seem?'

'Fine.' She hesitated. 'Is something wrong?'

'She was here earlier.' He looked hard at Elizabeth. 'I had a difficult time talking to her. She doesn't seem to understand why I have to leave Land's End without her. She thinks it's because of Addy.'

Elizabeth sat down slowly. 'You're leaving without her? But she told me . . .'

'What did she tell you?'

'She told me that she was going with you.' There was a note of alarm in her voice.

'When did she tell you that?'

'Yesterday. And again this morning. She said you had worked everything out.'

'Jesus,' he said. 'Why would she tell you something like that?'

'Maybe because she wants so desperately to believe it,' Elizabeth said quietly. 'Rachel has never been able to deal very well with adversity.'

Judd narrowed his eyes. Something was gnawing away at the edges of his brain, something that didn't make sense. He came straight to the point. 'Did you know that Rachel was never divorced?'

Elizabeth nodded.

Judd exploded. 'My God, what kind of people are you? How could you have let her believe she was?'

Elizabeth flushed. 'What are you talking about?'

'How could you have stood by and allowed your mother to manipulate Rachel like some kind of a brainless pet? Were you so afraid of her that you didn't have the courage to tell Rachel the truth? Or didn't you give a damn?'

'I . . . I don't know what you're talking about.' Her eyes filled with tears.

The last thing Judd had wanted was to hurt Elizabeth. She had never done a thing to deserve it. He softened his tone. 'You didn't know that Rachel thought Peter had divorced her?'

Her face went white. 'Rachel told you that?'

'Of course she did,' he said, trying desperately to make things connect. 'No one else would have.'

Elizabeth's next words chilled him to the bone. They were spoken very quietly but with such conviction that they left little room for doubt. 'No one else would have told you such a thing because it's not true.'

Judd stared. 'Are you trying to tell me that Rachel made it all up? That she knew all along that she was still married to Rostov?'

Elizabeth met his gaze straight on. She didn't answer but the stricken look in her eyes was answer enough.

Judd suddenly felt as if all this time he had been walking on thin ice and it had finally given way under his feet. His anger vanished, leaving him numb. He collapsed back against the pillows and closed his eyes. As much as he wanted to deny it, he knew in his gut that Elizabeth was telling the truth. Rachel had been lying all along. 'What's wrong with her, Elizabeth?' he asked quietly. 'Why did Priscilla send her to an institution?'

Elizabeth stood up and began to pace. 'I wish I knew what to do,' she said, wringing her hands. 'I wish I knew what to do.' She stopped and sat down hard on the edge of the bed. 'I suppose it's useless to tell you to ask Rachel.'

Judd nodded. 'Useless.' He suddenly felt a million years old. 'I might have once. But not anymore.'

'Why not?'

'Because I don't think she knows the answers,' he said quietly. 'At least not the real ones. So I'm asking you. No. I'm begging you. Rachel needs help. I think she's going to pieces and if I don't help her I don't know who will.'

'Damn it all. If only Mother were here. She'd know what to do.'

'I don't need your mother!' he snapped. 'All I need is the truth.'

'I'm afraid there's only one person who can give that to you,' Elizabeth said quietly. 'And unfortunately that person *is* my mother.'

Judd groaned. 'You're right. I know you're right. But still you know a lot more than I do.' He paused. 'I've come to depend on you, Elizabeth. More than I care to admit.' He reached out to touch her hand, then pulled back, and took a deep breath. 'But that's another subject altogether. For now, I have to help Rachel. So please, for whatever it's worth, tell me what you know about her breakdown.'

Elizabeth straightened her shoulders. Her whole body tensed, but oddly enough the planes of her face relaxed. It was as if she had suddenly accepted the fact that the battle was finished. 'All right,' she said. 'But remember, what I am to tell you now is between you and me. Rachel must never know.'

'Understood.'

She sighed. 'You must also understand that I was at Land's End so rarely during those years that my knowledge is superficial at best. I was told only what my mother wanted me to know. Nothing more.'

'Understood.'

Once Elizabeth began, she spoke rapidly, as if she had

253

plunged into a pool of icy water and couldn't wait to get to the other side. 'The year after Peter and Rachel were married they had a child,' she said. 'A little girl. And when she was five years old she died in a horrible accident. Mother sent for me and I came home at once but I never saw Rachel. She had already been hospitalized. In shock, Mother said. But she never came out of it. Later they transferred her to the Englewood Clinic. She was there for three years, and after her release she never came back to Land's End again until she came with you.' She shivered, then spread her hands as if to signal that she was finished. 'And that's it.'

Judd didn't move. He heard her words, he saw her face but he could only stare, the way a man stares who has suddenly come upon a grisly wreck and is unable for a moment to assimilate the full extent of the horror.

'Judd?'

He opened his mouth but the only sound that came out was a low moan. He groped for the words and finally found them. 'Rachel had a child.' It wasn't a question.

Elizabeth nodded. 'Rachel had a child.' She paused. 'Which brings me to the original point of my visit. Although I'm no longer sure I ought to mention it.'

Judd's mouth twisted into a bitter smile. 'What difference could anything else possibly make? You might just as well let me have it all at once.'

She stood up and crossed to the chair where she had left her handbag. She opened it, took out a piece of paper and handed it to Judd. 'Last night the kids were making get-well cards for you.' She told him about Addy's strange silence and the sobbing. 'That's what she made.' She pointed to the paper in his hand.

Judd looked down. *HELP ME!* he read. And a child's

254

shaky signature: *Lilith*. 'What the hell . . . ' he said. 'Addy wrote this?' He shook his head. 'Emma must have done it for her. Addy can barely print her own name.'

'I was right there. Emma had nothing to do with it.' She sank down on the edge of the bed. He could tell that she was trying to keep her voice steady but it quivered. 'I know that your psychiatrist says that Addy is having emotional problems. That because of her anxieties she's doing things she normally wouldn't or couldn't do, but . . . '

Judd could hear something in her voice now that hadn't been there before. It was fear. 'But what?'

'Rachel's child.'

'What about Rachel's child?'

'Her name was Lilith.'

twenty-two

'So,' Dr Roth said, settling himself beside Emma on the sofa in the library at Land's End. 'Tell me about Addy. I understand from your father that she scared you again. Both of you in fact.'

Emma looked at him over the top of her glasses and nodded. 'She scared me all right.' She paused for a minute, then looked away. 'I don't want you to think I'm mad at you or anything,' she said quietly, 'but remember when I told you something bad would happen?' There was the faintest hint of reproach in her voice.

Dr Roth made a sort of clucking noise. 'I remember, Emma. Although to be fair, there wasn't much I could do to stop it.' He frowned. 'Was there?'

She thought about it for a minute, then shrugged. 'No. I don't suppose there was.'

'And I did tell your father that I thought it would be a good thing if you all went back to New York.'

'That's true.' She patted him lightly on the arm. 'Don't worry,' she said, then sighed. 'I know it wasn't your fault. There wasn't anything anyone could have done. Lilith told me it was too late and she was right.'

'Lilith told you?'

Emma nodded.

'Using Addy's voice?'

'No. It was her own voice. But she used Addy's mouth.' Emma frowned. 'But then before that she told me all by herself.'

'How did she do that?'

Emma tilted her head to one side, remembering. 'She whispered. Out in the garden. I know she doesn't have a mouth of her own so I'm not sure just how she did it, but she told me all the same. "Too late, Emma." That's what she said. "Too late." But that's not all. Sometimes she sings.'

'She sings?'

Emma nodded, then shuddered. 'It's always the same. A sort of echoey little lullaby. And I can tell you one thing for sure. It scares me to death.'

Dr Roth didn't say anything. He just seemed to sink further into the sofa. Finally he cleared his throat. 'Hmmmm,' he said, then 'Hmmmm,' again. He took a pack of gum from his jacket pocket, offered a stick to Emma, and they both began to chew.

'You should always chew gum with your mouth shut,' Emma said, and then, 'How do you think she does it?'

'Does what?'

'Sings and talks without a mouth.'

The doctor looked pensive. 'I'm not sure, Emma. It's a real mystery. It truly is.'

Emma smiled a halfhearted smile. 'Well, at least you didn't say it was all my imagination.'

'That would be a dumb thing to say, don't you think?'

'Yes it would. But people say dumb things all the time.'

'They do indeed.' Dr Roth pulled himself out of the soft cushions and sat on the edge of the sofa. 'So. After Lilith spoke to you, exactly what did she do out there in the pasture?'

Emma hesitated, still not absolutely certain how much she should tell this man. She liked him but . . . Finally she said, 'What did my father tell you?'

'He told me that Addy didn't look like herself.'

Emma folded her hands and placed them carefully in her lap. 'That's because it wasn't Addy,' she said patiently. 'It was Lilith.'

'I see. And did Lilith say anything?'

'She just told me she couldn't let us leave.'

'Did she say why?'

Emma nodded. 'Because she had waited too long for us to come here. And then she scared Clarissa and the horse trampled my father.'

This time Dr Roth looked startled. 'You think Addy scared the horse?'

'Not Addy. Lilith.'

'But how could she?'

Emma couldn't help but be impatient. 'Everyone knows that animals are afraid of ghosts, Doctor Roth,' she said.

He made the clucking noise again. 'I have a lot to learn about ghosts, Emma. I hope you'll bear with me.'

Emma patted his arm again, then sat straight up, setting her feet together on the floor so that both sneakers were precisely aligned. 'You know what else?'

'What?'

'Last night we were making get-well cards for my

258

father.' She paused, not taking her eyes off her shoes. So far Dr Roth had seemed as if he believed her but she still wasn't sure what he was really thinking. All of a sudden she had to ask. 'Do you think I made Lilith up?'

Dr Roth made a steeple with his fingers and put it across the bridge of his nose. 'No, Emma, I don't think you made Lilith up.'

Emma pushed. 'So you believe that she's real?'

He didn't say anything right away, but when he did Emma knew that he was telling the truth. 'I'm going to answer you as honestly as I can. I do think Lilith is real.' He held up a cautioning finger. 'I'm just not sure exactly what she is.'

Emma considered for a long minute, then nodded solemnly. 'I guess that's good enough.' Then she told him about Addy's card.

'And Addy didn't write it?'

In spite of the seriousness of the situation, Emma couldn't help but smile an uneasy smile. 'Of course she didn't. Addy can't hardly print her own name. I don't mean her first name. She does that okay. I mean Pauling. She never spells it right and most of the time she does it backwards. You know.' She made a printing motion in the air with one hand. 'She makes some of her letters like you were seeing them in a mirror.'

Dr Roth smiled. 'I know exactly what you mean.'

'But then she's only five,' Emma said in her sister's defense. 'And Mommy said I used to do the same thing. But I don't anymore. Now I write in cursive.' She paused. 'But that's not really what you want to know.'

Dr Roth nodded. 'No, it isn't. Where were we? Oh, yes. So Lilith wants you to help her.'

Emma nodded. 'But I don't know how. And I don't

know why.' She shivered. 'Besides I'd be too scared to even try,' she said miserably. 'I just want to leave here, that's all.'

'Well, I'll tell you what. How would you and Addy like to come with me?'

Emma jerked her head up and stared at him. 'Come with you? Where?'

'To my clinic. It's not far from here. It's sort of like a boarding school and your father has already agreed to let you come for a week or so. Maybe longer if you like. If you want to, that is. You and Addy could share a room. And we can try to work together to see if we can't get rid of Lilith. Whoever or whatever she may be.'

Emma jumped up. 'Oh, Doctor Roth, that would be the answer to all my prayers. I don't care where we go as long as we can get out of here.' She clapped her hands together, hardly able to contain herself. She didn't know what this clinic place was and she didn't care. All she knew was that Dr Roth was going to take them away from Land's End. 'And guess what?' she said, jumping up from the sofa. 'Our suitcases are still all packed.' She leaned over and took the doctor's hand. 'Thank you, Doctor Roth,' she said solemnly. 'You're a very nice man.' Then she ran to the door. 'It won't take any time at all to get ready. I just have to go get Addy and we'll be back in a jiffy.'

'Slow down,' Dr Roth said. 'I'm not going anywhere without you.'

Emma didn't look back. She flew across the foyer, feet barely touching the floor, and took the stairs two at a time. Down the hall she went, not stopping for anything, past Mrs Daimler's room, through the gallery, finally bursting through the door into the bedroom where she had left Addy only minutes earlier.

Her eyes swept the room but she didn't see her sister. 'Addy! Addy, come quick! We're leaving! Can you believe anything so wonderful?' She crossed to the closet, took out one empty duffel bag and began to stuff the few things left in the room inside. The last thing she jammed in was the puzzle she and Addy had been working on earlier. 'Addy, come on. We have to hurry.'

She crossed to the bathroom door and looked in.

No Addy.

She turned around. 'Addy,' she said, her feeling of elation fading. 'This is no time to play games. Doctor Roth is waiting.' She bent down and looked under the bed, then behind the curtains. 'Addy, stop fooling around.' She squinted. Where the heck could Addy have gone? Emma had told her not to dare leave the room until she came back.

'Addy!' she shouted. 'Where are you?'

Still no answer.

Emma stamped her foot. She wasn't going to let herself get upset. No way. She wasn't going to let herself get upset *or* scared. Instead she was going to get darn good and mad. Here was Dr Roth, waiting right downstairs to take them away from this awful place, and where was Addy? Probably wandering around looking for Maude. Or maybe upstairs playing with the dollhouse. Or worse – Emma gulped – maybe she went to the nursery. She ran out of the room and down the hall, calling Addy's name as loudly as she could.

It didn't take her long to cover the second floor, partly because most of the doors were closed and partly because deep down inside, Emma knew that Addy wasn't there.

If she was anywhere in the house, Emma knew with mounting dread where she would be.

Down the corridors she went, her footsteps padding silently on the thick carpets, but no matter how loudly she called Addy's name, for some queer reason her cries sounded muffled. Nobody can hear me, she thought, shuddering. Nobody at all.

And for some reason the thin, empty stillness seemed far more ominous than all the ghostly breathing and soft sobbing of the past put together. Her teeth began to chatter and her resolve to keep calm vanished, swallowed up in the threatening silence. 'But Doctor Roth is waiting downstairs,' she reminded herself. 'And unless I find Addy, he won't be able to take us away from here.'

She took a deep breath. She wasn't going to let her fear ruin their last chance to get away from Land's End. She straightened her shoulders, pushed her glasses firmly up on the bridge of her nose, and headed down the hall. In slow motion she turned the last corner, then stopped, standing paralyzed at the foot of the shadowy stairway leading to the third floor. 'Addy?'

Crushing silence.

She took one trembling step forward. Don't go up there, a small voice inside told her. Go get someone. Get Dr Roth.

'That's what to do,' she said out loud, letting her breath out in a rush. 'Go get Doctor Roth.' She whirled around and raced back to the main hall.

At the head of the stairs she stopped to catch her breath and put on a brave face. No way did she want Dr Roth to know what a scaredy-cat she was. She put her hand on the bannister to steady herself and was about to start down when suddenly, through the window just opposite the main staircase, something caught her eye. It was a splash of color. Nothing more, but it made Emma back up and rush to the window at the far end of the hall. From there she could see the path that led up from the gardens, along the edge of the bluff, and down to the stables.

She squinted. There it was again. The splash of color. Yellow. And then for one single moment, just at the top where the path curved out of sight, she saw it clearly. Her breath caught in her throat. It was Addy's yellow slicker, just disappearing over the crest of the hill.

Emma whirled around and flew down the stairs, nearly knocking Dr Roth over as he came out of the library. 'It's Addy!' she panted, pointing toward the bluff. 'She's out there chasing that darned cat!'

Without another word she raced to the front door and threw it open. 'Don't worry, Doctor Roth,' she called over her shoulder. 'We'll be right back.'

twenty-three

It wasn't cold outside. The chill was in Judd's bones. They drove in silence, Elizabeth turning only once to ask if he was all right.

He nodded, then went back to his own confused thoughts. Life had taken on a nightmarish sense of unreality and he could only grope for some small measure of understanding. Rachel had been married before. She had even had a child. Those vital parts of her hidden past had been concealed from him in spite of the great love they shared. But knowing the events didn't help him know the person any better. If anything, he realized now that he didn't know her at all.

He turned and pressed his forehead against the car window, concentrating on the feel of the glass. Was all this his own fault? Had he been too willing to accept her as she was, without any questions asked? If he had pressed her from the beginning, would she have told him about Peter? About her child? Or would she have simply walked away from him without a backward glance at the first hint of inquisition? He guessed the latter.

His head began to throb, keeping pace with the throbbing in his rib cage. He leaned back against the headrest and closed his eyes. He didn't have any of the answers. He wondered bleakly if he ever would.

'What are you going to do when we get there?' Elizabeth asked, turning up the long drive that led to the house.

'I'll be damned if I know.'

'You won't tell her I told you about Lilith. You promised.' Her voice was anxious.

Judd looked over at her. 'Are you afraid of Rachel?'

She smiled an embarrassed smile. 'Did I sound frightened? I guess I did. Well, I'm not afraid exactly. I guess I'm just never sure how she'll react.'

Judd nodded. 'I know what you mean.'

Elizabeth sighed. 'It seems as if ever since my father died we've all been programmed not to upset her. As if she were still a child.'

'Maybe she is,' Judd said. He was silent for a minute. 'I wonder.' He was beginning to realize how little even Elizabeth knew about Rachel. Probably the only one who really does, he thought dismally, is Priscilla Daimler.

Elizabeth seemed to read his thoughts. 'Maybe Mother will come through for us. She always has before.' She paused. 'But then, Henry says that's not likely. Maybe you ought to talk to him. He always knows an awful lot about what goes on at Land's End. And I'm sure he knows more than I do about Rachel.'

Judd nodded. 'The only question is whether or not he'll tell me anything.'

She thought about it for a minute, then said, 'I think he will. Now that Mother can't be hurt anymore.'

As they came around the last bend in the drive, Judd watched for that first glimpse of the house that always made him feel an over-whelming impulse to whistle. 'It never ceases to amaze me,' he said.

'What does?'

'The house. Land's End. I once thought I'd like to paint it. But no more.'

She smiled a rueful smile. 'You wouldn't believe that anyone would dare be unhappy living here, would you?'

'No, I wouldn't.'

They pulled up in front. 'I wonder who's here?' Elizabeth appeared apprehensive. 'I don't recognize the car.'

'It's probably Doctor Roth.'

'Doctor Roth? What would he be here for?'

'He's going to take Emma and Addy under his wing for a few days. To observe them.'

Elizabeth breathed a sigh of relief. 'Well, that's certainly a step in the right direction. I don't think they ought to be here a minute longer what with all this hellish mess going on.' She frowned. 'There is one thing I have to ask before we go in. It's been bugging me for a while now.'

Judd waited.

'Where did Emma really hear the name Lilith?'

Judd shook his head. 'I haven't any idea. Except that I saw it myself in a book down in the old summerhouse, so maybe Emma saw it written in one of the books in your mother's library.'

'Of course,' Elizabeth said, switching off the ignition. 'I'm sure you're right.' Her tone was casual enough but underneath Judd could detect a faint note of anxiety.

They met Dr Roth coming out of the library. 'I heard the front door open and I thought it was Emma,' the doctor said with surprise. 'What are you doing here?'

Judd was equally startled. 'You thought it was Emma? Why? Where is she?'

'She just dashed out of here a few minutes ago looking very cross. It seems that young Miss Addy went out searching for a cat without bothering to check with her sister first.'

'And you let Emma go?' Judd realized that he sounded paranoid, but he couldn't help it.

'Easy,' Dr Roth said quietly, putting a hand on Judd's arm. 'Emma is a very sensible young lady. She went to get Addy and she's coming right back.' He lowered his voice. 'There is no ghost, Judd. Remember?'

Judd turned and headed back toward the door. 'I'm going to get them.'

'You're in no shape to go anywhere,' Elizabeth said. 'I'll go. They're probably down at the stables. That's where Addy thought Maude had her kittens.'

Judd wanted to go himself but his chest was on fire. 'How would I manage without you?' he said.

'Very nicely, I imagine,' she answered, not smiling. 'Very nicely without any of us for that matter.' Then she was gone.

'There goes one very special lady,' Judd said almost to himself. She had come through for him more times than he cared to remember.

He let Dr Roth lead him into the library. 'Have you seen Rachel? Does she know you're here to take the children?'

Dr Roth shook his head. 'I was told that she was resting and was not to be disturbed.'

Judd sat down heavily and put one hand over his eyes. 'How did it go with Emma?'

'Very well. You were right. She's perfectly willing to go anywhere as long as it's away from Land's End.'

'Did she tell you about Addy's get-well card?'

The doctor nodded.

'What do you think?'

He shrugged. 'Nothing. Just more of the same kind of disordered manifestation we've already seen.' He sat down next to Judd on the couch. 'I'm eager to begin working with Addy. I really think if we can get her to express her anxieties in a play situation, she'll be well on her way back to good mental health.' There was a confidence in the doctor's tone, but still Judd had his doubts.

'I wish I could feel as optimistic as you do.'

Dr Roth smiled sadly. 'If you'd seen as many emotional disturbances as I have, you wouldn't be so skeptical.' He leaned back and Judd noticed a sudden tightening around the corners of his mouth. 'There is one thing about this case however that really has me stumped.'

'And that is?'

'In almost every other patient I've ever treated, somehow the anxiety slips over into their everyday life.' He frowned. 'With Addy, except when she's having one of her seizures, no one has seen anything to indicate that she is disturbed in any way. That's why I want to observe one of her episodes firsthand. If, in fact, it is hysteria of some kind . . . ' He stopped and looked toward the door. 'Good,' he said. 'It sounds as if they're back.' He stood up and held out a hand to help Judd just as the door opened.

Judd turned and stared. This is impossible, he thought, thunderstruck. This is absolutely impossible.

'I have to talk to you,' Priscilla Daimler said from the doorway. 'Now.' She came into the room slowly, walking with a strangely rigid gait as if each step had to be considered carefully before her legs would move. Halfway across the room she faltered, but before either man could help her, she stopped them with a sharp jerk of her head. 'Please,' she said, her voice weak but firm. 'I have to finish this myself.' Her face was empty, devoid of expression, but in the slope of her thin shoulders and the turn of her head, her pain was evident. She eased herself into a chair by the window and sat for a minute motionless except for the clenching and unclenching of one hand.

Dr Roth made a move toward the door but Priscilla stopped him. 'I wish you would stay, Doctor Roth,' she said but it was not a request. It was a command. 'Since you are a psychiatrist, perhaps you can explain what I can't.' She clutched the arm of her chair and Judd could see the bones of her fingers through the transparency of her skin. 'Sit down, gentlemen,' she said. 'Please.'

She leaned back and closed her eyes. 'I tell you this now,' she began, her voice flat and lifeless, 'because I have been given a last chance before I die. I make no excuses for what I have done in the past. But someone has to know. Someone has to help.'

She looked over at the two men who had seated themselves across from her on the sofa. 'Do you believe in God?' She didn't wait for an answer. 'I do. And I believe He has given me this last chance. Not to right any wrong, mind you. That can never happen.' Her voice trembled but she kept on. 'But it must never happen again.' She gasped for breath.

'Are you sure you're all right?' Judd asked, alarmed. She seemed to be shrinking before his eyes.

She nodded impatiently. 'Don't worry about me. I'm dying and there's nothing to be done about that. It's not my concern any longer. My concern is for my child. My Rachel. I've thought about it and thought about it, wondering how to tell you. So you would understand. So you wouldn't judge too harshly. So perhaps you could help.' She spread her hands out in an uncharacteristic gesture of appeal. 'I ask only that you try to imagine what it was like, loving her as I did, with all my heart and soul. But seeing her so . . . so pathetically incapable of functioning in the real world.'

She leaned her head back and closed her eyes. 'How can I describe Rachel? A rare child? An angel? Trite, perhaps, but true.' A faint smile touched the corners of her mouth, remembering. 'We loved Elizabeth but our lives were made perfect with Rachel. Until she was twelve years old and her father died. Everything changed after that.

'There was a fire in the stables, you see. Rachel and Nicholas tried to get the horses out. He was trampled to death and Rachel was badly hurt. A head injury among other things. But she survived. At least part of her did.' She winced as if the memory was causing her real physical pain. 'On the surface she was still the same sweet, charming girl we all adored. Still an able student. Well-liked. Seemingly happy. But underneath there was something different about her.' She shrugged. 'I can only describe it as a loss of some kind. A loss of some mechanism inside. Like a part of her soul.' She shook her head.

270

'I don't know how else to describe it. A loss.' The word echoed through the room.

'Incomprehensible things began to happen. Small bothersome things that at first I ignored. Or made excuses for. But one afternoon one of the neighbor's dogs wandered onto our property and chased Rachel's cat. The dog did no harm. He treed the animal and sat there howling until one of the gardeners finally chased him off. We all forgot about it. But Rachel didn't.' She shuddered. 'Two days later someone poisoned the dog. It was Rachel.'

Judd stared in disbelief. 'I don't believe you.'

The old woman silenced him with a glance. 'Don't be so hasty, Mr Pauling, and don't be a fool. I didn't make this up. It happened.'

'How did you know it was Rachel?' Dr Roth asked.

'Because she told me. In all seriousness, she came to me and told me. I never asked. I would never have considered such a thing possible. But Rachel was very proud of what she'd done. No remorse. No guilt. In fact, at first she was very open about the amoral things she did. She stole from her classmates. She cheated. For no reason other than that she wanted to. But worse, I began to see subtle streaks of cruelty when she was displeased. Clever little things she did that hurt, things that only I noticed, because I was the only one who knew her so well.'

She took a breath that seemed to shake her whole body. 'It was as if she had lost the ability to judge right from wrong. But as time went on, I realized that it wasn't because she didn't know any better. It was simply that she had ceased to care.'

She drew her lips tight across her teeth. 'Somehow

something dreadful had happened to Rachel. Where once there had been nothing but kindness, now there was a grand indifference to suffering. She had become a cripple as surely as if she were paralyzed. And I couldn't bear it because I knew it wasn't her fault. So I protected her. I covered for her whenever I could. And I took her to an army of doctors. Every neurologist, every psychiatrist worth mentioning. They examined her, they tried to treat her. Always the same results. Nothing. "We're sorry, Mrs Daimler."'

She lowered her voice in an effort to maintain control. 'They said it might have happened in the fire, that sometimes head injuries can cause such changes in behavior. Or that it might have been a latent disorder that hadn't been noticed before because she was so young. But in the final analysis there wasn't anything to be done. They were all sorry. Sorry.' She laughed a bitter laugh. 'They were sorry, and in the end the only thing that was accomplished by it all was that Rachel learned to lie. To make excuses. To deny. To blame everyone but herself. And, to add to the tragedy, she was brilliant at it. She became aware of the consequences of her actions, of people's displeasure, but it didn't keep her from doing things. She just learned to cover her tracks. She became an exquisite liar. But more than that, she was the consummate actress. She could make you believe anything at all. In the flash of an instant she could turn night into day. Black into white. She could faint or cry or grieve on cue, so that living with her was like living with a phantasm, never knowing where the substance ended and the shadow began. On the surface she was still my dear, sweet daughter. But underneath . . . ' She looked up as if suddenly remembering that Dr Roth was sitting there.

'Are you familiar with something called constitutional psychopathic inferiority, Doctor?'

He nodded.

'Well perhaps you can explain it to Mr Pauling. So he'll understand.'

Dr Roth pursed his lips. 'I suppose the simplest term I can use to describe the disorder would be "moral insanity." A great indifference to matters of right and wrong. A complete absence of a sense of responsibility for one's actions. A distaste for ordered reasoning.'

Something clicked in Judd's brain. A distaste for ordered reasoning.

'It may be caused by trauma of some kind, or it may be a hereditary weakness. Each case has its own fingerprints.' He held up a cautioning finger, temporizing in the air. 'But don't be misled. It is not insanity in its most recognizable form. Most psychopathic personalities are absorbed into the mainstream and are rarely hospitalized for long if at all, mainly because there is no confusion in the psychopathic mind. No loss of contact with reality. No disorientation.' He frowned. 'That's what makes it so devilishly difficult to diagnose. I make no excuses for my colleagues, Mrs Daimler, but in addition, a psychopath feels no motivation to get better. Therefore, we are faced with a very difficult if not impossible disorder to treat.'

Judd didn't want to believe what he was hearing. He had wanted answers, but this? Jesus Christ, this was a nightmare. He turned to Priscilla. 'I've lived with Rachel for four months. She's insecure. She's frightened. She's confused. She's stubborn. But she's not a psychopath. She's not.'

'I'm sorry, Mr Pauling,' she said softly. 'Truly I am. I

273

know you love her. But I have all of her medical records. You may see them if you like. Wait until you've read what all the experts have had to say, and then perhaps you'll understand. I do. I know how irresistible she can be. How sweet, how vulnerable. But it's all an illusion. The only real thing about her is the intangible air of tragedy she carries in her eyes. The one thing that makes it impossible not to want to help her. Sometimes I tell myself that it's because somewhere in the farthest corners of her mind she grieves for the part of her that's been lost.'

Judd's ribs were still throbbing and now his breath was coming in shallow gasps. He had to stop this. He had to go upstairs and get Rachel. Make her listen to her mother so she could tell him that none of this was true. But deep inside he felt despair. As if he were going through the motions of denial out of loyalty, not out of conviction. He stood up. 'I don't know whether any of this is true,' he said quietly. 'But I can't listen to anymore unless my wife is here to defend herself. To hear what you're accusing her of.'

He wasn't sure what effect he had thought his words would have on Priscilla. Anger? Reluctance? Fear? Perhaps a little of each. But her expression never changed. She simply nodded. 'I had hoped to spare Rachel this final indignity, but I cannot protect her any longer.' The words were spoken in a monotone, without emotion, a final acceptance of something she could no longer avoid. 'Go get her then. Bring my daughter here so you can judge for yourself. Then Heaven help you both.'

twenty-four

It wasn't until Emma stepped out of the shadowy coolness into the warm summer sunshine that she realized how scared she had been and how relieved she was to be outside. She hadn't allowed herself to think about it while she was in the stable looking for Addy. If she had, she would have thrown up. As it was, she hadn't given herself time to think. She had simply plunged into the darkness, driven by one single thought: find Addy and leave Land's End.

She had searched through every stall, calling her sister's name, but there had been no answer. The stable had been empty. No horses, no stable boys, no cats, no Addy. And again she had felt the silence. The thin, awful silence.

Now she leaned against the fence and tried to figure out where to look next. She had been so certain that she would find Addy here, that for the moment she was stumped. She had run all the way from the house, sure that she would catch up to her sister. Now it was clear that she had misjudged. Addy had not come to the stables.

Maybe if she was following Maude, Maude led her somewhere else. But where? Emma racked her brain, then suddenly remembered the day they had gone on their picnic and Maude had left the path and gone down through the brambles to the old summerhouse. Maybe that's where Maude had hidden her kittens, Emma thought.

'Of course,' she said. 'That would be the perfect place.' With a last sidelong glance at Clarissa who was peacefully grazing under the old apple tree with two other horses, Emma skirted the pasture, then broke into a run and headed up the path away from the stables.

At the top of the bluff she stopped for a moment to tie her sneaker, then ignoring the underbrush that tore at her legs, she left the path and made her way down the side of the ridge.

The wind had picked up and she could hear the sound of the waves crashing on the rocks. 'You better not have gone near that water, Addy Pauling,' she said under her breath, then suddenly realized that she was doing something their father had expressly forbidden them to ever do. She was going down to the ocean without an adult.

She hesitated, but only for a minute. After all, Daddy had also told her not to dare let Addy out of her sight. Besides, Dr Roth was waiting.

She broke through the last of the tangled underbrush and followed the thread of a path downhill until she came to the summerhouse. 'Addy?' she shouted. 'Are you in there?'

The only answer was the roar of the waves and the low whistle of the wind.

She made her way across the overgrown terrace, through the nettles to the door. She pushed.

It didn't budge.

'Addy!' she called. 'I'm not going to yell at you. I promise. Just answer me.'

There was no reply.

Emma pushed again and this time the door swung inward. Cautiously she stepped into the room and looked around. The sun was filtering through the broken windows, and she could still see their old footprints in the sand where she and Addy had followed their father across the floor that day that seemed so long ago.

'Ads?' Her voice was a whisper, and for the first time since she caught sight of Addy's yellow slicker disappearing over the crest of the hill, something terrible occurred to her. What if something bad had happened to Addy? Something really bad?

The sound of the ocean was roaring and angry now, and Emma sank down on her knees and stuck her fingers in her ears. 'Where are you, Addy?' she cried. On the brink of panic, she closed her eyes and tried to think. To imagine if she were Addy where she would have gone. There was only one other place either of them had ever been and that was down to the dock near the boathouse where Rachel kept her sailboat tied.

But why would Addy go there? She thought about it for a minute, then jumped to her feet. What difference did wondering make anyway? You never could tell what Addy might do. And she did have her slicker on so maybe she was thinking she might get wet.

Emma sucked in her breath. She couldn't believe that Addy would be so bad. She knew perfectly well that Daddy said never to go near the water without a grown-up. But then sometimes Addy didn't pay much attention to what people told her.

Emma's heart began to pound. What if her sister *had* gone down to the cove? And what if she had fallen into the water?

Without another look around the summerhouse, Emma shot out the door and took off back up the hill toward the path that wound around the trees and back down to the shelter of the cove. Once she tripped and scraped her knee, but she paid no attention. She was driven now by the worst fear of her life. A fear that something terrible had happened to Addy. Her eyes hurt with tears and her vision blurred, but she kept on running until she was almost to the boathouse.

And all at once she saw her. Addy, in her yellow slicker, sitting in the front of Rachel's boat. 'Addy Pauling, you get out of there right this minute!' She was half-choking, half-sobbing, and the wind carried her words away.

Addy didn't turn to look at her sister. In fact, she didn't move at all. She just sat where she was, hunched up on the seat as a frantic Emma pounded down the path toward her.

Emma was almost there when suddenly she realized with a shock of horror that the sailboat wasn't tied to the dock anymore. Somehow the lines had come free and the boat had begun to drift away. 'Addy!' she shrieked, throwing her arms out. 'Come back here!'

Still, Addy didn't move.

And then the mainsail swung around and Emma saw Rachel at the tiller. Overwhelmed with relief, Emma dropped to her knees. 'Rachel, come back,' she panted. 'Addy has to come with me. Doctor Roth is waiting.'

But Rachel paid no attention. Instead she headed the boat into the wind and the gap of open water between them yawned wider and wider.

Emma panicked. 'At least take me with you!' she cried.

Still it seemed as if Rachel hadn't even seen her. But Addy did. She sprang off the seat and began to jump up and down. 'Rachel! Wait! Go back! There's Emma!'

Rachel turned and stared for a moment at the little girl, but she made no move to change course.

'Rachel!' Emma wailed, then watched in desperation as the gap of dark water widened between them and the sailboat slid silently away across the waves.

Judd came back into the library. 'Rachel's not in her room,' he said. 'Do you have any idea where she might be?'

Dr Roth was standing next to Priscilla Daimler's chair, holding her wrist. 'I think we ought to call an ambulance, Judd,' he said quietly. 'I can't get a pulse.'

'Jesus,' Judd said. He moved away from the door but stopped when he saw her face. It was as if the flesh beneath the skin had fallen away, leaving only a transparent tissue covering her skull. He was sure she was dead until suddenly she opened her eyes and looked straight at him.

'Please,' she whispered. 'I have to finish.' The last was an anguished plea.

'Rachel isn't upstairs,' Judd said stupidly. He had never seen anyone who looked so dead still breathing.

'Come close, Mr Pauling. Don't speak. Just listen. You said you knew my Rachel. Well, you don't. She can be as lovable and sweet as anyone alive. And that side of her you do know. But there is another Rachel. The dark side of the mirror. And although that Rachel is to be pitied, to be sheltered, she is also to be feared. That's what you have to hear. What you do when I have finished is up to you. The burden can no longer be mine alone to bear.' She closed her eyes. Her lips continued to move, but only her lips. It seemed as if the rest of her were already in the grave.

'Rachel and Peter had a child. A daughter. And her name was Lilith. In the beginning, Rachel treated her like a treasure. She was fascinated by her, the way a small child is fascinated by a baby animal. Lilith was a darling, a plaything to be dressed up in beautiful clothes. But she was also expendable. After all, a plaything can be put aside with no harm done at the first sign of inconvenience. And after the novelty wore off, neither Rachel nor her husband had any time for her, pathetic little waif, what with Peter flitting off with his horses and sailboats and ladies. And her poor, pitiable mother unable to function herself, never mind provide nurture for a baby.

'More and more frequently Peter left them alone, although to be fair to Rachel, even when he was here he had little time for either of them. And typically, Rachel began to look around for someone to blame for her unhappiness. She never would admit that Peter was just a scoundrel, pure and simple. That she never should have married him. He didn't love her. He never had. Certainly not enough to try to understand her. Or help.

'But I knew Peter, even if she didn't. They lived here at Land's End and I could see what he was. A user. As much of a misfit in his own way as Rachel was in hers.' She broke off in a fit of coughing and when she finally got control, the only thing left to her voice was a shredded whisper.

'When the child began to walk, she was completely ignored. Rachel and Elizabeth's old nanny took care of her. Old Nellie. She knew Rachel almost as well as I did and she loved her, so she kept the little one out of sight. Rachel rarely saw her, so intent was she on trailing after Peter. Her devotion to him was obsessive.

'But as Lilith grew older, Rachel suddenly seemed to rediscover her. But not in the way one would have hoped. Instead of growing together as mother and child, Rachel seemed unable to understand what her role ought to be. She was most immature, most intolerant when she was with Lilith. As if the child were an envied playmate instead of a daughter.'

She shook her head and tears began to seep from the corners of her eyes. 'She demanded more and more from the child. "Please your daddy, Lilith. See if you can make him proud of you." "Stupid child, can't even play the simplest notes." "Lilith, do this. Lilith, do that." '

She lifted her head and looked straight into Judd's eyes. 'Do you remember the seven deadly sins, Mr Pauling?' She didn't wait for an answer. 'I do. But somewhere I once read that the deadliest sin of all is none of those. Rather it is the mutilation of a child's spirit. And that's what Rachel did to her daughter. She mutilated her spirit. While I – dear God forgive me – I stood by and watched.'

She covered her face with her hands. 'I have no defense. The more time Peter spent away from Land's End, the more demanding Rachel became of the child. In the wasteland of her own mind she blamed Lilith for his absence. And the more difficult the tasks she set for the child, the more she seemed to delight in Lilith's failures.

As if in some bizarre way Lilith's inabilities made Rachel all the more successful.'

Her body suddenly stiffened up as if someone had dealt her a death blow, and Judd held out his hand. She grabbed it and squeezed, as if it were the only thing keeping her alive. 'Please God,' she gasped. 'Give me the strength to finish.'

Dr Roth crossed to her side. 'I think we ought to get Henry,' he said.

She shook her head voilently. 'I haven't time. Please. Just listen.' And Judd knew from the awful tonelessness of her voice that this was the part she had dreaded telling the most. 'The swimming lessons,' she said. 'Lilith was deathly afraid of water, but Peter and Rachel were avid swimmers and sailors, and Rachel was determined that the child should learn to do both.

'Each day during those dreadful summer months, rain or shine, she took the child down to the beach or out in the boat. And Lilith would come back a trembling, pathetic wreck. It became more than even I could bear, and I finally spoke to Rachel about it.

'My poor daughter threw her arms around me and cried as if her heart were breaking. She begged me to understand. She was only doing it so Peter would love Lilith. She was going to teach the child to swim and sail, and then he'd be proud. Then he'd come home for good. And as usual she was brilliantly convincing. And as usual I was willing to believe, to hope that maybe she had changed.

'That weekend Peter made a rare stopover on his way to God knows where, and Rachel decided that it was time for Lilith to perform. We all gathered on the beach by the summerhouse to watch. The whole event was like some kind of nightmarish sideshow.' Priscilla was weeping openly now, tears rolling unimpeded down her sunken cheeks. 'Poor little Lilith was beside herself. In water up to her knees the child was incoherent with fear. Too frightened to go forward, terrified not to, sobbing her heart out until even that wretch Peter was finally moved to protest. "God, Rachel," he said. "Surely you don't consider this amusement?" '

'Rachel was devastated. She snatched Lilith out of the water, and carried her back to the house. Later I discovered the child in the cubby under the stairs. Rachel had sent her there to sit until she could apologize for being so mean to her mother and father. I'm not sure what happened after that but I do know that Peter, with his own impeccable sense of timing, chose that particular evening to tell Rachel he was leaving her. He didn't want a divorce, mind you. He simply needed some time away. Though Lord knows he spent little enough of that with her as it was. In any case, in the morning he was gone.'

Up to this point, Priscilla Daimler's words were almost toneless, but now every trace of expression left her voice. 'It rained that day. All day. Rachel never left her room and I could hear her pacing, pacing like a caged animal. But when she finally came downstairs she was as controlled, as calm as I had ever seen her. And I knew – dear God, I knew in my heart – that something terrible was going to happen. And it did.

'Rachel told me that she realized that she had been far too indulgent a parent. That Lilith had been allowed to behave like some poorly trained puppy, and it was mostly because I was continually interfering. Tomorrow, she said, it is all going to change.

'And sure enough. The next morning Rachel dressed

the child in her bathing suit, packed her slicker and deck shoes, and off they went. I watched them go from my window. I never saw Lilith alive again.'

Judd felt his mouth go dry. 'Lilith drowned,' he said flatly.

Priscilla nodded. 'Rachel came back to the house, hysterical. She told me she had made a terrible mistake. That she had read that the only way to teach a reluctant child to swim was to force him. So she had taken Lilith out in the sailboat. And had dropped her over the side. That by the time she realized that the child was in trouble, it was too late.'

Judd was stunned. 'My God, no wonder she had a breakdown.'

Priscilla Daimler reached out a skeletal claw and dug her fingers into his arm with incredible strength. 'That's what I thought, too,' she said. 'Rachel was grief-stricken. She was beyond consolation. And my heart was broken. For her, for the child, and for myself, because I knew I was to blame. For that, there will never be forgiveness. Never.'

No one spoke. The only sound in the room was the terrible rattling of the old woman's breathing.

Judd fixed his gaze on a spot on the carpet just to the left of her foot. He was numb. 'I'd better go find Rachel.' His voice echoed in his ears, as flat and toneless now as Priscilla's had been. He stood up and was about to turn away when she spoke again.

'I'm afraid it's not over, Mr Pauling. You have to hear the rest.'

Judd heard himself groan.

'I asked Rachel where Lilith's body was. Rachel said she couldn't find her. That she had looked and looked but the child was gone. The next morning the poor baby washed up on the beach by the summerhouse.'

She stopped and all of a sudden Judd felt the hair stand up on the back of his neck. 'Lilith had on her deck shoes and her yellow slicker.'

And then it came, the end of the story in words that filled him with profoundest horror. 'The pockets of Lilith's slicker were filled with rocks.'

Judd felt the nausea sweep over him, knew it was visible on his face, but he didn't fight it, nor did he look at either of the other two people in the room. He stood staring at the same spot on the carpet and then suddenly the door crashed open and a frantic, sobbing Emma threw herself into his arms.

'Oh, Daddy,' she gasped, fighting for breath. 'Rachel took Addy away. In the sailboat. I tried to stop them. I told them Doctor Roth was waiting, but Rachel paid no attention.'

Judd felt as if he had just hit a brick wall head-on. 'Who went where?' he breathed.

'Rachel has Addy. They went out in the sailboat.' She burst into a fresh flood of tears. 'I knew it. I just knew it,' she sobbed. 'We're never going to get away from here now. Never.'

twenty-five

Rachel has Addy. Rachel has Addy. Through the incoherent rushing of words, those were the only ones that Judd fully understood. There were other things Emma was saying, things about Rachel paying no attention to her and Addy jumping up and down, but the only words he really heard were three: Rachel has Addy.

Without the faintest notion of what he was going to do, he bolted out the door, Emma right behind him. 'Don't leave me here, Daddy!' she wailed. *'Please!'*

He stopped just long enough to grab her by the hand and together they ran from the house, nearly knocking Elizabeth over on the way out.

'Good,' Elizabeth said. 'You found her.'

'Don't ask anything,' Judd said. 'Just tell me if there's another boat. Besides Rachel's.'

The urgency in his voice must have been explanation enough, because Elizabeth didn't question him. 'There's one other,' she said. 'In the boathouse. I'll show you.'

Together the three began to run.

As they went, Judd prayed. Please God, don't let this be true. Don't let any of this be true. With his free hand he wiped the sweat away from his eyes, and realized suddenly that it was tears. His ribs were pounding and as they came up along the ridge, the pain became so intense that he was sure he was having a heart attack. He stopped just long enough to suck in an agonized breath of air, then turned down the path after Emma and Elizabeth.

The small sailboat heeled over and came about, throwing a fine spray of salt water across the bow. Addy sat huddled on the seat across from Rachel, silent now, eyes red and swollen from her tears. She put her thumb in her mouth.

'How many times do you have to be told?' Rachel said quietly. 'Or do you do that just to defy me?'

Addy shook her head and let her hand drop quickly to her side.

'Well?' Rachel's voice was still quiet but there was an edge to it. 'Can't you answer?'

Clearly bewildered, the child's lower lip began to tremble. 'I . . . I don't know what I should say,' she stuttered.

Rachel smiled a cold smile that touched her mouth but not her eyes. 'Of course you don't,' she said. 'Because you and I both know what you're up to.'

With one smooth motion she let the sheets out and instantly the sails began to flutter. The boat came around and headed into the wind. There was no more forward motion.

They sat for a moment, gently rocking back and forth with the motion of the waves. Rachel stared silently at the child, her head tipped to one side as if she knew a secret she wasn't sure she wanted to share. Finally she spoke. 'You are a very naughty girl, Addy,' she said softly. 'Naughty and mean.'

For a moment Addy looked as if she thought Rachel was teasing her. Then her face puckered up and she began to cry.

'Stop that sniveling at once!' Rachel snapped. 'That nonsense may work with your father but it will get you nowhere with me.'

Addy rubbed her eyes furiously with her fists and tried to stop, sucking in a few hitching sobs. 'I'm . . . I'm sorry,' she managed finally.

'You're sorry?' Rachel's eyebrow flew up to form a perfect arch over one eye. 'Of course you're sorry now that the damage is done. Now that you've turned your father against me.' She was no longer calm. Her voice was filled with venomous rage.

Terrified by her stepmother's tone, Addy pulled back and huddled over, trying to make herself as small as she could. Trembling, she stared back at Rachel, wide-eyed, the tears still dribbling slowly down her cheeks.

Rachel looked away and took a few deep breaths. 'I mustn't let you upset me,' she said almost to herself. 'After all, I'm the adult here. And I know how to punish naughty girls.' She turned back and fixed Addy with a determined gaze. 'You don't know how to swim, do you.' It wasn't a question.

Still wary but obviously encouraged by the fact that Rachel had changed the subject, Addy wiped her nose on her sleeve and shook her head. 'I'm sort of scared when I'm in over my head.'

'Well, I'm going to teach you,' Rachel said. Her voice was quiet now, almost pleasant.

Addy looked around at the vast expanse of deep, open

water. 'Way out h . . . h . . . here?' she stuttered. 'But . . . '
She made a motion to stick her thumb back in her
mouth, then jerked her hand away and sat on it.

'Way out here,' Rachel said. 'And just to make certain
you don't cheat, I brought something to put in your pockets.' She opened the vent in her slicker and took out a
handful of large, round stones.

Addy stared in abject fear and total bewilderment.
Then she shook her head frantically and burst into a
fresh flood of tears. 'I want to go home!' she wailed. 'I
want my Daddy!'

'Come here at once!' Rachel snapped, reaching out to
grab the child.

In a desperate attempt to get away, to hide, Addy
jerked back and tumbled off the seat. On all fours, she
scrambled across the deck toward the front of the boat.

'You malicious little brat,' Rachel exclaimed. 'Don't
you ever dare run from me.' She reached out and seized
the terrified child by the legs, pulling her back. Then she
jerked her around, lifted her into the air, and slammed
her down hard on the seat, holding her there.

Addy was crying and gasping, trying desperately to
wiggle free, when all at once she stopped. She stopped
crying. She stopped struggling. She sat perfectly still,
head bowed, absolutely still.

'Good,' Rachel said quietly, loosening her grip. She
seemed to be in complete control once again. 'Now then.
Put these stones in your pocket.' She held out her hand.
'I've got lots more right here.' With her other hand she
patted the bulging pockets of her own slicker.

For a single moment there was a complete absence of
sound. No whistle of wind, no splash of the waves, no
crying of the gulls. Perfect, bone-chilling silence. And

then, faint at first, borne on the barest breath of air, came the sound of a child's high, sweet voice singing a soft, hauntingly sad lullaby.

Rachel froze, her lovely face registering stunned surprise, then sheer horror, as slowly, deliberately, the child lifted her head. Her pale, dead eyes like empty caverns stared back at the woman who once had been her mother.

Rachel jerked back, her own eyes opened wide in sudden terrified recognition.

'Hurry, Daddy!' Emma cried over her shoulder. 'I know something bad is going to happen! I just know it!'

'You wait on the dock,' Elizabeth said. 'I'll get the boat.' She disappeared into the boathouse and moments later he heard the motor start up.

It wasn't until the three of them had pushed off from the dock that Elizabeth finally asked where they were going.

'I'll be damned if I know,' Judd said, covering his face with his hands. 'Rachel took Addy out in the sailboat.'

Elizabeth looked first from Judd to Emma, then back. 'And?'

'We have to find them,' Judd groaned. 'We have to bring them back.'

Elizabeth held up one hand. 'Well, I don't know why the urgency, but I think you're in luck. With this wind against them, and the tide running in they can't have gone very far. Maybe once we get out around the end of the cove we'll spot them.'

Judd felt Emma edge closer to him on the seat. 'Daddy,' she said, her face red and swollen from crying. 'What's happening to us?'

'I don't know, Emma. I just know we have to find them and bring them back.'

'But why did Rachel take Addy away?'

Judd could only shake his head.

'Does Rachel want to hurt Addy?' she asked gravely. 'Is she the one who hurt Lilith?'

Before he could think how to answer, a blast of wind and spray hit him full in the face and he realized that they were out of the shelter of the cove and into open water. He squinted his eyes against the force of the sun, scanning the horizon, but could see nothing but blue sky stretching endlessly above an empty blue sea. He felt a sick lump come into his throat. This was madness. They weren't going to find them. He should have called the coast guard.

'There's a sailboat,' Elizabeth said, pointing. 'But I can't tell if it's *Windward*.'

Judd started up, then sat back down. 'Jesus Christ, can't we go any faster?'

Elizabeth shook her head. 'I have it on full throttle. But don't worry, their sails are luffing. It doesn't appear that they're going anywhere.'

In slow motion, Judd watched as they came closer and closer to the boat.

'It's *Windward*.' Elizabeth's voice floated back to him, and she had been right. The sailboat wasn't going anywhere. It was rocking gently over the swells, the sheets loose, the sails flopping in the wind.

Judd stared. The sailboat was drifting with the tide. There was no one on board.

Elizabeth circled and tried to bring the motorboat closer but *Windward's* boom, swinging free, forced her to cut around to the other side. 'I don't see anyone!' she yelled, panic coming into her voice. 'What's happened?'

'Addy! Rachel!' Judd shouted.

No answer. No sign of life except for a solitary gull that wheeled in over the top of a wave.

'Addy!' Emma cried. 'Where are you?'

Elizabeth brought the motorboat around. 'When I get closer, you see if you can grab on.'

'Jesus, Elizabeth,' he said, the spray stinging his eyes. 'They're gone.' He reached out and painfully caught hold of the side of the sailboat, pulling it toward him with an excruciating effort until the two boats came together.

Judd stared up across the bow.

There was not a soul on board.

He swung his leg over the side, every movement an agony, and dropped onto the open deck. 'Addy!' he screamed. 'Rachel!' They must be here somewhere, he thought wildly, even though he could see that there was no sign of life. All rational thought left him and he began to rush from one side of the small boat to the other, calling their names. He was dimly conscious of Emma and Elizabeth holding tight to the sailboat, their eyes wide in disbelief and horror, and he felt himself sink to his knees on the deck. 'They're gone,' he groaned aloud. 'My Holy Christ, they're gone.'

Minutes passed in which he wasn't conscious of anything but black despair. And then faintly, 'Daddy, I'm scared.' A pathetic whisper.

He heard it but for a moment he didn't react. And then he was on his hands and knees, crawling toward the front of the boat. 'Addy?'

And all at once, he was looking into his own blue eyes staring back at him from the tiny crawlspace under the bow. 'Addy,' he breathed and gathered the small, shivering body into his arms.

She leaned her head against his chest.

'Addy,' he said softly. 'Are you okay?'

She nodded.

'Where's Rachel?'

'I don't know,' she whimpered. 'We were going to the stables to look for Maude, and then Rachel said wouldn't it be fun to go for a sail. But then all of a sudden she got so mean. And she said I was a bad girl. And she was . . . she was going to make me swim over my head.' The last words rose in a wail as she remembered her terror. She buried her face again in his chest.

'And then what happened?' he said gently.

'I tried to hide and then she grabbed me. And then . . . well, that's all, Daddy,' she whispered. 'That's all.'

He sat cradling his child, not thinking, not even trying to make sense out of what right now was incomprehensible. All he knew was that Addy was safe. And his poor crippled Rachel was gone. Somehow the rest would follow.

epilogue

During the night a thunderstorm rolled up from the south and washed all the soft baby-green of early summer away, leaving the gardens bathed in deep, lush, vibrant color.

Emma sat on the terrace trying to read, but it was impossible. She kept finding herself looking up and listening to the normal, regular old sounds of summer. Birds and crickets and the warm wind moving lazily through the trees. Somehow she knew that Lilith was gone. She hadn't had time to figure out just why or how, but it was true all the same. Lilith was gone, Addy was Addy, and Emma wasn't afraid anymore. Not one tiny little bit.

'Come on over here,' Addy called, breaking into her thoughts.

Emma sighed. Addy had been bugging her all morning. Ever since one of the servants brought Maude and her kittens up from the stables to the house. Right now they were all sleeping peacefully in a box on the edge of the lawn, Addy kneeling right beside them.

At the first sight of the babies Emma had been just

as enchanted as Addy. The two children had spent most of the morning on their knees, watching Maude nurse the five tiny kittens.

Finally Emma lost interest, but her sister didn't. Addy was still sitting right beside the box. She hadn't moved one inch. 'I wonder how long it will take them to get their eyes open,' she asked for the fourth time.

'I told you, I'm not sure,' Emma said, still trying to be patient. 'Maybe a week or so. Ask Elizabeth.'

'Maude loves to lick them,' Addy said. 'But her tongue is really scratchy.'

'How do you know?'

'She licked me by mistake.'

'I thought Elizabeth told you not to touch the kittens.'

'I didn't.'

'Then how did you get licked?'

'My hand got in there on an accident.'

Emma sighed and went back to her book. A beautiful orange-and-black butterfly fluttered across the terrace and stopped on the edge of the page she was reading. Emma held her breath and after a minute, *flitter-flutter*, it was off again.

Emma gave up and closed her book. She couldn't concentrate. She looked out across the garden again, trying to make some sense out of the things that had happened. So many bad things. Like that awful scene when they found Addy alone in the boat. Daddy called the coast guard and the police, and lots of boats came to search with sirens wailing and lights flashing. They finally found Rachel's body washed up on the beach down by the old summerhouse.

Emma overheard some of the servants talking about it, and what they said made her feel sick. They said that

Rachel killed herself, because when they found her, her slicker pockets were full of rocks. And that it wasn't surprising because Rachel used to be crazy. And then Kate said wasn't it weird how they found Rachel in the very same spot where they found poor little Lilith all those years ago.

Emma shivered. She had a million questions buzzing around in her head but she didn't ask any. Daddy said what happened to Rachel was just a terrible accident and he was very, very upset. And so was Elizabeth. So Emma kept still.

And then the very next day poor Mrs Daimler died. Emma felt really sad about that, too, because Mrs Daimler never got a chance to hear her favorite part of *The Secret Garden*.

But there were good things that happened, too. Like not being scared anymore because she knew that Lilith was gone. And like knowing that after they left Land's End, they would still see Elizabeth. Because she was going to come to New York for a while. And Daddy promised that before school started in the fall, they could all go to Maryland to visit her and see her horses. Emma could hardly wait.

She looked over her shoulder at the house but all was quiet and she guessed that Dr Roth hadn't arrived yet. She and Addy were going to stay with him at his clinic for a few days while Daddy and Elizabeth straightened things out with the funerals and everything. Emma had told her father that it wasn't necessary because Lilith was gone and Land's End didn't scare her anymore, but he still wanted them to go. At first Emma couldn't figure it out, but then finally it came to her. It was because he was still worried about Addy. He never did understand about Lilith. Oh well, she said to herself, he'll just have to see for himself that Addy is perfectly fine, and she always will be as long as I'm around to take care of her.

Suddenly Emma heard her father call. 'Come on, Ads,' she said. 'Doctor Roth is here.'

'Oh, nuts,' Addy said, sticking out her lower lip.

Emma walked over to her sister and held out her hand. 'Don't worry,' she said softly, taking Addy by the hand and pulling her to her feet. 'Before you know it, the kittens will be old enough to leave their mother. And don't forget, Elizabeth said you could even have two. So they won't be lonely.'

'It's going to be the most fun in the world, isn't it, Emma?' Addy began to skip across the terrace toward the house. 'And I'm going to pick out the best names ever. What do you think about Weenie? Wouldn't that be a good name?'

'I thought you were going to name one of them Mr Freddy?'

'Oh, yeah. I forgot.'

Emma pushed her glasses up on her nose. 'I think you should make a list,' she said. 'You tell me the names and I'll write them down for you so you won't forget again.'

Addy stopped at the door and took her sister by the hand. 'You're so nice to me,' she said.

'I know,' Emma replied solemnly. 'But after all, Ads, that's what big sisters are for.'

Judd waved them off, then stood watching until the car disappeared around the last bend in the drive. 'Please let Ads be okay,' he whispered.

'She'll be fine,' Elizabeth said from behind him. 'I just know she will.'

Startled, he turned to see her at the top of the steps, and with a jolt he remembered that it was exactly there that he'd first met her. Slowly, she came down the stairs to stand beside him. 'I thought you'd left,' he said.

'I was going to, but I decided to wait for you. I thought we could go to the cemetery together.' She paused, then touched him gently on the arm. 'I didn't think you'd want to go alone. I know I don't.'

He looked down at her and felt a sudden wave of sadness. For a minute she looked so much like Rachel. There had been many times before when he had caught glimpses of Rachel in her face. But somehow, curiously, he never really thought they looked alike. And all at once, he knew why. Elizabeth's eyes were always full of kindness. His poor Rachel didn't know the meaning of the word. 'Thank you,' he said softly.

Puzzled, she tipped her head to one side. 'For what?'

He smiled. 'I'm sure I'll think of a reason.' He turned, took her by the arm, and together they walked back up the steps and into the house.

Stranger in Savannah
Eugenia Price

The hearts of three families and the soul of a nation – torn by the passions of the civil war.

Stranger in Savannah continues the saga of the Browning, Mackay and Stiles families as they, and their country, are torn by civil war. Here are the turbulence and passion, drama and heartbreak, of a nation struggling within itself. For, as the Civil War shatters the United States, it also brutally tests the strength, love and faith of the Savannah families as they come face-to-face with the conflict that threatens to destroy them – and their way of life – forever.

The Savannah Quartet:

Savannah
To See Your Face Again
Before the Darkness Falls
Stranger in Savannah

are all available in Fontana Paperbacks

FONTANA PAPERBACKS

Virginia Andrews
The Dollanganger Series

FLOWERS IN THE ATTIC
PETALS ON THE WIND
IF THERE BE THORNS
SEEDS OF YESTERDAY
GARDEN OF SHADOWS

When *Flowers in the Attic* was first published, it rapidly became an international publishing sensation, establishing Virginia Andrews as one of the most popular and biggest selling authors in the world.

Her spellbinding story of four children who spent days, and then years, imprisoned in an airless attic – just so that their mother could gain her inheritance – proved so irresistible that it was made into a chilling film, and was soon followed by four more bestselling books continuing the story of those loveless, forgotten children and the terrible effect their harrowing ordeal had on them and their own families . . .

FONTANA PAPERBACKS

Virginia Andrews
The Casteel Family Saga

HEAVEN
DARK ANGEL
FALLEN HEARTS
GATES OF PARADISE
WEB OF DREAMS

Virginia Andrews' second compelling series is the heart-breaking story of four generations of the Casteel family and their desperate fight for happiness. Again and again tragedy threatens to overwhelm them as they struggle to escape the awful shadow cast over the family by the Tattertons and their mysterious, magical home, Farthinggale Manor.

FONTANA PAPERBACKS

Fontana Paperbacks: Fiction

Fontana is a leading paperback publisher of fiction. Below are some recent titles.

- [ ] ULTIMATE PRIZES Susan Howarth £3.99
- [ ] THE CLONING OF JOANNA MAY Fay Weldon £3.50
- [ ] HOME RUN Gerald Seymour £3.99
- [ ] HOT TYPE Kristy Daniels £3.99
- [ ] BLACK RAIN Masuji Ibuse £3.99
- [ ] HOSTAGE TOWER John Denis £2.99
- [ ] PHOTO FINISH Ngaio Marsh £2.99

You can buy Fontana paperbacks at your local bookshop or newsagent. Or you can order them from Fontana Paperbacks, Cash Sales Department, Box 29, Douglas, Isle of Man. Please send a cheque, postal or money order (not currency) worth the purchase price plus 22p per book for postage (maximum postage required is £3.00 for orders within the UK).

NAME (Block letters)_____

ADDRESS_____

_____